Totally Bound Publishing books by Jennifer Luna

Emerald Mafia
Dove

Emerald Mafia

DOVE

JENNIFER LUNA

Dove
ISBN # 978-1-80250-546-7

Interior text design by Claire Siemaszkiewicz
Totally Bound Publishing

Published in 2023 by Totally Bound Publishing, United Kingdom.

Totally Bound Publishing is an imprint of Totally Entwined Group Limited.

DOVE

Dedication

To my little Irish mutt,
Mommy wrote this story on her phone in one hand
while breastfeeding you with the other.
Now go do your homework.
There aren't any dinosaurs in this book.

Acknowledgements

First and foremost, to you, the reader. Thank you for supporting debut and indie authors, small press and independent publishers. There are so many amazing stories out there that deserve to be seen and heard. I am beyond grateful to every single one of you.

I'd like to thank my husband for being so supportive, for listening to my crazy ideas about sexy underground fighters and criminal overlords, for trying not to speed-read through the steamy scenes. But mostly, for giving me the two greatest gifts of all—your love and our son.

Breanne and Autumn, for proving that thousands of miles can't come between fifteen years of friendship. To my alpha readers—Heather, Tissa and Sebrina—I couldn't have completed this story without you. Your encouragement and unfiltered opinions feed my creative soul.

This is my debut novel, so I needed all the editorial help I could get. Lexie Eldridge at Morally Gray Edits, your manuscript critique is a godsend. Tiffany Tyer, my developmental editor, *Dove* wouldn't be what it is without your guidance. You pushed me outside of my comfort zone and I am forever grateful that you did. It may've taken a few glasses of wine, but I got there. Kimberly Steinke, for finetuning this manuscript before I sent it to publishers. Laura Apgar, for helping me perfect the headache that was my original query letter.

To Totally Bound Publishing for taking a chance on a new author. The publishing process can be complicated and overwhelming, but you helped every step of the way. Specifically, Anna Olson and Rebecca Scott for your guidance and attentiveness.

Lastly, to the Smuthood, thank you for being such a supportive group of individuals. Your recommendations are on point. I really enjoyed going down the rabbit hole with everyone and can't wait to continue exploring romantic literature. Your open-mindedness, inclusivity and humor are a breath of fresh air.

Prologue

The air was sweeter this time of year.

My lungs filled with the saccharine scent of petunias and violets. The soft dirt beneath my feet had been baking in the sun all day, but I pushed my soles into it, longing for the heat rising from the ground. The wind began to pick up. Wide maples leaves rustled, the trees whispering secrets to one another, telling tales from decades ago.

The weatherman had predicted one last summer storm to round out the season. The rain would remind us that school was just around the corner. Our days of lounging at the pool and eating snow cones were over. The sleepovers in the backyard, the tan lines and the sound of flipflops slapping against the asphalt would be tucked away in our memories.

But not for him and me. We always spent the last few hours of summer in our private spot, two and a half miles outside town, away from the prying eyes of nosy neighbors.

My eyes snapped open, my heart hammering an erratic rhythm inside my chest.

This is just a dream, I reminded myself. I was safe in my bedroom in the city. The symphony of car horns and squealing tires guided me back to sleep. My mind drifted and I was there again, trapped in my own reverie.

His hair was lighter than it had been a few years ago. He'd ditched the boyish cut at the end of last summer in favor of a shorter chop. Although there always seemed to be a spiral curl that escaped, drooping over his left eye. He looked up at me, his smile brilliant and set in a youthful face that'd been tanned by two months of outdoor activities. His long lashes cast shadows over caramel-colored eyes. The sinewy muscles in his forearm twitched as he beckoned me to follow him before diving into the pool of dark crystal water. Nate…

My chest ached, knowing I'd have to wake up.

Still, I needed to see him again and I knew where he was going. There was a small cave set into the rock at the back of the pond. It was covered by thick ivy, a tree jutting out of its entrance. We'd discovered this place by luck three summers ago, before high school had started.

As I braced myself for the dive, cold fingers suddenly wrapped around my throat. No, this wasn't right. This wasn't how the dream went. This was supposed to be a safe one. Good, even. The new addition was unwanted, tainted. His breath hit the back of my neck, the smell rancid and bone-chilling. My memories were colliding, racing over one another without any regard for the linear flow of time.

I tried to scream for Nate, but an arm crushed my windpipe. I struggled, but the man was too strong. My lungs burned, panic quickly setting in. I reached backward, but my attacker grabbed my arm, pinning it to my side.

Just when I thought I was going to pass out, his lips pressed against my ear. I knew what he was going to say. I'd had this nightmare before, but its effect wasn't lost in redundancy. An icy shiver skated down my spine as the voice hissed at me in the dark.

"Luca sends his best."

Chapter One

Emma

The subway screeched to a halt at Canal Street, but I was used to the various bends and lurches of the NYC underground. A few tourists stumbled, giggling as if they were on an amusement park thrill ride instead of an underfunded transit system.

My last class of the day had run long and I was already late to a place I had no desire to be. *If I'm late enough, maybe they'll just give up on me.*

As exhaustion set in, the resentment I'd been harboring toward my roommate dissipated. I'd known from the beginning that Ava Davis' sole purpose in our shared apartment was to keep tabs on me. I also had a feeling that my mother was subsidizing her rent in exchange for updates on my mundane life. I didn't blame Ava. If I were in her shoes, I'd do the same. The Davis family didn't have as much money as mine.

Now that I was on my way to a self-defense lesson at ten o'clock at night after a full day at school, I was starting to see my roommate's reports for what they were—a hindrance. It was still better than returning to my therapist, which had been my mom's first suggestion. I'd been doing better, but the attack had triggered old emotions and the painful dreams attached to them. The nightmares had undoubtedly scared Ava enough to rat me out to my mom.

As I stood outside an unimpressive building with a sign saying nothing more than "GYM" in neon-green lettering, I wondered whether I should just turn around and call it a day. There didn't seem to be any lights on inside. I was more than thirty minutes late and bone-tired. I didn't feel like learning useless self-defense moves from an overweight man in his fifties.

"Most likely has a limp, too," I muttered, turning back to head toward Fulton Station. I hoped enough time had passed for my MetroCard to reset itself so I could get through the gate.

"I hate to disappoint you."

I spun around, fumbling inside my book bag for the canister of Mace I'd purchased a few days ago on my father's order.

"Relax, darling." The hooded figure raised his hands when I found the spray and pointed it at him. He was almost a foot taller than me, and his frame wasn't slight by any means.

"G-get away from me," I stammered, arms trembling as I used both of them in an attempt to steady my aim. It hadn't yet registered that if the man wanted to attack me, he'd already had ample time to do so.

He glided into the neon light emanating from the sign and I took an involuntary step backward. He was wearing black joggers and a sweatshirt with some sort of logo on the right breast. His green eyes all but glowed in the dark, staring me down. He was a little older than me and incredibly handsome, but I squeezed my hands tighter on my one line of defense—the pepper spray. Predators could be handsome, too.

"First of all," he began, taking a cautious stride in my direction. His voice was masculine and commanding, but its low timber put me at ease. "I'm the owner."

He pointed to the logo on his hoodie, which I now saw said "Emerald Gym." He continued forward, reaching for my hands, which were now frozen in place with shock.

"Second of all, you've got the nozzle facing the wrong way."

It was then that I put his words together. I tore my eyes from his and glanced at the canister, which was indeed pointed straight at my own face.

"Shit!" I squealed, dropping the Mace altogether.

"Jesus!" he cursed, scooping the canister from the sidewalk and putting the safety tab in place with practiced agility. "You scared the shit out of me, lass!"

I made a mental note of the undercurrents of an Irish accent.

"Me?" I fired back with scrutiny, releasing the breath I'd been holding. "What are you doing sneaking up on a girl in the dark?"

"Sneaking up, was I?" His hood fell as he laughed, revealing messy, dark brown hair and a thick scruffy shadow along his jawline. His white teeth gleamed wolfishly in the artificial light. "Was standing here thirty minutes, waiting for a client, when you walked up muttering something about a man with a limp."

Had I been so lost in thought that I hadn't noticed someone right in front of me? I hoped I wasn't beginning to lose track of time again.

"You need to be more aware of your surroundings, sweetheart," he scolded, turning around to open the door to the gym. There had been lights on inside all along, but the windows were blacked out so that no one on the street could see them.

"Well?" he demanded.

I literally jumped out of my thoughts and looked at him yet again, trying to slow the pace of my heart. It thudded against my ribcage, refusing to let me calm down. He was standing with his back holding the door open, gesturing for me to enter the gym.

"I'm assuming you're here for self-defense, yeah?"

I nodded, aware of the warmth radiating from his body as I passed close by, entering the gym.

"Good," he muttered. "Because, by God, if anyone needed it…"

The gym was more impressive on the inside than from the storefront. It was open concept with dark marble floors separated every so often with rubber mats. At the center was a sunken area dominated by a large octagon ring. Two sweaty men were exchanging punches, surrounded by a group of onlookers yelling encouragement or advice. There were three rooms around the ring, each housing different types of equipment ranging from cardio to weightlifting. Everything was state-of-the art.

After changing in the empty female locker room, I followed directions to a private room at the back of the building. I felt oddly exposed in my workout gear, which I'd stolen from Ava's dresser on my way out of the door this morning. She'd already left for rehearsal and wouldn't miss an extra pair of leggings and a Lycra vest. Besides, she owed me.

I'd tried to grab the largest size from Ava's drawer, but even that was a bit tight. Ava and I had very different body types. She was one-hundred-percent muscle crammed into a tiny dancer's body, whereas the past few years had taken their toll on mine. I'd dropped a couple dress sizes and was used to wearing my old, baggy clothes to hide the weight loss.

The tightness of the elastic blend made me uncomfortable. I pulled at the hems and seams, hoping to hide some of the curves I hadn't noticed since high school. Come to think of it, I hadn't worn anything this skintight *since* high school.

Giving up with a sigh, I used the wall-length mirror to tie my dark hair into a loose ponytail, feeling jittery as I waited for the instructor.

"Right, so I'm Jack and I'll be teaching you self-defense twice a week until…"

I spun around at the familiar lilting tones of the man I'd met outside. As the owner, I had figured he wouldn't be conducting my session. Admittedly, somewhere deep in the back of my mind, I'd been hoping to get a look at him in better lighting.

He was peering down at a sheet of paper on a clipboard as if reading from a script. "Well, I suppose I'll be your teacher until you're sick of me or the checks stop coming in the mail, to be frank."

He still hadn't glanced in my direction, so I felt less shame as I eyed him from the corner of the room. My earlier assessment hadn't done him justice. His features looked like they'd been chiseled from a piece of Renaissance-era marble. He was all sharp angles and soft skin, apart from the jaw, which was dusted with dark hair. His eyelashes were thick and long, shielding his eyes from view. He'd taken off his hoodie and was wearing a simple black thermal, the sleeves pushed up to reveal intricate tattoos on his right forearm. The smoky designs stretched to his middle finger, which housed a series of faint Roman numerals. I couldn't quite make out the rest of his arm before I noticed he'd gone silent.

When I looked up, his piercing gaze was studying me as well. An odd heat ran over me as his intense stare slid from my feet to my mouth, which he paused at shamelessly before meeting my eyes for a few agonizing moments. Cheeks burning, I dropped my head and crossed my arms over my stomach, once again aware of how revealing my borrowed clothes were.

"Shit, I'm sorry." He set the clipboard onto a nearby bench, running his tattooed hand through his hair. My palm itched, and I wondered what his curls would feel like. "You caught me off guard. Let's try that again. I'm Jack O'Connell."

He closed the sizable gap between us with purposeful strides, his long fingers outstretched toward me. *God, even his hands are sexy*. Clean and hard, like he was used to working with them. Shaking off the nerves rooted deep in my belly, I reached out, willing my hand to feel as sturdy as his looked.

"Emma Marshall," I replied, my voice ringing strong and clear. *Congratulations, Em. You remembered your name.*

His hand was much larger than my own and surprisingly warm. His skin seared against mine when our hands met, but I didn't pull away until he did.

"All right, Miss Emma Marshall, have you warmed up yet?"

"Um..." I glanced around the room. "I walked a couple blocks to get here. Does that count?"

I expected a polite smile at my stupid joke, but he furrowed his brow instead. Had I upset him? I couldn't imagine how. Was it normal to warm up before a self-defense class?

"Okay, we'll do it together, then." He recovered his polite tone so quickly that I wondered if I'd imagined the slight dip in his mood.

Jack O'Connell's warm-up was longer than I'd anticipated the lesson being. After forty-five minutes of stretching, jumping rope and lifting kettlebells, I thought we had to be close to done for the night. I was burning through my exhausted stage, bordering on comatose. I'd been athletic in high school—tennis, soccer, dance—but hadn't so much as jogged a mile in years. My breathing was becoming embarrassingly labored.

Jack was a very fit person. *He should be on a billboard in Times Square, not a small gym teaching physical fitness.* I couldn't help but think I wouldn't be as self-conscious if he were a little harder on the eyes.

"Easy, easy!" Jack warned, pulling the water bottle away from my mouth. "You'll make yourself sick if you drink too fast."

I snatched the bottle back, trying my hardest not to glare at his smug face, but I didn't take another sip. Instead, I slumped onto a cool metal bench and focused on normalizing my heart rate.

With my head between my knees, I watched as Jack organized the room, moving weights and medicine balls into place with ease. He hadn't broken a sweat during my so-called warm-up even though he'd been right beside me through it all. I studied his features as he moved gracefully around the room—the way his brow furrowed and his eyes darkened. A few times, he licked his lips and I averted my gaze, discomfited by the way my body responded. Could he hear my heart racing from across the room?

Jack turned to face me. "I think that's a good start, Emma."

I stared at the floor, hoping he hadn't caught me studying the way the muscles moved over his expansive shoulder blades.

"That's it?" I asked, stuck somewhere between shock and relief. Yes, I was exhausted. But I hadn't thought I'd be leaving so soon either. I stood, brushing my hands over my thighs. "But I didn't learn any self-defense."

Jack smiled lopsidedly as he approached, his pupils widening. The effect was magnified now that he was looking right at me. Something whirled around deep in my belly. I swallowed, trying not to break eye contact. It felt as though I'd been caught in his crosshairs, like he could see straight into my brain.

This is all in your head. He's not into you. Get a hold of yourself.

He was less than a foot from me now, heat pulsing from his body. Goosebumps erupted along the nape of my sweaty neck. He hadn't been this close throughout the whole lesson. My mind was screaming, begging me to touch him, to break the magnetic tension under my skin. I imagined reaching out and poking his chest to see if he was real.

"Lesson one," he said. I held my breath so I wouldn't miss what he had to say. "Aim the nozzle *away* from you, darling."

His arm was stretched to the side, pointing my can of Mace toward our reflections in the mirror.

Chapter Two

Jack

Holy fucking mother of Mary.

Fate was showing its cynical sense of humor by sending this one into my path. Hell, if she didn't walk and talk so convincingly, I'd think she was just a figment of my imagination.

You're not that creative, Jackie Boy. I sat on the bench she had just vacated, head in my hands. *What the hell just happened?*

I obviously hadn't gotten a good look at her beforehand. Maybe then I wouldn't have made a complete ass of myself during the introductions. Then again, if I'd seen her clearly from the beginning, I would've assigned her to Mickey. I never mixed business with pleasure.

And Emma Marshall was all pleasure. With her waist-length brown hair and innocent eyes, her pouty pink lips and soft frame.

I forced myself to keep a safe distance during the lesson, which didn't make sense seeing as it was a one-on-one defensive class. The irony wasn't lost on me. The most dangerous thing in Manhattan for her over the past hour had been me and me alone.

The carnal thoughts wouldn't stop bombarding my brain as I came up with new exercises for us—anything that would keep my hands busy and her body well out of arm's reach. It was one of the single most difficult things I'd done in a while. I was a man of instant gratification. If I wanted something, odds were I would have it within the following ten minutes. And I couldn't recall ever wanting anything more than I wanted Emma.

"Ey, Mick!" I called across the octagon to the one person I would ever consider a best friend, a short, stocky man with dark red hair. He was wrapping his wrists for the next fight. "Since when do we teach self-defense?"

"Since when do we turn down a check?" He shrugged, grinning to reveal a chipped incisor. "Besides, by the looks of her, I did you a favor, mate."

A few of the fighters whistled their agreement.

"Watch it," I warned.

Something about that girl had my emotions bouncing from light to dark over the past hour. Still, I trusted Mick more than anyone in the city, apart from my brothers. I gestured for him to follow me into the hall, my mood plunging as the remaining men started to talk.

"Everything okay, boss?" Mick asked once we were out of earshot.

"No," I replied, harsher than necessary. "We don't get many women in this gym."

"Aye, that we don't."

"The last thing we need is those bastards harassing the poor girl…scaring her off or something."

Mick nodded, his heavy brow knit with confusion.

"I know our men. They'll be chomping at the bit to get a minute of her time." My blood boiled at the thought. "But she's a client. Hands off."

That last part was for my own benefit.

It wasn't normal for me to feel so possessive, but the girl was in need of help. She seemed jumpy. She couldn't even aim a can of pepper spray. As if that weren't enough, she admitted to walking the streets of Manhattan alone at night. Combine all that with the way she looked, I was surprised someone hadn't taught her a few defensive moves beforehand.

"So basically, you need me to tell the men not to fuck her?" Mick clarified.

My anger was reaching an apex at the idea of anyone taking advantage of the girl. I clenched my jaw to keep from yelling. My hand itched to form a fist, but this was Mick I was talking to. I'd known him most of my life. We'd grown up together. He didn't mean any harm, and I was being irrational at best.

"I don't want any of them so much as lookin' at the girl." Whenever my composure waned, my accent became more pronounced. "Or they'll have to answer to me. Got it?"

Mick's periwinkle eyes widened at my unexplained rage. "Heard, boss."

"And pass it along quick," I commanded as the door to the women's locker room opened.

Ignoring the initial shock to my system that was Emma Marshall, I ushered her outside while the men resumed their routines, hoping she wouldn't notice the shift in my attitude, or how the room quieted upon her reappearance.

"Where're you headed, Miss Marshall?" I asked, holding open the door to my gym.

She wrapped her blue suede cloak tighter around her. I wondered if I should grab her an extra jacket from inside. It wasn't very cold, but she didn't have a lot of meat on her bones. Her hair—now down and framing pale, delicate features—blew in the wind as she pointed east.

"The A train is my ride home." Her voice was soft and feminine but clear enough despite the breeze making its way down Sixth Avenue.

If this woman stood at the other end of a crowded room and began to whisper, hers would be the only voice I heard. How did she command my attention after an hour of knowing her, and was she aware of it?

"I'll accompany you," I offered, stepping out from under the cover of the Emerald. I'd already been upset to hear she'd walked the few blocks from the station to the gym in the dark. I wasn't about to let her do it again.

"I'll be fine," she protested, shaking her head as a faint shade of pink rose in her cheeks.

"Then I'll just walk ten feet behind you to make sure you get on okay," I replied, shoving the ever-present sexual thoughts into the recesses of my mind. My attempt at covering my attraction to her was making me out to be a dick, but I couldn't help it.

Her mouth popped open for a moment before turning into a smile, her lips stretching over a set of white teeth. *Fuck, how would that mouth feel around my—*

Groaning inwardly, I tore my eyes away and set the pace, which was much too slow for the average New Yorker but not suspicious for two people on a casual late-night stroll.

"You going up or down?" I was more than curious about where this woman had come from. Meeting someone of her caliber in my gym seemed unceremonious. It would've been less shocking if she'd approached me on the street and slapped me across the face.

"Upper West Side."

I eyed her from my peripheral vision. Her hair was long and sleek, dark but with natural honey-colored highlights. Based on the little time I'd known her, she didn't seem the type of girl to spend hours in a salon chair. Her clothes were designer but understated so it would be hard to tell with an untrained eye.

I'd been trained by the age of seven to spot a nice coat from two hundred feet. It was the only way to get money for food since my father had drunk all of what little we earned. Luckily, Uncle Henry didn't have children of his own and took us under his wing. In his will, he had handed his accumulated wealth to my eldest brother, much to my father's vexation. This move put us in the realm of upper-class life. Based on the last hour with Emma, she didn't act like someone from Manhattan's high society.

"Where are you from?" I asked.

"That obvious, huh?" She glanced at me with a sly grin. I noted it was only the second time I'd seen her smile. "I'm from a small town in Connecticut. Moved here for school a couple years ago."

College girl. Still, two years in the city would make her a junior. She'd be twenty, maybe twenty-one. Four or five years younger than me. *Stop it,* I commanded. *She's a client.*

"Which university?" I asked, wondering why I was putting so much thought into the statistics of a relationship with this woman when it could never happen. Emma Marshall was off-limits for more reasons than one.

My line of work didn't make for easy relationships with outsiders. It didn't make for easy relationships with anyone, which was why I never kept a lass around for more than twenty-four hours. Any longer and they'd start asking questions I couldn't answer.

"Columbia." Emma looked down at her boots as if ashamed to admit she attended one of the best schools in the country.

"Ivy League." I whistled. "Your parents must be proud of you." I imagined what my father's reaction would be if I told him I'd gotten into any college. He'd probably just grunt and ask me to bring him another drink.

"I guess," she mumbled, fiddling with the cuff of her sleeve as we neared Fulton Station. We still had a block to go, and I couldn't help but slow my pace. I had more questions.

A picture of her membership form popped into my head. I'd fumbled through it while she'd gotten changed for the session. It had been faxed in from an out-of-town area code that I hadn't given much thought to at the time. It'd been filled out in neat cursive with basic information, but the check was signed by a Mr. Gregory Marshall. Maybe her father? There wasn't a ring on her finger. She wasn't wearing any jewelry that I could see.

"So, why the interest in self-defense?" I probed. "Despite the fact that you are in desperate need of it."

She sighed and a thermal current raced through my fingers. I wanted to reach out and make her face me so I could see her expression head-on, but I kept my hands in my pockets like a good boy.

"My parents told me it was either this or back to therapy…and since I've already been to therapy, I thought I'd try my luck at these classes." She bit her lip, seeming to regret her words the moment she spoke. Maybe, like most people, blatant honesty didn't come naturally to her.

"I don't see how the two are related," I wondered aloud.

"I was sort of mugged last week. My parents think the city is dangerous. They figured I either need to toughen my mind or strengthen my reflexes."

I stopped walking. "What do you mean, you were mugged?"

The fury was back. My hands balled into fists, regardless of the absence of immediate danger. But it was the mere mention of a threat that infuriated me. Why was it angering me so much? Plenty of people got mugged on the streets. This was New York, for Christ's sake!

"Well, I suppose it was more of an attack than a mugging." She turned around, realizing she'd left me behind. "He didn't actually *take* anything."

A few silent moments passed before I cleared my throat. "What did the fucker do?"

She was quiet. Those X-ray eyes studied me, but I refused to look. If she didn't speak soon, I would grab her and shake the answer out. *Please don't let it be what I'm thinking,* I begged no one in particular.

"He must've been deranged or something. It's possible he thought I was someone else. He held me around the neck for a few seconds and…and then he just took off. Maybe he got spooked."

The air I had been holding left my body in a hiss. Emma took a hesitant step away. Her reaction pulled me back from my own murderous thoughts. The desire to find this man and wrap my fingers around his throat was strong, but I didn't want Emma to be frightened of me.

"Where was this?" I asked, walking faster to burn off the excess energy. She matched it, taking two strides for one of mine. "Did you get a look at the piece of shit?"

"No, he stood behind me. I was too shocked to notice anything when he ran off. It was outside of that nightclub in Hell's Kitchen called the Drop. I used to work there but my parents made me quit. Another stipulation to avoid therapy."

"I can see why they suggested both. Only someone without an ounce of self-preservation would walk around Hell's Kitchen alone at night looking the way you do."

I hadn't meant to snap at her, but how could someone who seemed as smart as she not know the basics of street safety? Did they not teach women how to protect themselves at Columbia?

Emma's face fell, and she focused on her boots again. As we walked down the steps into the underground station, I tried to turn the conversation back in my favor.

"Listen, your parents already prepaid for three sessions." I jogged down the last few stairs to catch up with her. She'd started to move fast and I didn't care for the distance between us. "And you're light as a dove, so I think we should work on leverage techniques in our next lesson."

I'd never taught self-defense to anyone. In my mind, the best defense was a good offense. I never shied away from taking the first punch, metaphorical or not. All I knew was that I needed to get these three sessions over with and send Emma Marshall on her merry way. I didn't like being attached to anyone. And that was exactly how Emma made me feel—attached.

"Whatever that means." She stood at the turnstile, sifting through her bag for what I assumed was her MetroCard.

"What are you doing tomorrow?" I asked, trying not to sound too antsy.

She hadn't said when she would return to the gym. Now that I was watching her disappear into the city that had recently harmed her, my heart raced with an uncomfortable anticipation. The sooner I could ensure she had proper training, the sooner I could get this girl out of my gym and forget about her.

She looked up at me, MetroCard in hand and at the ready. "I have class, then I need to go job hunting. Preferably somewhere that isn't a shitty nightclub."

An idea popped into my head and it slipped out before I could think it through. "I hear Roisin's is hiring."

Why the hell had I said that? I was trying to get her away from me, not integrate her even further into my life. I was at war with myself—the physical desire to draw her in and the emotional need to push her away were both fighting for a front-row seat.

She narrowed her eyes, that magnetic pull between her body and mine snapping to attention. "Row…sheens?" Her tongue struggled over the Irish name. I fought the urge to smirk, despite being turned on by the Gaelic leaving her mouth.

"Nice restaurant. Upper East Side. A bit classier than your average nightclub."

She slid her card, stepping onto the other side of the turnstile. Her hips swung around the metal dividers, her hair dancing along as she turned to face me.

"Thanks. I'll check it out."

I reached my hand across the turnstile, silently thanking and cursing the divider for preventing me from following her onto the platform.

"It was a pleasure meeting you, Emma."

Her hand was so much smaller and cooler than mine. The contact sent a vibration down my side and straight into my groin. My imagination ran wild with all of the things I wanted to do with her—to her. *Client*, my inner monologue hissed.

"The pleasure is all mine, Jack."

My lips parted in surprise as she walked onto the A train, which had just arrived. I was beside myself with this woman.

Fucking hell.

Chapter Three

Emma

The pleasure is all mine? The *pleasure* is all *mine*!

What the hell was I thinking? Who says that kind of thing?

You, apparently.

Maybe it was the fatigue. It had to be. When I'd gotten home after the self-defense lesson, I had crashed into bed, falling asleep with my purse tied around my waist and my boots on.

The following morning, I recalled every detail. The lesson with Jack, the walk to the station. Oh, and the awkward handshake where I'd suddenly become someone sultry and desperate. I washed my body twice, hoping to get the remnants of that woman off my skin before starting the day.

It was hard to focus in class. No matter how many times I shook my head to clear it, I couldn't stop thinking about him. His fit body, lean and muscular underneath those dark clothes. The way his stubble sounded when he ran a hand over his jaw, forcing my eyes to zero in on his mouth. The inky skin on his arm that moved when he did, stretching and relaxing as he worked out beside me. How his pupils dilated when he looked at me, those green eyes melting into pools of emerald.

It wasn't until the professor ended class that I realized my notes weren't up to my usual standards. I'd stopped typing halfway through the last piece of information. *"The fall of the Huns was unprecedented because it characterized the..."*

Leaning over, I asked my nearest neighbor if he could share his notes. He looked startled—I wasn't one for many words—but obliged with a smile, emailing them to me on the spot.

After school, I grabbed a panini from a street vendor, which I ate on the subway back to my modest apartment in Lincoln Square. I changed into a respectable outfit for job hunting and was out of the door in under twenty minutes with a list of local establishments programmed into the notes on my phone. I'd added Roisin's last night after Jack O'Connell's suggestion, but it was further down on the list.

Two hours and a series of uninterested snubs later, I rounded the corner of Park Avenue and East Sixty-Third, impressed. The address for Roisin's had brought me to a swanky apartment building on the Upper East Side. The entrance of the building, called the Shannon, was a huge glass wall. The rest of the imposing skyscraper was made of sturdy reflective metals, rising far above my line of sight to commingle with the rest of the towering block.

As I neared the dark awning, a large, sharply dressed man wearing a clear, inconspicuous earpiece approached.

"Welcome to the Shannon, ma'am. May I be of service?" he asked, holding open the glass door.

"Uh." I was still a little jittery when speaking to people, especially doormen who appeared more Terminator-like than the average human. "I'm looking for a restaurant called…Roisin's?"

The man smiled, which transformed his face into that of someone ten years younger. "Right this way."

The Shannon's lobby was tastefully minimalist. Although the chandelier, marble flooring and imported white area rug screamed luxury, they were easy on the eyes. I was wondering how they kept the carpet at the center of the room so clean when another suit-clad man greeted me.

He stood behind a massive marble counter situated in front of a long, well-lit hall of elevators. It didn't take a genius to conclude that the layout of the lobby was strategic, designed to ensure the privacy and safety of its residents. It was impossible for someone to walk in off the street and enter an elevator with Terminator One and Terminator Two standing guard.

"You must be Emma Marshall," a female voice sang.

Turning toward the sound, I was met by a striking woman. She stood outside of a large entrance to what I assumed—but had somehow overlooked earlier—was the dining room of Roisin's.

She had a figure with curves in all the right places, and curly red hair—with vivid lipstick to match. Her skin was fair, her eyes a brilliant shade of green. She wore a black button-down tucked into a coordinating pencil skirt and Louboutins. As she appraised me, her smile was genuine.

"I'm Shannon," she continued and I shook her hand.

"You own the building?" I asked, incredulous. Was it normal to meet the owner of a building upon entrance? Not in my experience. And she didn't look more than five years older than me.

"Oh, heavens, no! The name is a coincidence. I just run the restaurant." She pointed behind her at the dimly lit eatery. It looked classy in an understated way.

"I'm Emma." I winced, realizing she'd already said my name. How did she know? "I was hoping to drop off my résumé. I heard through the grapevine that you were hiring."

"Of course! Jackie told me you'd be stopping by." Her teeth were straight and as white as the marble accents around the room.

"Jackie?" I asked.

"Mr. O'Connell. The owner."

I put what she was saying together. "The Jack O'Connell who owns Emerald Gym?"

She nodded. I tried to picture the man from last night—it wasn't hard, seeing as I'd been fighting to rid my thoughts of him all day—with his sweats and stubble owning both a fancy restaurant on the UES and a rundown gym in the Financial District. I didn't see the connection.

"Mr. O'Connell owns this restaurant too?" I clarified.

"He and his brothers own the entire building." She handed me a sheet of paper. "Here's a list of our schedule. We run three overlapping shifts from open to close. Mr. O'Connell has informed me that you are a full-time student and attend lessons at the Emerald, so you can just let me know if you'll be arriving late or leaving early the day of."

"W-wait," I stammered. "I'm already hired?"

"Yes, of course!" She seemed shocked by my bewilderment. "A recommendation from Mr. O'Connell doesn't come often. In fact, I don't think he's ever sent us a waitress for hire. He likes to stick to his duties at the Emerald."

The surprises just kept coming. Not only did I have a job at a high-end establishment on the Upper East Side, but Jack—a man I'd met yesterday—hadn't been merely mentioning that the place was hiring. He knew for a fact they were because he owned it, as well as the entire building above.

To top it off, I would get to pick and choose shifts to suit my schedule. I even had permission from the manager to arrive late and leave early if and whenever I damn well pleased.

"...is minimum wage, but the tips are generous,"—she was still going on while my mind raced—"I'll have some uniforms sent over to your apartment by tomorrow. Jack already emailed me your contact information from the gym. I'm guessing a two?"

"Excuse me?" I asked, breathless. Things moved fast in the city, but this was a little wild.

"For the uniforms. Your dress size?"

A two. "Oh! Yes, thanks."

"And shoe?"

"A seven."

"Great!" She shook my hand again. "Unfortunately, I have to get back before our executive chef decapitates the sous, but it was a pleasure meeting you, Emma. If you have any questions, feel free to call me. I'll send over my card tomorrow with your clothes."

"Wait!" I yelled, seeing as she had already spun around on her red-soled heel and was heading toward the restaurant. "Is this normal?"

She turned to face me, an unreadable glint in her eye. "Like I said, Emma. Jack has never recommended someone for hire. You must be very special."

* * * *

It was the beginning of autumn, but the air was starting to bite at any and all exposed skin. As the sun made its way across the sky, the temperature took a nosedive. A few trees in Central Park were already turning color, the burnt orange and bloody red leaves contrasting against the cloudy backdrop.

After grabbing a much-needed hot coffee, I sat at a stone picnic table near the baseball fields, listening to the shouts from a nearby game. A few dogs with relaxed owners sniffed at my coat, hunting for food. I indulged in a quick pat on their heads, but remained focused on my laptop.

I had three papers due the following week, each on a different race of people from different periods in history. I chose to start on the easiest class first—Myth and Fact in American History. It was an essay on the glamorization of Native American burial grounds in Hollywood.

When I was halfway through my argument, a notification popped up in the right corner of my screen. Someone was calling me from a local number. Assuming it was one of the establishments where I'd dropped my résumé, I fished through my purse for my cell, prepared to let them know I'd found other work.

"Hello?" I answered.

"Emma," a familiar voice said, eliciting a zip of warmth down my spine. He hadn't phrased my name like a question, but it wasn't a statement either, more of a given. As if the call had been planned by both of us, but we'd only just remembered.

"Jack," I replied, sliding my laptop back into its case. "I mean…Mr. O'Connell?"

He chuckled, deep and raspy. I felt it in my knees, stumbling as I rose from the table and slung my bag over my shoulder.

"Jack is fine. Congratulations on the job."

"Thanks, but it wasn't much of a challenge." I bit my lip, stifling my own laugh. "You didn't tell me you owned the joint."

"With my brothers," he clarified. "It's a family business."

"Quite the family business." Tossing my empty cup in the recycling bin, I joined the queue forming at the West Sixty-First crosswalk.

"We make it work," he joked. I could hear men yelling and something hard being dropped in the background. He must've been at the gym. "I called to let you know I have an opening tomorrow if you don't have plans."

My calves ached at the thought of returning to the gym so soon. "I don't know if my body can handle exercise for a few days."

He hummed, the sound emerging from deep within his throat. "I'll go easy on you."

Jesus, why did everything he say sound sexual? And why was I flushed? I nearly ran face-first into a woman walking in the opposite direction. She flipped me off, so I didn't apologize.

"Okay," I squeaked, my airway dry. "What time should I swing by?"

More noise in the background. Based on the clapping, someone had just won a fight. A door clicked and I assumed Jack had stepped into another room to avoid the commotion.

"Does nine work for you? I have a meeting at noon in Harlem."

"Perfect."

As I walked the few blocks back to my apartment, I pulled my scarf over my nose to hide the smile stuck to my face.

Chapter Four

Emma

The next morning, I was riffling through my nightstand, searching for a hair tie, when my thumb brushed against a thin manila folder. The air caught in my chest, my eyelids shuttering. The contents of the envelope were long gone, but I could picture the anonymous note, clear as day.

You know what I did
Please know I'm sorry

Three weeks ago, I'd returned from grocery shopping to find a small package stuffed into my mailbox. My name was written on the envelope, but there was no return address or stamp.

When I got into my apartment, I'd opened it with trembling hands. As well as the ambiguous note, the contents had included a black-and-white photograph taken from a security camera. The image was too zoomed in to make much of, but I knew the woman in the photo well. The resemblance between Maria Ranucci and her son was so great that pain lanced my abdomen.

It took me a full five minutes to recover. Then I had noticed the blurry man standing behind Maria, his hand resting on her shoulder. She was looking back at him, fully aware of his presence. In the corner of the photo was a location and time stamp. It had been taken at the Booker Hotel in Little Italy two weeks before Maria was murdered.

A few hours later, I had been standing on the fifteenth floor of the same hotel, having deduced which room Maria and the mystery man were entering. I didn't know what I was expecting to find, but it didn't matter. Apart from the faint smell of cigarettes and a Bible beside the bed, room 1523 had been empty.

I'd left the photograph next to a bowl of mints on the weathered desk, anger brewing in my belly as I exited the hotel. When I'd reached the sidewalk, I had tossed the cryptic sticky note into a trash bin and never looked back. I didn't have the mental coping skills to take a trip down memory lane. For God's sake, I'd slept with socks on my hands for the first six months of my freshman year to prevent me from shredding my skin during the nightmares. It'd taken years to recover from my depression and I had no intention of returning to the black hole in my mind.

Whoever had sent the package must've been playing a sick joke, but it didn't change the fact that Maria's life had been taken too soon. The events that occurred after her murder still haunted me at night.

Icy skin, purple fingers, loose pills…

"Emma, let go!"

Now, I slammed the drawer shut, stuffing the manila folder into my gym bag before heading out of the door. By the time I made it downstairs and onto Columbus Avenue, I'd tossed the empty envelope into a dumpster, my reverie long forgotten. During the train ride downtown, I welcomed a new, tingling wave of anxiousness.

You're going to see him soon, I kept thinking. Then, almost right after, *Calm down, Emma.*

I hadn't had a crush in… Well, I'd never had a crush to be honest. With Nate—I still winced just thinking his name—everything had been so simple. I'd never been nervous or scared with him. There were two days in which I was alone until he came into the world. After that, I hadn't known anything different.

As I walked down the sidewalk, dodging the occasional passersby, I shook my head of the painful memories. Remembering how things had been with Nate made me feel terrible about being attracted to Jack.

Which, I begrudged, was the truth. I was attracted to him, as I imagined most women were. It was impossible not to be affected by his immaculate face, those enigmatic eyes and what I'd pictured multiple times to be a very chiseled body.

Once inside the Emerald's locker room, I forced myself to acknowledge the strange sexual tension that existed when we were close. The memory of it had my fingers slipping as I tugged a brand-new white sports bra over my head. I'd purchased it yesterday along with a pile of expensive and downright naughty athletic wear. The sales associate had picked everything out for me, greedy for a hefty commission.

I was painstakingly aware of what I was doing but didn't know how to stop myself. It'd been over three years since I'd had sex. Even then, it had always been so innocent and easy with Nate. Something told me sex with Jack would be far from innocent.

I didn't know if that was what I wanted. Or him, for that matter. I wasn't terrible looking, but I wasn't a supermodel either. There'd been one boy interested in me throughout my life and he was gone now.

Comparing sex with Nate to how I imagined it would be with Jack just made me feel more ashamed about my actions. I wished I'd brought a hoodie to cover my revealing ensemble, but I hadn't because I knew I'd chicken out. And I couldn't wear my overcoat to work out in.

"Man up, Em," I said to myself in the mirror, tucking a tendril of hair into my long braid. "You're a single, sexy twenty-one-year-old woman. You're allowed to be attracted to people."

I twisted my lips to the side, my pep talk falling on deaf ears.

On the walk from the lockers to the private room in back, a few gym members glanced in my direction but busied themselves before I could feel self-conscious. I assumed it was rare to have a woman in this gym, as I still seemed to be the only one. None of the lockers in the women's room were in use.

As I stretched in privacy, I wondered why they offered self-defense classes if women never came to the gym. Then I realized how sexist it was to assume just females needed self-defense and chastised myself for the next thirty seconds.

"Good morning, Emma," Jack said, entering the room. I straightened, the blood rushing from my head after touching my toes. "How are you today?"

"G-Great," I stammered. "I mean good…thanks. You?"

Control yourself, Em.

It was difficult to do. He looked even more mouthwatering than I remembered. Everything about the man screamed, "Out of your league!" Dressed in a gray thermal and joggers, he looked casual and cool.

"Never been better." His grin was crooked, eyes twinkling with mischief as he gave me a quick once-over. His expression spelled trouble for me. I turned my head to hide my flush.

Luckily, Jack didn't waste any time starting the lesson. We warmed up for fifteen minutes, stretched for five then began leverage work, as he called it.

"Right, so leverage is just using your opponent's weight against them," he explained in the voice that'd been ringing through my head since the night he'd walked me to the subway. "We'll cover how to get out of holds next class but for now, I want you to knock them down before they can even get that close to you."

As he talked, I tried to focus on what he said as opposed to the way his accent seemed to come in waves. There were times he sounded almost American, but his dulcet Irish tongue would return in the following sentence.

"…first, I want you to attack me."

"Wait, what?" I asked, looking from his mouth back to his eyes.

He smiled and spread his arms out wide, welcoming me. "Come on, darling. Give me your best shot."

My heart hammered at the thought of getting that close to him. "I'm not much of a fighter."

"Mmm," he wondered aloud, looking at me with curiosity. "You're a right little over-thinker, aren't you?"

My flush crept up again, but he was right. As usual, I was overthinking. I lived most of my life trapped within the confines of my skull. It was as useful as it was maddening.

With an intake of breath, I charged, reaching out an arm to grab onto him—I was imagining something along the lines of stealing his wallet—when he stepped to the side. There wasn't much I could do as he snaked my outstretched wrist and pulled it down behind him. My own momentum brought my belly onto the mat hard and fast.

"Jesus!" I flipped over, glaring at him.

Jack stood over me, a cocky grin stretched across his face. He offered a hand to help me up. "Now, normally, you wouldn't assist your opponent after the fact, but I think we'll make an exception in your case."

I took his hand, angry that he'd let me fall so hard. "Oh, ha-ha."

"There it is," he murmured, making sure I was steady on my feet before letting go and stepping back a few paces.

I rubbed my shoulder more to make a point than to relieve a sore muscle. "There what is?"

"That fire I've seen flickering in your eyes."

"I have no idea what you're talking about." Heat skittered across my skin. Was he flirting with me? I told myself no. Jack could have anyone he wanted. Models, actresses, et cetera. He was probably just one of those guys who couldn't talk to women without sounding flirtatious.

"I think there's more to you than meets the eye, Ivy League." He shrugged with confidence, as if he'd discovered my secret. "That's all."

"Well, trust me, there's no—ahhh!"

He came out of nowhere. One second, he was grinning. The next, he was all seriousness, running toward me faster than I could switch gears. He swung my body around like a sack of potatoes and planted me on my feet within seconds, pacing backward a few yards.

"What the *hell* was that?" I asked, my outrage growing.

"That was you doing a piss-poor job of using leverage." He knelt, straightening the tongue on his black high-tops "Some bloke off the street isn't going to tell you he's about to kidnap you before he does it."

"Oh, so I'm being kidnapped now, am I?"

He went from adjusting his shoe straight into a crouch before I could react. He charged again and I had a chance to step out of his way but no time to grab his arm and pull him down. He spun and picked me up from behind, his arms wrapped around my middle. He let me down achingly slow, my body sliding along his. I was hyperaware of how solid he was, his muscles tense as he held me to him. Time moved at a glacial pace, but he released me too soon. My lungs refused to work long after he let me go. The exposed skin between my sports bra and high-waisted leggings burned where his iron-like arms had just been.

"Plenty of time to shove you in the back of my van." As he made his way across the room, I noticed he was somewhat breathless. He watched me from his peripheral vision like an animal stalking its prey.

"Stop doing that!" I ordered, recovering my composure. I was getting tired of being tossed around, albeit kind of turned on. Lord, why was it turning me on? This class was nothing like what I'd expected. How many self-defense instructors harassed their students like this?

"Make me," he teased.

This time, I was ready. My anger—at both myself for lack of discipline and my teacher for lack of social boundaries—clarified things. He sprinted toward me. I stepped to the left, grabbed his arm and yanked it down as hard as I could. His powerful frame hit the mat with a loud *thud*.

"Finally!" I shouted, elated, fists above my head.

Without warning, I lost my footing and was lying on my back, spreadeagled on the mat. Jack had kicked my ankles out from underneath me.

"What was that for?" I fumed, trying to catch my breath. "I did it right!"

His face was suddenly inches from mine. "You forgot to run, dovey."

A warm, sweet maple syrup seeped into my skull. *Holy shit*. I couldn't think. I couldn't breathe. All I could do was stare.

Jack held himself off the ground six inches above me, his arms bent at either side of my shoulders. His legs rested between mine and a rhythmic thumping began somewhere in my lower belly. His green eyes appeared hooded and dark as he surveyed me from above, curiosity and something else—frustration?—fighting for the spotlight on his face.

At first, I was too shocked by his proximity to move. The heat from his body scattered my senses. The only thing that seemed to be working inside me was my heart, which beat so fast it was a mere vibration in my chest. The small amount of air between us was frigid and electrified at once. I felt a deep ache to close the gap.

Then, as his tongue trailed a line across his bottom lip, I lost control.

I launched my face into his, our mouths crashing into one another. Wrapping my arm around his neck, I dragged him closer until his statuesque form was pressed against mine. The electricity that had hung in the air between us now sizzled through my skin, seeping into my veins. Like powder to a flame, my entire being sparked to life, responding to him. I hooked my leg behind his thigh, pulling him to the place where I craved friction. My senses soared when he moved his hand to my hip.

Until I realized he was gently pushing me away.

"Oh my God!" I screamed, falling back to earth. "I'm so sorry!"

I jumped up from the floor quicker than I had landed, covering my impulsive mouth as I ran out of the room, leaving Jack kneeling on the ground, looking shocked and somewhat resigned. It was incredible my legs even worked.

What the hell is wrong with you?

If it were possible to die of humiliation, I wouldn't have been surprised to see a ghost in the dusty mirror of the locker room. I threw my coat on and grabbed my purse. There was no time to change. I had to get out of there—*now.* I needed to put at least sixty blocks between myself and Jack O'Connell. Hell, even that might not be enough. I wouldn't know for sure until I was in my apartment and under the covers, hiding from the world.

"Upper West Side, right?"

Exiting the Emerald, I spun around to find the source of my humiliation standing there looking as unaffected as ever. Jack held open the back door to an electric SUV, a sexy curl of chocolate hair dusting his forehead.

My mouth opened and closed a few times before I remembered my vocabulary. "I just… You want…" I took a deep breath and focused on my sneakers. It was easier to speak to him if I stared at something else. "I just attacked you."

Was he *laughing*? I refused to take a peek for verification, sure that the flush in my cheeks was hot enough to melt my skin.

"I think you're being a bit dramatic with your choice of words."

"I just attacked you and you want to give me a ride home? You should be filing charges or something." I glanced at him through a few strands of hair. He *was* laughing, a vein at his temple appearing with the effort. "At the very least I should be banned from your gym!"

He leaned on the door for support, unable to contain himself any longer.

"And I should also be fired from your restaurant."

He straightened, doing a terrible job at hiding his amusement. "Just get in the damn car, Emma."

I shuffled to the other side of the shiny Tesla, opening my own door. I didn't want to chance what would happen if I got near him again.

"I really am sorry," I whispered as the driver of the vehicle edged into traffic. Mortified, I kept my eyes on my hands, intertwining my fingers into knots on my lap.

"Hey." Jack lifted my chin with his thumb and forefinger, then dropped his hand. "Don't think on it. It's been a while since I got to kiss a lovely lady such as yourself. But I think, for our purposes, we should just stay friends."

I nodded, shocked by my luck. He wasn't firing me from his restaurant even though it was within his power to do so. He also wasn't canceling our lessons, although I didn't know whether I could show my face at the Emerald ever again.

Still, I couldn't help but be a little disappointed that he had no sexual interest in me. It was the first kiss I'd had in years and I couldn't imagine sticking my neck out like that again.

Well, you didn't exactly plan this one either.

I tried to ignore the visual of Jack declining my advance like I was a naughty child reaching for candy in a shop. Or, more accurately, an alien life form trying to invade his body. The emotions I felt toward him were foreign enough to be from another planet. Was it lust? I'd never experienced lust this powerful.

At the same time, I was relieved at having been rejected. I didn't feel guilty about finding him attractive now that I knew for sure the feelings weren't reciprocated. I could go back to my life as it had been—school, study, work and sleep somewhere in between.

"You're overthinking again," Jack admonished. When I looked up at him, it appeared as if he'd been analyzing my profile. Glancing out of the window, I noticed we were entering Midtown.

"Where are you from?" I asked, hoping to steer the subject away from me and my rambling inner monologue. *Just get through this car ride and you never have to see him again.* I already planned on bailing out of my last lesson. I would make up an excuse to my parents later. All that mattered was surviving in the here and now.

"Boston," he replied. Seeing the confusion on my face, he continued. "My dad and my brothers and me left Ireland when I was seven years old. Only moved to Manhattan four summers ago."

"What about your mom?"

Because I'd grown up in a little town like Stonerose, my childhood had been quaint but sheltered. That was, until all hell broke loose and I'd decided to move to the city, ditching my plans for Yale Law. Even so, I hadn't experienced as much of New York as I should—or any of it.

"We convinced Mum to stay behind in Ireland." He looked out of the window as a police cruiser blew by. "Our parents don't get along very well."

"I'm sorry." My mom and dad had rarely argued growing up, but Nate's parents had sometimes had it out. It had taken its toll on him at times.

After Maria's death was ruled a homicide, her husband was the primary suspect, even though he was the one who reported finding her body at the bottom of the stairs that fateful afternoon. However, Mark Ranucci had a solid alibi. He had been working at his chop shop in New Haven, then had stopped for a bottle of wine on the way home. Maria had been dead at least thirty minutes before Mark got there, according to the medical examiner's report.

The ME discovered something else whilst combing Maria's body for clues. Apart from her broken neck and fractured skull, there was semen in her vaginal canal, but it didn't belong to her husband. The DNA evidence led them to her killer.

"Well, that's the Irish for ye," Jack joked, his accent present in full. I snapped out of my rumination. "If there's two things we're good at, it's drinkin' and fightin'."

I smiled, looking down at my hands. *We've got to be above Fortieth by now,* I pleaded.

"What are you studying?" he asked, sounding sincere in his interest.

"I'm going for a major in history and a minor in archaeology."

"Why the interest in things that've already happened?"

"With history, there are no surprises because everything is in the past. There are so many times when humanity thought the world was at its end—the Crusades, plagues, atomic bombs—but we persisted. It's both a comfort and a privilege to learn about the events in an academic setting." I rubbed the cuff of my sleeve between two fingers, continuing my ramble. "I'm supposed to be studying law at Yale. That was always the dream."

Jack was enraptured while I talked, his lips parted. "Why aren't you at Yale, then?"

I shrugged, uncomfortable under the weight of his scrutiny. "I guess...my dreams changed when I did."

Stiff hands, frozen cheeks, purple veins...

"Emma, let go!"

I turned toward the window, hiding my flinch from Jack. Thankfully, he didn't belabor the topic.

"I was always shit in history growing up," he jested, lightening the conversation. "Well, if I'm being honest,

I wasn't quite good at school in general. It's a miracle I even graduated."

"I'm sure that's not true." I couldn't imagine a successful man like Jack not having had some sort of degree in business.

"I suppose I did all right in gym," he mused.

"So, what do you and your brothers do, then?"

"We buy and sell real estate, mostly. We dabble in trade. My older brother, Connor, has been pulling the strings since we left Boston. I prefer to be a silent partner."

Intriguing as Jack was, the familiar storefronts and buildings on my block came as a relief. I had to fight the urge to press myself against the door, antsy to get out of the vehicle. I couldn't wait to be free from his pity. *"We should just stay friends."* I shuddered. There was no way an affluent, sexy man like Jack O'Connell wanted to be friends with a little schoolgirl like me.

"You didn't have to take me home," I began, gripping the handle as the driver pulled to the curb outside my building. "But thank you."

Jack shrugged, eyeing my hand on the door. "I was heading to Harlem anyway."

"Oh." I stepped out onto the busy street. "Cool. Well, thanks again."

Before he had a chance to respond, or make it any more awkward, I shut the door and ran across the sidewalk, losing myself in the rotating glass of the lobby entrance.

I didn't feel safe until I was locked in my room and under the duvet with a pillow over my face.

You never have to go back. I would think of a way to get out of the arrangement with my parents. I'd find another instructor at a different gym if I had to. Hell, therapy might not be such a bad idea if I was launching myself onto nearby men.

You never have to see him again.

But that thought didn't make me feel any better. In fact, I felt remarkably worse.

Chapter Five

Jack

The meeting with the McKenzies had been torture to sit through. I couldn't stop replaying that moment with Emma. The way she'd latched herself onto me. How her lips had moved in tandem with mine, soft and supple but ravenous and consuming all at once. She tasted so sweet, like green apples and lavender. I still felt the pressure of her petite figure against my body. Her soft curves contrasted perfectly with my unforgiving frame.

Friends.

Lord, help me.

I couldn't be friends with Emma. Especially not after she'd given me her explicit opinion on the matter. She wanted more than someone like me could offer. Emma was a good, kind person—warm and innocent. She was the type of woman who expected something from men.

At the very least, she needed a gentleman who would stick around the next morning to pay for a cab.

I'd never been very caring. I was selfish and downright vicious at times. I would destroy her and hate myself for it, which was a surprising revelation. *I don't want to hurt her,* I'd remind myself every time my thoughts strayed into dark fantasies.

She was testing me, though. I'd give her that. A small voice in the back of my head cursed the woman who was challenging my self-control, whether she was aware of it or not. In a world that was constantly changing, I never allowed myself to be a variable. Too many people relied on my concentration and skillset. Sure, I was hot-headed, but I channeled my aggression into appropriate outlets. Emma was not going to be one of them.

If I couldn't be friends with her and I refused to be more, why was it so hard for me to let her go? She couldn't seem to get away from me fast enough this morning. Her entire body had been pressed up against the door like she'd planned to jump out of the car before the wheels came to a complete stop.

Fuck. Seeing her run had made me wince. It was the smartest thing she could do, but it didn't make it any easier to watch. I relished the thought of having her close, of keeping a protective eye on her. If I still felt the need, I could check on her at Roisin's from a safe distance. I wouldn't allow anything more than that.

I'd even called Mick on the way to Harlem, informing him that he needed to take over any future self-defense lessons. I didn't trust myself to be alone with her now that I knew she was open to my advance. When that hazy look had come over her, when she'd pulled my leg into the apex of her thighs, she had been begging me to fuck her.

"Jack, where the hell have you been today?"

Glancing up from my untouched dinner, I realized my eldest brother had been talking to me for quite some time. My younger brother, Kieran, watched me from his side of the table, a spoonful of stew held in the air as he waited for my response.

"Sorry, what?" I asked, wiping a hand over my forehead to clear my mind of Emma Marshall.

Connor narrowed his eyes in suspicion. We were seated in the private dining room at Roisin's, having just been served our meal. A waitress entered to deliver the bottle of wine Kieran had ordered.

"You've been drifting all day." Connor speared a piece of steak on his fork and shoved it into his mouth.

"Yeah, I think I may be coming down with something." I coughed, emphasizing the effect of my lie.

Kieran laughed, pouring himself a glass of red. "You haven't been sick since you were three years old with the pox."

"I'm not buying that excuse either, Jackie Boy," Connor added.

"Come off it, Kieran," I fumed, busying myself with my own food. "You were still growing in Mum when I was three years old."

"I bet I could still hear your bloody whining from inside the womb, though." My little brother chortled into his stew. Connor was trying to hold back his laughter as well, but they both knew better than to push me on the subject.

"So what did you think of the McKenzies' offer?" Connor asked a few minutes later on a more serious note.

I took a sip of wine, taking advantage of the pause it enforced to think back on our meeting with the McKenzies, which I'd struggled to pay attention to. "I think they're shite and I think their offer's shite as well."

"It's a lot of money," Kieran noted.

I glared at him, tightening my fist on the glass. "It's a lot of heat as well."

"We didn't have a problem moving the shipment from the Sweeneys," Connor pointed out.

"That was a different product." I turned my focus on him. "And it was two years ago. Things are heating up between the Murrays and the Nicolettis again."

"What does that have to do with us and the McKenzies?" Kieran asked.

"Heat for them means heat for us, *Willie,*" Connor teased.

In our family, the name Willie meant someone who was new to the crew—someone who still needed to be taught lessons. Most of the grunt work went to the Willies. From the hand gesture Kieran shoved at Connor, he didn't care for being referred to as such, nor should he.

"I don't understand why you took the meeting with them," I continued, getting us on track. "You know how I feel about it. I've been trying to get our name out of this trade since we left Boston."

"It would've been a snub not to take the meeting, Jack. You know that."

I sighed, leaning back in my chair. "I vote no. A hundred percent no."

"I agree," Kieran piggybacked.

Connor nodded, his face indifferent. If I didn't know him well, I wouldn't be able to discern whether he was disappointed. But he was being truthful. He'd taken the meeting with the McKenzies to keep the peace between our families. He didn't want anything more to do with the drug trade than I did, but deals like this always came down to a vote between us brothers.

"All right, then. I'll contact Peter tomorrow with our answer. Anything else we need to discuss?"

Kieran was silent, but a thought popped into my head as another waitress walked by, her heels clicking on the stained-wood floor.

"Do you think we could make their dresses longer?" I nodded toward the server, lost in thought as I pictured Emma. I didn't like the idea of her wearing anything as short as the rest of the waitresses at Roisin's.

At least, I didn't like the idea of anyone other than myself seeing her in it.

Chapter Six

Emma

After ample time spent wallowing in self-pity, I finished the essay on Native American burial grounds and made macaroni for dinner, which I ate out of the pot with a serving spoon. My parents called to check how my self-defense classes were going and I gave them half of a lie. It was boring—lie—but I was learning some useful things—truth. I was certainly discovering some new things about myself, like the little harlot that'd somehow snuck in and made herself known.

For the first time in a long while, I missed my parents. I hadn't been home since deciding to leave for college, but my family visited the city over major holidays. We were two hours apart, but the distance was refreshing enough to recover in peace. I feared returning to Stonerose would worsen my symptoms, even after all the progress I'd made. The one problem with shunning the town was that my family happened to be a part of it.

Mostly I missed my little sister, Ella. She was turning into a force to be reckoned with. Unlike me, she was an extrovert and made friends everywhere she went. She was head of the drama department and the newspaper at Stonerose High, not to mention student body president.

We spoke every so often. Since she was a teenager and born in the era of smartphones, it was over text. After I'd left home, Ella had been getting more and more into filmmaking. She'd always been a bit of a shutterbug, annoying the hell out of me by taking candid photos. She had albums of me stuffing my face with food, looking a wreck while sleeping and even biting my nails while I studied, a habit I'd gotten over in high school, thank God.

After speaking with my parents, I opened the package from Shannon at Roisin's, which took some time to sort through. She'd sent over five exorbitant little black dresses. They were all similar in length, but the styles and materials varied. She included three pairs of black Louboutin heels and, as promised, a sleek business card with her phone number scribbled on the back. I tried on an off-the-shoulder number with a pair of matching shoes to make sure they fit. The dress was a perfect size, albeit a tad shorter in the leg than anything I owned.

With Ella already at the forefront of my mind, I snapped a photo in my floor-length mirror, my hair an absolute mess but my outfit pristine. I captioned it *"New job, who dis?"*

Her response was immediate.

Omg, luv the dress! R u leaving ur hovel?

A second message swooped in directly after the first.

Btw, random question. What was the core meaning of Ellison's Invisible Man*?*

I rolled my eyes, checking the time on my watch. My parents had mentioned Ella was taking an AP Literature practice test. She was about thirty minutes in and, given her messages had popped up green, her Wi-Fi was offline. She couldn't use the internet.

Really, El? Cheating on a practice exam?

Her reply was a challenge.

Really, Em? Not helping me cheat on a practice exam?

Like my father, I was a stickler for academic integrity. Still, I had a soft spot for my little sister. When I thought of her, guilt entered my heart. I had wanted to apologize for that night on multiple occasions but just couldn't find the words. Now that I was outside the events, I realized I hadn't thought about the effects my actions, or lack thereof, might've had on Ella. I stared at my sister's question, then caved, giving her the answer.

She thanked me, then made a joke to lighten the mood.

Sounds like a good book. Might even read it.

From the moment I was born, I'd shared a playpen with Nate. We spent so much time together, the citizens of Stonerose referred to us as "the twins," but Ella was my true sister. Despite that fact, we couldn't be more different if we tried. Introvert, extrovert. Bookworm, social butterfly. Brunette, blonde. Ella hid her intelligence behind a façade of ignorance, but she was more cunning than she let people believe.

Chuckling to myself, I plugged my phone into the charger, then climbed on my bed, armed with my laptop. If designer dresses and $3,000 shoes were considered a normal uniform for Roisin's, my waitressing skills needed to be sharp. I researched the establishment online and studied the sophisticated menu, which was a mixture of traditional Irish foods and upscale American dishes. The prices weren't listed. I didn't want to know what the average dinner would cost someone like me. My parents were considered wealthy in Connecticut, but this clientele had to be in a different stratosphere.

At the bottom of the menu, I followed a link to a webpage for the Shannon, which boasted luxury apartment living within a five-minute walk from Central Park. The building was ten years old but had been purchased by its current owner five years prior. Although the name wasn't listed, I assumed it was referring to the O'Connells.

Around nine o'clock, a blip in the corner of the screen alerted me that I had a new email. I didn't recognize the name, but the website tag caught my eye.

Emma Marshall,

My name is Mick. I'm the manager at Emerald Gym. I will be taking over your self-defense lessons, as Mr. O'Connell has been called out of town on business. Just let me know when you want to come in next. Any time works.

Mickey Kelley
Emerald Gym
Financial District

Even though I was disappointed I would never see Jack again—except maybe in passing at Roisin's—I was relieved that I wouldn't have a reminder of my shame and blatant rejection face-to-face. On top of that, I still hadn't come up with a solid excuse for my parents. Arguing with Gregory Marshall, top of his class at Yale Law, was next to impossible. But if push came to shove, I was probably the one person on the East Coast who stood a fighting chance.

Already invested in my internet stalking, I visited the Emerald's website. It was simple, just one page with no scroll bar. The menu didn't even offer a list of classes. How had my dad found this place?

There was a roster of employees, but Jack wasn't included amongst the headshots of thick, muscle-bound men. I clicked on a photo of Mickey Kelly, a short, brutish man with light eyes and a scowl. His bio was packed—twenty-six years old, Army veteran, trained in seven different fighting techniques. Suffice it to say, I was overwhelmed, but he couldn't be more intimidating than his boss.

I shot a quick reply to this Mickey character to set up a time for Thursday, which was one of my lightest lecture days, then sent a text to Shannon to ask about working a few shifts the following weekend.

Ava came home after I'd finished the dishes. I was sitting on the red IKEA couch in our living room reading a novel about Attila the Hun, but figured it was a respectable time to hit the hay.

"Long day?" I asked, shutting the book as I stood to stretch. My muscles were still tight from falling on the mat.

Ava paused before hanging her keys on the rack. Her eyes widened as she shrugged out of her long puffer jacket, but she smiled. For being roommates, we weren't very talkative. We'd both grown up in Stonerose, but had run in different circles.

"To say the least," she joked.

I had no idea what the average day at Juilliard entailed. I was assuming a lot of exercise and memorizing choreography. We'd been in the same ballet classes as kids, but Ava had surpassed the rest of us within a year. Her parents had started driving her to New Haven for a more rigorous program by the age of eight.

"How's Columbia?" Ava asked, standing awkwardly by the door.

"Good," I answered, my voice light.

"Cool."

I sucked at my bottom lip, feeling just as uncomfortable as she looked. Ava folded her hands together and twitched her feet, like she couldn't keep them still after moving them all day.

"Well, good night," I said right as Ava opened her mouth. "Oh, sorry…"

"That's just what I was about to say." She chuckled, tucking a thick strand of hair behind her ear, her dark skin glowing in the dim lamplight. "Good night, Em."

"Yup," I muttered, retreating into my bedroom. Wow, I needed to work on my small talk. At least I'd bridged the gap, although it had taken me two years to do so.

After kicking off my jeans, I set my reading glasses on the side table and crawled into the safety of my bed. Pale yellow sheets and a paisley quilt enveloped me as I drifted into sleep. I didn't have any nightmares, but I did dream of Jack O'Connell. I dreamed things I had no right to dream and, when the sun woke me up the next day, my skin was flushed and my inner thighs were throbbing.

* * * *

I went to three more self-defense classes before my parents let me call it quits. Although my lessons with Jack had been interesting, I learned more with Mick because I was able to focus. I felt comfortable knowing I could somewhat defend myself on the streets of Manhattan if need be. I hated to admit it, but my parents were right to encourage me in the first place.

Mick turned out to be less imposing in person than the Emerald's website had led me to believe. He smiled when we met, shaking my hand in his firm grip. As he guided me through the lesson, his periwinkle eyes put me at ease. He was much more professional than his boss. For instance, he didn't pick me up and slide my body sensually down the length of his torso.

During my final class, he taught me how to escape a chokehold. Mick held me from behind, his forearm over my windpipe. Reminded of the attack in Hell's Kitchen, my panic rose. It took me a few tries, but I managed to break the hold. That night, however, I went home and dreamed of the attack for the first time in weeks. On this occasion, I remembered the blur of a tattoo on my assaulter's arm. It was intricate and dark, with thick lines crossing the back of his hand. Every time I got a clear picture in my head, it slipped away again. When I awoke, I had the vague recollection of a skull imprinted on the backs of my eyelids.

My schedule at Roisin's was becoming routine. The staff were welcoming, which wasn't customary in my experiences with both NYC and food service in general. The servers at my previous job had been cliquey, but the environment at Roisin's was almost familial. The award-winning chef explained the ins and outs of dishes to me so I could better present them to guests. The waitresses—all female and, of course, sexy as sin—helped each other if it got busy, which it did most nights. The place was popular—tables were booked months in advance.

We were paid minimum wage, but the tips were incredible, as Shannon said they would be. In fact, the lowest I'd been tipped on a bill so far was thirty percent.

That wasn't the only bonus.

When my first shift ended and I threw on a coat to leave, a waitress named Anna linked arms with me on the curb outside, pointing to a dark SUV parked a few feet away.

"That's us," she said, walking toward the vehicle.

Apparently, waitresses were required to use a chauffeur service provided by the O'Connell family to get home after each shift. Anna told me it was in response to a waitress being harassed a couple of years ago by a guest who'd been removed from the premises. The kitchen and support staff were offered the service to use whenever they liked, but we servers were required unless we left a shift early and it was light out.

Over the course of my employment, I noticed that just a few waitresses were ever assigned to serve the private room, which I'd seen the inside of once. Shannon had given me a tour of the restaurant before my first shift, mentioning the room toward the back. She said it was reserved for people who wanted to pay extra for privacy. Besides the door connecting the exclusive room to the dining area, there was another one on the other side that went straight through to the kitchen. Just when I was about to ask Shannon why there were locks on the insides of both doors, she hurried me into the hallway to continue the tour.

Still, my curiosity got the best of me. Instead of pestering Shannon, I checked the reservation book and kept an eye on the door to the private room in the hopes of catching a glimpse of what sort of clientele required such confidential dining. Even though the room was never booked for reservations, I didn't see anyone but Anna enter, apart from Shannon herself.

By my fourth weekend at Roisin's, I ceased being nosy and kept to myself, which was hard when my coworkers were so sociable. Shannon, in particular, had taken a liking to me, which I found exciting. I hadn't made any friends since moving to the city. Those I had back home had all drifted away after the incident. Shannon was the only other person in the world I could consider a new friend. Although she was my boss and we never saw each other outside of the restaurant, I thought she considered me one as well.

During the week, it was difficult to come up for air in between classes and essays and skimming through notes. I was studying so many different eras in history that I forgot to pay attention to my own. I recorded and downloaded lectures onto my phone so I could relisten while I ran errands, afraid to let even an hour pass without studying. I started to get up early and jog around Central Park before my first class of the day, which was something I'd never dreamed I would do. But with my nightmares mostly gone and my appetite revitalized, I had excess energy that I could harness toward a greater personal good.

On a laidback mid-October night at Roisin's, I was in the employee break room scrolling through a few notes on my phone about bridal ceremonies in Ancient Rome. I had an exam coming up and was trying to solidify some facts that kept slipping from my mind.

"Hey." Shannon surprised me, rounding a corner in high heels and a lovely Gucci dress. She was grinning and looked impeccable, if not a little excited.

"Sorry," I stammered, slipping my phone into my locker. "I have that group of seven that's in no hurry to leave, so I ran back to cram."

"Oh, don't worry about it. School is more important anyway." She waved her hand dismissively. "I have to do an emergency order for a supplier. I was wondering if you could take the drinks to the private table for me. They've already eaten."

I straightened, intrigued at the mention of the exclusive room. "Sure. Am I allowed?"

"You are if I say so." She winked, sashaying out of the employee lounge. "Drinks are ready behind the bar!"

Ancient bridal ceremonies flew from my mind. I skipped to the bar, thrilled that Shannon trusted me enough to serve whatever stuffy Wall Street execs who had undoubtedly booked the room for the night. There were quite a few waitresses working this evening who had been around longer than me. She could've chosen any one of them.

Balancing the tray of drinks in one hand—it was much easier to do here than at a nightclub—I backed into the room, knowing that with higher-paying clientele, seamless service was expected.

"—should move in on pier twelve soon," a man with a thick Irish accent was saying.

"I think we should give it another week," a familiar voice argued. "I know the bastards will come down."

The room was occupied by three young men and a fourth older gentleman. They had half-empty plates in front of them and appeared to be in the middle of a business meeting. The older gentleman wore a three-piece suit, while two of the younger men were at home with their ties loosened and the sleeves of their button-downs pushed to their elbows. The fourth man, who had been the last to talk, was wearing fitted black jeans, a white T-shirt and a denim jacket. He balanced casually on the back legs of his chair and had just finished draining his pint when he glanced up at me.

His chair came down with a loud thud, but Jack O'Connell didn't take his emerald eyes from mine.

A moment passed before the others caught on to Jack's silence and looked in my direction as well. I couldn't seem to peel my gaze from his. The way he looked at me was both surprise and something else entirely. Whatever it was, our second and last meeting replayed in my head. I had been trying to forget it over the past month. I'd almost convinced myself that our kiss was a mere figment of my imagination...until now.

I flushed and cleared my throat, continuing my work.

The other men at the table—two of which must've been related to Jack in some way based on their resemblance—smiled and thanked me as I set their next round of pints in front of them. Jack's thermal stare followed my movements as I circled the table, placing his drink down last. Thankfully, my hand didn't shake.

A part of me had been hoping to see Jack again, but now I couldn't get away fast enough. Avoiding Jack's gaze, I checked with the other members of the party to see if there was anything else I could get them.

"Are you Emma?" the man sitting farthest away asked. He was maybe a couple years older than me and smiled as if someone had just told a joke.

My cheeks burned with the fire of a thousand suns. Had Jack told these men—perhaps his family—about our awkward encounter? Had he told them that I was crazy and desperate? Because that was how the story would sound. In fact, that was how I'd felt for two full weeks before I'd decided to save my last shred of dignity by blocking it from my memory.

Now, I could now kiss that shred goodbye.

"Um, yeah," I muttered before making a swift exit.

After dropping the tray on the bar, I was heading toward the bathroom to splash water on the back of my neck when Jack stopped me in my tracks. He must've appeared from thin air because I hadn't heard him follow me.

"Emma," he stated, matter-of-fact. Even though I felt humiliated, the sound of my name coming from his decadent lips made my stomach flutter. I recalled exactly how those lips felt against my own.

"Mr. O'Connell." I chose to look at his suede Chelsea boots rather than his face.

"Call me Jack," he muttered, but it sounded more like a command. "How have you been?"

"Fine," I replied shortly, then felt bad about coming off as rude. Silent partner or not, he was still my boss. Worse, he was my boss's boss. "And you?"

He sighed, but I didn't look up. "I'm fine as well, thank you."

He was silent for a while and I continued to study his shoes, which were a mere foot from mine. I interlocked my hands behind my back, ignoring the crackle of electricity in the air between us. How was it that, after what happened last time, I still had to fight the urge to jump him? Why were images of us naked and intertwined flashing across my mind? Had I not done enough damage to my self-esteem?

"Well, I've got tables, so…" I trailed off.

Jack gently grabbed my wrist, preventing my escape. His strong fingers sent a strange, welcome jolt through my body.

"My brothers only know you by name." He kept his grip on my wrist. Could he feel my rapid pulse there? "I told them there was a waitress here that took self-defense at my gym. They made fun of me because women aren't known to frequent the Emerald. Besides Shannon, of course."

That had me confused. I looked up into his brilliant eyes. God, his face was even sexier than I'd remembered. I bit the inside of my cheek, the same way one would pinch themselves to check if they were dreaming. "Shannon? My boss?"

He smiled and I swore my heart skipped a few beats. "Shannon's my sister-in-law. She occasionally comes to the Emerald to harass me about something or other."

It made sense that Shannon was married to someone as affluent and handsome as an O'Connell. After all, she was a breathtaking businesswoman and her name was on the outside of the building.

"Oh," was all I could say in response. His hypnotic gaze roamed my face as if trying to commit it to memory, but I knew that couldn't be true. Was my mascara smeared or something? "Well, it was good to see you, Mr. O'Connell. Glad to know you've made it back from your business trip."

He seemed bewildered, but I chose to end the conversation on a solid note for an employer-employee relationship. When I turned a second time, my wrist slid from his grasp, his fingers leaving a trace of heat across my skin as I made my way to the dining room.

* * * *

Jack

I found Shannon sitting behind the marble desk in her office. She had a laptop out in front of her, but the screen was off. When I walked in, she began rummaging through a drawer in an unconvincing attempt to appear busy.

"That little stunt had your name written all over it," I grumbled, trying to sound menacing. I plopped down in the leather chair across from her, leaning back to marvel at the modern painting hanging on the wall. It was impossible for me to be upset with Shannon for very long, but she had the uncanny ability to get right under my skin.

"What little stunt?" she asked, her green eyes wide and lips pouted. "I was just filing paperwork in here."

"Uh-huh." I stretched my legs out, crossing one ankle over the other to show I wouldn't be leaving any time soon.

Her face brightened. She was a good actress, but I'd known her too long. Connor had started dating her in high school and hadn't let her out of his sight since.

"Oh, you mean the waitress?" She smiled conspiratorially. "Was there something about her you didn't like?"

I groaned, putting my elbows on my knees. "Those aren't the words I would use."

She clapped her hands in victory. "I knew it!"

"Do you mind keeping it down?" I glanced toward the hallway, but Shannon's office was far removed from the kitchen. Besides, with the chef spewing expletives and pans being dropped, no one would overhear.

"Jackie Boy, are you *smitten*?" she teased, putting her heels on the desk and twirling a lock of fiery hair.

I cringed at the audacity. "When have you ever used 'smitten' to describe my relationship with women?"

"I've never known you to be in a relationship long enough to comment on it."

I cast her a dark look. "I am not…smitten."

She rolled her eyes. "You've been doing a good job hiding it, I'll give you that. But over the past month you've been in the restaurant twice as much as usual and every time you *are* here, it's during Emma's shifts. How very convenient for you."

I dropped my head into my hands, pinching the bridge of my nose. If Shannon had noticed, had anyone else? I'd been trying my hardest to keep away from the girl, but something kept pulling me in. The longer I went without catching a glimpse of her, the more space she inhabited in my head. It was borderline obsessive.

"Don't worry. No one's noticed," Shannon continued, reading my mind. "And Emma hasn't seen you. How could she? You move like a ghost and stay tucked in the shadows, you creep."

"I'm not a creep." I was. That was exactly what anyone would call me. I needed another drink. Or a swift punch to the gut.

Shannon sighed in exasperation, setting her elbows on the desk. "Just go ask her out!"

I winced. "No."

"I don't understand you."

"She's not my type," I argued.

"Clearly. She's sweet and has more than one brain cell."

"I'm not talking about this." I stood to leave. I'd had enough of Shannon poking around my private life. I didn't even like admitting to myself that stalking Emma Marshall was part of my private life.

"You're scared." Her voice was quiet, as if she were speaking to herself, but her gaze dug into my back.

I turned to face her, wanting to put an end to this subject. "I'm not scared. I'm being honest. You're right. She is attractive. But she's not like the other women I've been with and I don't want to treat her like she is. So, I've decided to ignore it. It's better for her."

Shannon processed my words, then opened her mouth to say something, but I cut her off.

"End of story."

She sighed and whirled past me toward the kitchen, flicking her hair in my face for good measure.

Chapter Seven

Emma

Running into Jack at Roisin's solidified the fact that there was nothing between us, not that I hadn't gotten the memo when he'd rejected me at the Emerald. But the awkwardness in our most recent encounter made it all the easier to wipe my mind of Jack O'Connell. Yes, I hadn't been attracted to a man since my high school boyfriend. Yes, it was long overdue for me to move on with my life. But no, Jack was not the man for me.

Keeping that in mind, I went to class the following day with my head held high and a brighter disposition. I'd been making enough money at the restaurant to purchase clothing that fit my smaller frame. I was eating better and my new exercise regimen was making a significant impact on my mood.

After a pop quiz in my last lecture, I was in desperate need of caffeine. I grabbed an iced latte and a slice of pizza from a takeout near campus—satisfying the requirements for my major food groups—before heading home to get ready for my shift.

It was the last Friday night in October and Roisin's was buzzing. I had seven tables to myself at any given moment from the minute I clocked in, taking over for an exhausted Anna. Thankfully, I'd grown accustomed to jogging in five-inch heels during my employment because tonight felt like a marathon. My sole communication with the other waitresses was the occasional frustrated sigh or surreptitious eye roll. Just before ten o'clock, I was pulled aside while walking past the private room.

"It's time for a night out, I think."

Shannon was dressed in a long-sleeved white crop top and high-heeled boots that disappeared beneath a leather miniskirt. In that outfit, coupled with her curves, she looked to die for.

"I'm sorry?" I asked.

"You're going out with me tonight whether you like it or not." She flipped her long red hair over her shoulder, leaning back to perch on the edge of the dining table.

"It's packed," I replied. Coming from a manager, her request was insane. "I have, like, a dozen tables."

"That's an overstatement." She rolled her eyes, approaching me with a wry smile. "Besides, Shay came in unexpectedly and I already assigned her your section."

I floundered, looking for another excuse. "I have a test to study for."

"It's *Friday*," she sang, holding my shoulders in each of her hands. She gave them a reassuring squeeze. "And you study too much as it is."

"I don't have anything to wear." I didn't know what a night out with Shannon looked like, but I was guessing my black collared dress and Louboutins, designer or not, wouldn't fit in where we were going.

She winked. "Already taken care of."

* * * *

Thirty minutes later, a pair of Terminator men were driving us south through the streets of Manhattan, muttering into their earpieces. The lights of the city blurred past the window as I tugged at the hem of my see-through chemise blouse, failing in my attempt to tuck it into the waistband of a dark pair of skintight leather pants. Leather *pants,* for Christ's sake. Were we auditioning for a punk rock band?

I didn't know how or where Shannon had acquired clothes that seemed to fit me perfectly, but I was beginning to regret going out with her. I knew I should be more open to a social life—which, at my age, included partying—but I'd been up since five and my bed was calling my name.

"Where are we going?" I asked Shannon. She was sitting across the middle seat from me, looking down at her phone with a smile. I wondered who she was texting, then recalled she was married to one of Jack's brothers.

She glanced up, the glow from her smartphone casting a blue light over her exquisite bone structure. "Soho."

I was hoping for more of an answer than that, but the driver had just pulled to the curb in front of a modest high-rise. Shannon hopped out of the vehicle before the man in the passenger seat could open her door. Instead, he held it ajar for me as I scrambled after her onto the sidewalk.

"She's here," the man barked into the wire hanging from his ear, standing very close to us.

A few seconds later, a metal door along the building's façade opened and we were ushered inside. When it shut behind us, we were left in near pitch-black. Shannon grabbed my hand and led me across the floor of an empty warehouse, our footsteps echoing ominously.

"Through here," she encouraged, cracking open another door just enough to let us both through.

The white light was blinding. I barely had time to blink as we weaved through a massive group of people. Stage lights were suspended from the rafters in the center of a large room. Everyone faced the same direction, hollering at something in front of them.

A tall man with thick blond hair tied into a bun guided us through the crowd, which split once they took notice of us. We were deposited at the bottom of what I assumed to be a stage. My eyes were still adjusting, and my ears were ringing with the sound of at least fifty people yelling at once.

"Kieran!" Shannon squealed, releasing my hand to hug a familiar young man. He had light brown hair and red stubble, icy blue eyes and a youthful expression. He returned Shannon's embrace, holding his bottle of beer off to the side and smiling in my direction.

"Emma, Kieran. Kieran, Emma," Shannon introduced us and I realized where I knew him from.

He was wearing distressed jeans, a black hoodie, matching boots and had a large diamond in his earlobe, but he had to be one of the men I'd seen in the private room at Roisin's. The one that had asked if my name was Emma. Which, I reminded myself, meant he was most likely Jack O'Connell's brother. Although Kieran was younger and much less built, I recognized the subtle similarities. He was striking but in a luminous way. Nothing like his intimidating older brother.

Part of me wished Jack was here so that I could catch a glimpse of him, but a much larger, self-preserving part wished harder that he wasn't.

Kieran reached out his hand and I shook it, hiding my nerves with a smile. I was feeling a little shell-shocked going from almost no social contact with the outside world to whatever this was.

"I've heard about you," Kieran said, leaning forward so I could hear him over the rabble. The warmth drained from my cheeks. Jack said he hadn't told his brothers about my stolen kiss. "You work with Shannon at Roisin's, right?"

I smothered a sigh of relief. "Yeah, that's me."

He grinned, wrapping his arm around Shannon in a brotherly way that indicated she must not be married to this family member. By process of elimination, she and the eldest were shacked up.

"Shannon has been bossing us around since I was nine," Kieran went on, making Shannon roll her eyes. "I bet she gives everyone at work hell."

"She's great," I answered. The noise had died down and I no longer had to shout to be heard.

"See?" Shannon shoved Kieran playfully. "I do my job well."

"Is your husband coming?" I asked, aiming to steer the conversation to family and, in particular, the one O'Connell brother I both hoped and dreaded was here.

Shannon shook her head, pouting. "He's in Boston for the weekend. Terrible timing too. Jack rarely fights these days."

My heart performed acrobatics at the mention of his name, but the context confused me. "Fights? I don't understand."

Shannon nudged her chin to my right. I followed her gaze, realizing what I thought had been a stage was actually an elevated octagon ring. The surrounding audience was loud and energetic as they exchanged wads of cash back and forth. The rubber surface of the ring was covered in sweat stains and—*No, surely not*—blood. The chain-link fence enclosing it looked like it had seen better days.

At either side of the octagon, two men hopped on their feet. They were around the same build, wearing nothing but faded jeans and wrappings over their knuckles.

One of the men was Jack O'Connell.

Before I had time to process what was happening, a third man in the ring—a man I recognized as Mickey from the Emerald—yelled something and stepped out of the way. Jack and the other fighter went at each other, exchanging blows so fast I had to shake my head to keep up.

"It's a boxing match?" I asked. This didn't look anything like a boxing match.

"More like MMA," Shannon replied.

"With fewer rules," Kieran added, then shouted words of encouragement to his brother, who was too preoccupied to hear.

Jack and the other fighter were well matched. For every hit Jack took, he returned a blow in the same vicinity on his opponent's body. I couldn't tell who the crowd was rooting for more. Like the fight itself, they seemed to be split.

Despite the violence unfolding before my eyes, I couldn't help but admire Jack's physique. I'd imagined him without a shirt more times than I cared to admit, but my mind couldn't comprehend just how fit he was. I'd never seen anyone like him, except maybe in a Calvin Klein ad. There wasn't a lick of fat on him, just hard, unforgiving sheets of muscle that bulged and stretched with each blow. The balls of his feet danced over the mat, heels never touching the ground.

Jack was incredibly focused. If I squinted, I could see his line of sight shifting. He analyzed his opponent's every micromovement. Every flick of a finger, every twitch of a muscle, Jack's gaze darted to it, ready to react.

The fight had been carrying on for what felt like ages, but he wasn't laboring at all. His powerful frame was covered in perspiration, but his breathing remained controlled. Each time he dodged his opponent's attacks, a glint appeared in his eye like he was trying to hide a smile.

Then, so fast I almost missed it, his opponent launched a left hook to the side of Jack's face. It was the first time the other fighter had landed a blow above the neck. I covered my gaping mouth with my hands. Miraculously, Jack didn't go down.

"Don't worry," Shannon spoke close to my ear. "He let him have that one."

"Jack is a showman," Kieran added. I tore my gaze away from the fight just long enough to see him roll his eyes at his brother. "Such a flair for the dramatic."

According to them, Jack had allowed his opponent to almost break his face. I didn't understand why anyone would let themselves get injured.

I watched in disbelief as he ended the fight. His opponent had gotten cocky and wasn't guarding himself. Jack jabbed with such precision that his arm was just a blur. The other man dropped to the mat, limbs loose at his sides, eyes rolling once into the back of his head. He was out cold.

"TKO!" Mick yelled. I gnawed on my lip as he bent down to examine the man on the ground. His right arm was twitching reflexively, like he thought he was still fighting.

Jack held his fist in the air for a few seconds, a thick line of blood trickling down the side of his face. The majority of the crowd went wild. Money was exchanged and a few people argued over bets. Jack dropped his arm and walked through a chained gate at the opposite end of the octagon. He was engulfed by the mass of people as they laughed, slapping him on the back.

"Afterparty upstairs." Shannon was leading me again, but I wasn't paying attention. I was still trying to process all that I'd just witnessed.

Jack was some sort of underground street fighter. Shannon said he didn't fight much anymore, but he hadn't lost his skill. I knew next to nothing about fighting but from the ease of his takedown, it seemed Jack had been capable of a knockout from the moment the bout began. So, the whole thing had been for show on his part, like Kieran said?

The three of us huddled into an elevator, Shannon and Kieran chatting animatedly. I was lost in thought, recalling the cash exchange. Illegal gambling. Was that how Jack made all his money? But that didn't make sense. Maybe he could earn enough from fighting to fund his gym, but there was no way he could buy a skyscraper on the UES with it. He was a legitimate businessman, along with his brothers. The fighting must be something he did for fun on the side. It *did* look like Jack was enjoying himself.

The elevator bell dinged, announcing the twelfth floor and jerking me from my rumination.

"Afterparty?" I asked.

Shannon squeezed my hand in reassurance. "Family and friends only, don't worry."

Did I fit into that group? I cringed, recalling what Jack had said in the SUV before dropping me at home. The word *friend* had tasted acidic on my tongue. I got a feeling Jack didn't have a lot of female friends and he'd made it clear I wasn't going to fall into any other category.

That was when I realized I'd been overlooking another O'Connell standing right next to me. Shannon might be my boss, but she thought of me as a friend as well. The feeling was mutual. As her friend, I had every right to be here.

"Time to show Ivy League how the O'Connells party!" Kieran roared once the elevator doors slid open.

On cue, the bones in my skull started rattling from the vibrations of a rap song. The lights on this floor were muted and more forgiving than the warehouse below, but they were bright enough that I could see clear across the room.

It was a massive loft, at least four times bigger than my apartment. Like the Shannon, it was decorated in an understated way. There was an exposed copper ventilation system in place of a solid ceiling and a quintessential Manhattan brick wall. Leather couches were scattered around, a fully equipped stainless-steel kitchen glistened to my right and a massive entertainment system took up a portion of the living area. The wall opposite the elevator was made of thick glass. Two huge doors were propped open, allowing guests to flow through to the adjoining balcony. The outdoor area was filled with half a dozen wooden tables and sleek lounge chairs. Heated lampposts glowed red against the dark night sky and fairy lights drooped from one end to the other.

I didn't have time to ask Shannon who owned the place—although I could take a wild guess at their last name—before the music was drowned out by loud chanting. Kieran joined in. Parties were clearly his element. I followed his gaze, my mouth falling open.

"Emerald Devil! Emerald Devil!" the crowd boomed.

Jack O'Connell stood on a sturdy, weathered dining table in the center of the room. He'd been cleaned up from the fight but still wore blood-stained jeans and nothing else. His rippled abdomen glistened with sweat. He held a bottle of amber liquid in his lips. He had titled his head, draining what appeared to be the last of the bottle. When the decanter was empty, he threw it clear across the loft and glass shattered against the brick wall. The horde of a few dozen erupted, dragging Jack—who was grinning ear to ear—down from the table and, once again, engulfing him before my eyes.

"Jesus," I whispered.

"Oh, the many faces of Jackie Boy." Shannon shook her head in dismay, but there was a smile along her painted lips. "You need a drink."

Shannon grabbed my hand and led me to the kitchen, mixing and pouring something into two martini glasses. When she handed whatever it was to me, I didn't ask questions. It was gone in two gulps.

She raised her eyebrows, taking my glass and refilling it with her concoction. I still didn't know what was in it. I hadn't tasted a drop.

"The O'Connells are a bit rowdy," she explained, grinning at me in a knowing way. Kieran had said that Shannon had been bossing him around since age nine, so she was used to this.

I, on the other hand—being from a town with a population roughly larger than that of my apartment building—was not. I'd spent the first two years at Columbia living one rung higher than a recluse. I wasn't sure if I wanted that to change. Yet here I was.

"Rowdy is an understatement," I half-joked, my voice returning to my body. "If I drank that much, I'd be hospitalized."

I made a conscious effort not to search the room for Jack. Even now, I was on edge just knowing we were in the same vicinity. *Chill, Em.*

"He doesn't know you're here yet." Shannon snickered. When I froze, eyes widening, she tapped her French-manicured finger against the side of her head.

Okay, so she knew I had a tiny crush on her brother-in-law. Shannon seemed like a girl who could keep a secret.

"I think I'd like to keep it that way." I took another gulp of my drink, the alcohol starting to calm my nerves. *You're here with Shannon,* I reminded myself. *You didn't come to see him. You didn't even know he'd be here.*

She stepped closer, squeezed my hand and whispered in my ear, "Too late." She was looking over my shoulder, smiling wickedly at someone behind me.

If I were being honest, I could sense him a few seconds before she confirmed his presence. That strange, tether-like pull between us strengthened. I drained my glass, set it on the counter and steeled myself before turning around.

His dark hair—much darker than his brother's—was a mess from so many people congratulating him on the knockout. He'd thrown on boots and a black T-shirt, but it didn't help now that I'd seen what he looked like underneath. The inch-long cut above his right eyebrow was no longer bleeding.

I readied myself for his piercing gaze, but he wasn't looking in my direction. He was glaring at Shannon, who merely smiled back, calm as could be, as if the look he was giving her wasn't cold enough to freeze water.

"See you found a date." He inclined his head toward me, refusing to meet my gaze. His voice was chillier than his eyes.

"See you found a shirt." She was quick with the comeback. I got the feeling Shannon liked to tread on her brother-in-law's toes. I couldn't see why. His demeanor was making my stomach turn. Or maybe that was the two drinks I'd slammed back-to-back. I wasn't familiar with alcohol. A glass of wine here or there, sure. But whatever Shannon had mixed was stronger than that.

"Can we talk in private?" Jack asked her, gesturing toward a hallway I hadn't noticed before.

She sauntered forward and patted his shoulder twice. "No."

We watched as she sashayed away, her hips swinging back and forth in a beeline for Kieran and a group of people chatting across the room.

"She's intense," I managed to get through the dryness in my throat.

Jack faced me with reluctance, a muscle twitching in his jaw. "She's something, that's for sure."

He was laser-focused on me now, but I stood my ground. *You're with Shannon,* I chanted. *She invited you.* He tilted his head, studying me in that predatory way. His liquid gaze traveled the length of my body, taking in my appearance. My skin prickled with heat. *You have every right to be here.*

Okay, so maybe I should leave.

"I'm just gonna…" I trailed off, hiking my thumb at what I hoped was the elevator. "Try to… *not* be here…"

His icy gaze melted in an instant and I was staring straight into the deep emerald pools again. "Follow me."

Without waiting to see if I'd obey, Jack disappeared into the throng of people. My feet propelled me forward. I could just make out the back of his chaotic umber curls passing under the glass wall and onto the balcony. He made a quick right and ascended a steel staircase. Against my better judgment, I continued after him.

Jack stopped, pivoting in my direction. We were standing on top of the building, directly above the loft. The roof vibrated under my strappy heels, but that had nothing to do with how unsteady I felt. There were no lamp heaters to take the chill away from the October night. An icy breeze sent a few wavy strands of hair across my face.

He licked his lips, the intricate lines in his throat working on a swallow. "I didn't know you'd be here tonight."

"Shannon invited me." I said my mantra aloud this time, but it seemed silly now. Why had I come? I should've just told Shannon no, although I knew she wouldn't take that as an answer. "I didn't realize you'd be here, either. I thought she was taking me clubbing or something."

Jack's eyes softened a bit more. He took a step toward me, then stopped himself. "I didn't want you to see this."

"The fight?" I asked, trying to give him my best 'no biggie' smile. "So you like to play the Emerald Devil every once in a while. I'm sure your work is stressful. It's probably a good way to let loose."

He looked off into the twinkling skyline, the muscle in his jaw twitching again, but he didn't appear angry. "That's not what I meant."

Jack waited as I pondered his words.

"The illegal gambling?" I laughed half-heartedly. "I'm not a cop."

He smirked, but it didn't reach his eyes. "I wouldn't have been drinking if I knew you'd be here."

"I don't see how one has to do with the other." He just stared at me, as if I wasn't understanding something obvious. "Oh, because you're my boss? Honestly, I don't ca—"

Just as he moved like lightning during the fight, Jack was suddenly so close. I took a step backward out of shock and my leather-clad thighs hit an air-conditioning unit, unbalancing me further. I'd forgotten it was behind me, but Jack had stellar reflexes. He splayed his hand onto the skin at the small of my back, applying just enough pressure to steady me. Despite my flimsy attempt at a blouse, it didn't seem so cold on the rooftop anymore. In fact, his touch all but burned me.

He was struggling to mask his emotions, his conflicted expression inches from mine. "You make me want to lose control."

I furrowed my brows. "At the gym, you pushed me away."

He stared at my mouth, his pupils so dilated, I could barely see any green in them. "You seem to be under the impression that was easy for me."

I shook my head, attempting to clear the fuzziness in my brain. Was it the alcohol or him? Both seemed capable of inebriation. "But in the car, you told me you thought we'd be better off as friends."

He chuckled and my gaze flitted to his mouth as well. "That goddamn word has been fucking with me for weeks."

He'd been thinking about me for weeks too? "So…you *do* like me?"

"*Fuck* yes." He tilted his head back and sighed into the night, as if saying the words aloud had brought him some form of relief.

The static energy between us hummed. I'd been doing my best to ignore it. I didn't understand why Jack O'Connell was interested in someone like me, but I chose to disregard that voice in my head. I had spent the last three years cutting myself off from the world, spiraling into abysmal sorrow. I'd been terrified to close my eyes at night. I wasn't going to ruin another moment with self-sabotage.

He placed his right hand on my cheek, brushing a strand of hair away with his thumb. His eyes flickered between mine like he was inspecting a rare diamond. "From the moment you walked into the Emerald, I've wanted you, Emma."

My breathing shallowed. His smell was intoxicating. The world blurred as Jack leaned forward, his hungry gaze fixed on my mouth. My eyelids fell, but something caught my attention. The tattoo underneath Jack's forearm had me frozen in shock. The heat of our moment was replaced with an icy chill.

The rooftop vaporized beneath my feet. The buildings and lights of the city disappeared and transformed as I was sucked back to that night…

My heels clicked against the sidewalk, my stride brisk. The entrance to the subway was a block away, but my feet still protested. It was after two on a Saturday morning. I'd been working all night, serving drinks to people my own age who were well past the legal limit.

Apart from the occasional homeless person, the streets of Hell's Kitchen were empty. Whoever said New York didn't sleep hadn't stayed awake long enough, or had wandered into the wrong part of town.

It was the middle of August and humid, even though the sun was on the other side of the earth. The strap of my heel slipped from my sweaty ankle. I bent down, struggling with the cheap imitation leather.

Suddenly, I couldn't breathe.

Someone was holding me from behind, my back to his chest. His forearm crushed my windpipe, his other arm pinning one of mine to my side. I scratched at the man with my free hand, wriggling frantically. He had my arm at a painful angle. If I fought him too much, my shoulder would dislocate.

He grunted, the guttural sound making tears prick the backs of my eyes. When black dots floated over my vision, I knew I was done. Maybe this was what I deserved for failing Nate. Limbs tingling with numbness, I stopped fighting. I'd earned this ending. Tears fell, carving a path down my flushed cheeks.

The last thing I recalled was the man's hand, pale and sinewy. There was a pitch-black tattoo on the back of it. Intertwining circles with a smoky skull in the middle. Instead of black holes for eyes, two shamrocks.

"Luca sends his best."

"Stop!" I screamed.

I was on the rooftop again. Jack's face was a breath away, his eyes searching mine with alarm. At my command, he removed his hands and took a step backward, concerned.

"I'm sorry if I moved too fast." He was breathless as well, his chest rising and falling fast. I didn't know if it was from how close we'd been or from my reaction.

"Your tattoo," I choked, hand to my heart in a futile effort to settle it. "Is that a common design?"

"Which one?" he asked, bewildered.

His right arm was covered in them, so I pointed at the design I'd seen before. It was on the underside of his forearm, well-hidden near the crook of his elbow. "Is it from a band or something?"

His entire demeanor shifted, darkening like a cloud had obscured the moon. His eyes slid from the marking, rising to glare at me. "Why?"

"The man that attacked me. The reason I took self-defense at your gym. He had that exact tattoo."

There was no mistaking it. The skull with the shamrocks for eyes, the smoky color and solid black circles.

"Where?" Jack demanded.

"In Hell's Kitch—"

"Where was the *tattoo,* Emma?" he interrupted, nostrils flaring.

"On his right hand," I answered, frightened. "In the web between his thumb and forefinger."

And, just like that, Jack was gone.

Chapter Eight

Jack

I descended the rooftop, feet pounding the metal stairs. A few people on the balcony called out to me, offering a pint, but I ignored them.

"Mick, take Shannon home," I commanded, grabbing my leather jacket from one of the sofas and sliding my arms into it. "Stay there with her, Kieran."

Mick and my brother sprang into action, the party mode dropped from their faces by my tone of voice. They flew to Shannon, who was gossiping with a blonde nearby and hadn't noticed my return. My second and third lieutenants closed ranks, awaiting further instruction.

"Emma is on the rooftop. Tail her like a hawk but be discreet about it."

"I'll need a few more men." Eoghan, my second-in-command, stepped forward. He was tall and lanky but gifted with tracking. "She uses the underground more than she should."

"Take whoever you need, just no one she'll recognize." Eoghan nodded once, heading toward the balcony to find her. "Cathal, keep your ear to the ground. I want to know if any of my father's men are in the city."

"Anything we should know about?" Cathal asked, his beady eyes combing mine. He was the newest member of my personal ranks, but he made up for it with his uncanny ability to gather information.

I grabbed my helmet from beneath the sink, bypassing his query. "Keep everything on lockdown until I get back."

Two minutes later, I was in the underground garage, warming my bike for the trip. Shannon hadn't given Mick and Kieran a fight when they told her it was time to leave. She'd looked annoyed, but she knew the drill. I didn't have a chance to lay eyes on Emma before I bolted, but I trusted Eoghan to get her home safely, then disappear from sight.

Once my tires hit the city's streets, I called Connor. I would've preferred to sober up over an hour or two before driving, but I didn't have that kind of time. I needed answers now, so the cold air would have to do the trick.

"Little brother!" Conner's voice rang through my helmet. "How was the fight? Is the bloke still breathing?"

"Where are you?" I growled, going well over fifty as I wove through the traffic on Seventh. The engine of my Icon Sheene hummed. It was an expensive piece of metal but worth every penny. Navigating NYC was easier on two wheels, especially if I had a tail.

"Safe house off Quarterpath," Connor answered, the amusement vanishing from his tone. "Is Shan—"

"She's fine. Kieran's taking her home." I took a deep breath, rounding into Lincoln Tunnel. I would lose him soon. "Is Ghost with you?"

There was a pause on his end. "Yes."

I sped the bike to ninety in a matter of seconds, blowing past the other vehicles in the tunnel. "Keep him there. I'm on my way."

The speedometer rose steadily as I drove to Boston.

* * * *

Sunlight was just beginning to crest the horizon when the safe house loomed into view, a small warehouse in an industrial section on the outskirts of Boston. It was one of a few properties my father still owned, but he wouldn't be here. It was early Saturday morning and he'd be nursing a hangover at the trailer park he now called home.

When I entered the building, seven men stood from the dusty card table. For a safe house, security was lax. I hadn't been to Boston in over a year, but it appeared good ol' Dad had lost more than a few men during that time. He didn't protect his assets. Least of all, human life.

"Jackie boy!" Tom, a hairy Irishman in his sixties, announced. His cheerfulness grated my nerves. "Come to join us for a game?"

My sights narrowed on my target—the pale, thin excuse of a man standing in the corner, his teeth yellow as he grinned, his face marred with acne scars even in middle age. His hands were in the pockets of an old pair of jeans, but the tattoo glowed against his sickly skin. Right between his thumb and forefinger, like Emma had described.

Before anyone could react, I had Ghost pinned to the wall, my forearm on his windpipe. When he attempted to throw me, I pulled the revolver from the waistband of my jeans and held it to the stringy hair at his temple.

"What the *fuck*, Jack!" someone yelled, but the six men standing behind me all had their hands up by their shoulders, shocked.

Despite the pressure applied to his throat, Ghost smiled. "You think because you're Frank's kid you can just walk in here like you own us, huh?"

"Why are you roughing up girls in Manhattan, Ghost?" My voice was authoritative, but I felt so far away from it. I pressed the barrel into his skull.

Comprehension flashed through his small eyes. The fucker knew exactly what I was talking about. His smile turned mocking. "Is Jackie Boy all bent out of shape over a lass?"

I eased up, then slammed his head back again. Drywall cascaded onto our shoulders. One of the men—I didn't know who—stepped forward. I aimed my gun at him, cocking the hammer twice.

"Take it easy, Jack," the man said, attempting to defuse the situation. I didn't take my eyes off Ghost, who was beginning to realize I was one-hundred-percent not fucking around.

He raised his hands. It was a smart move. "Was just followin' orders, Jack."

My father's.

"Why would Frank order an attack on a girl in the city? She's innocent."

Ghost shook his head with effort, hardly able to move under the weight of my arm. "Frank asked me to do it, but it wasn't him who ordered the attack."

"Then *who*?" I demanded, hanging on to my last shred of patience. If I wasn't careful, I would lose my shit.

"Luca Nicoletti."

The entrance of my father stopped my mind from spinning out of control. I hadn't expected to hear his voice or that name. I released Ghost, not bothering to catch him as he slid down the wall, his breathing ragged. I clicked the gun's hammer back in place, letting my hand fall by my side.

Frank O'Connell walked in from a room at the rear of the warehouse, my brother not far behind. My father had been handsome once. He looked more closely related to me than either of my brothers, with his dark hair and green eyes. But time and alcoholism had taken their toll on him. His hair was peppered with white, his beard unkempt, his eyes bloodshot. A thick layer of fat resided over what muscle he had left, and his skin was red and splotchy.

"I called him after I spoke to you," Connor explained, eyeing the gun in my hand with mild concern. I was too upset to be ashamed, but I slid the weapon into my waistband regardless. "Figured whatever angered you enough to come back here, Dad must have something to do with it."

"Think we should go somewhere private an' have a chat," Frank croaked in his thick accent, words slightly slurred. I passed through a sea of silent scrutiny, following Connor and Frank into the room they'd just vacated. It was an ill-lit office with an old desk, a few chairs and peeling wallpaper.

"Why are you doing Luca Nicoletti's dirty work?" I asked once the door was shut.

Frank sank into a rickety chair behind the desk, propping his feet up. Connor, looking moderately disheveled in his Brioni suit, sat across from him. I remained standing, my nerves scattered.

Frank grumbled, unscrewing a dirty flask and pouring its contents into a black cup of coffee. "You haven' seen your father in ages...an' you don' even have the decency to ask how I am?"

"I have eyes," I fired back. "I can see how you've been."

"Answer the question, Frank," Connor demanded. "What's your business with the Nicolettis and why weren't we informed of it?"

"I don' have business with the damn Nicolettis." Frank took a sip from his mug with a grimace. "I had a debt. They paid it."

"How much?" I asked.

"It'll cost ye, boyo." I slammed a few hundred on the desk and Frank nodded that it was enough. "'Bout fifteen grand."

"They paid you fifteen grand to scare Emma," I clarified, dumbstruck.

"Wait, *Emma*?" Connor whipped his head toward me, alarmed. "The new waitress at Roisin's?"

"Don' say that name!" Frank erupted, slamming his boots to the floor. Even decades after their separation, he became irate at the mention of our mum's name.

"Shut it!" Connor yelled, now on his feet as well. "Is Shannon safe?"

"I told you she's fine," I fumed. Clearly, Emma was the one in danger. "This happened weeks before I even met Emma."

Whether he believed me or not, Connor left the room, cell phone pressed to his ear.

Frank rapped his knuckles on the desk. "Double it and I'll tell ye what I know."

I obliged, throwing a few more bills on top of his hand and sitting in the seat my brother had abandoned. "Now."

"Ye always were an impatien' little lad." Frank folded the bills and slid them into the breast pocket of his soiled flannel. "Ye have more o' me in ye than yer brothers. Do ye ever get so angry ye think ye'll burn alive if ye don' hit somethin'?"

A vein throbbed in my temple. "I am now."

Frank's gaze roamed my face, then he met mine and began to talk. "End o' las' summer, Luca Nicoletti hisself approached me an' said it was time to pay up. Thought he had plans to cut out me tongue when I tol' him I didn' have the money, but he had a different kind o' payment in mind."

I nodded, trying my best to be patient. My father liked to take his time with a story.

"Said there was a girl in Manhattan givin' him some trouble. 'Taunting' I think was the word he used. She was a student at Columbia by the name o' Emma Marshall. For whatever reason, he didn' want his men gettin' their hands dirty. Tol' me he just wanted to give her a scare, tha's all. Let her know to keep her nose out o' his business. 'Bout a week later, I sent Ghost to the city. He was there and back by the next mornin'. Told me he didn' even leave a mark on the girl, but there was no way she didn' get Luca's message."

I pinched the bridge of my nose, a thousand more questions flying through my head. What had Emma done to taunt Luca Nicoletti, don of the New York

Mafia? Why didn't he want any of his men involved? Was she aware of the danger she was in? *Was* she still in danger?

"Why don' ye stay and have a drink with yer ol' man?" my father asked, taking a swig from his flask.

I was already heading toward the door. "The sun isn't even out yet, Frank. Slow the fuck down."

Chapter Nine

Emma

"What the hell happened on that rooftop?"

Shannon's voice was too insistent and demanding at this hour. I pulled the phone away from my ear, squinting at the screen. I'd barely made it into bed the night before. I lay sprawled sideways across it, fully dressed, heels still on.

I kicked them off and curled my knees into my chest. "Jack said he liked me." That brought a small, sleepy smile to my lips. I almost forgot I was on the phone.

"Of course he does," Shannon snapped. "What happened after? Connor just called from Boston, frantic. He said Jack showed up out of the blue and Kieran insists I'm not allowed to leave my apartment."

The events of last night replayed in my mind like a roll of film. The fight. Jack throwing the bottle against the brick wall. The rooftop. How close we'd been to kissing. The tattoo.

Shit.

"What's the story behind Jack's tattoo?" I sat upright in bed, a headache pounding its way up my neck. Damn me and my low tolerance for alcohol.

"Which tattoo?"

"The skull with the shamrocks in its eyes." I could picture it in my head. The tattoo on the inside of Jack's arm matched the one on the back of my attacker's hand. The fact that I could never make it out from my memory had been haunting me since August. Now it was stuck, lodged into the forefront of my mind.

"I..." Shannon grew quiet, her annoyance vanishing. "I...I don't know. It's probably from some stupid Irish metal band or something."

"You're lying. What's its significance? What aren't you telling me?"

"I have to go. Connor's calling." There was a shuffling sound on her end of the line, then it went dead. She'd hung up on me.

Frustrated, I threw my phone onto the bed, changed into a pair of sweatpants, and grabbed my laptop. Once Safari was open, I typed in the description of the tattoo and searched the images. There were various tattoos of smoky skulls and bright green shamrocks, even a few Gaelic symbols, but nothing came close to what I was looking for.

With a dramatic sigh, I leaned over to my nightstand and took a long sip of water. New tactic. I typed in "Irish band tattoos." No match. "Irish skull rock band." Nothing. "Irish skull prison tat." A lot of sickening anti-Semitic ink, but still not what I'd seen. "Irish fight club tattoo." When I stumbled upon a shirtless Brad Pitt, I slammed my laptop shut and threw my head against the pillows, cursing when it hit my phone.

Why, *oh why*, did Jack have the same tattoo as the man who attacked me? It obviously wasn't popular. I couldn't find traces of it anywhere online. With the way Jack had disappeared after I'd made the connection, I knew this wasn't just a bad coincidence. Jack knew the man who had attacked me over summer – maybe even had something to do with it.

I didn't want to believe that but it was a probability I forced myself to consider. I'd walked into the Emerald by total chance. Jack hadn't seemed to recognize me, but I couldn't say for a fact that he didn't. He was stellar at hiding his emotions behind a schooled mask of indifference. Evasiveness came easy to him. Was he pretending to be attracted to me just to see if I knew anything?

But I hadn't even reported the incident to the police. The man hadn't left a mark and nothing had been stolen. This was Manhattan we were talking about. The cops would've just laughed it off.

Feeling too jittery to stay in bed any longer, I threw on an old Columbia University hoodie, a beanie and my running shoes. I left the apartment. With my AirPods in and The xx threatening to burst my eardrums, I tried to leave all thoughts behind as well.

* * * *

That night, I dreamed of Nate.

It was more of a memory, as most of my dreams of him were. Instead of the nightmare I usually had, this one was sweet.

We had just finished practicing penalty kicks. I wasn't much of a goalie, so we stacked a few cones outside the net to help with his aim.

It was the summer before senior year and we were dressed accordingly, Nate in denim cut-offs, me in a floral romper. Our feet were bare and covered in shreds of wet grass. It'd stormed the night before but was bright and sunny this afternoon.

"What are you wearing to Kira's party?" I asked, breathless from dodging his powerful kicks.

Nate grinned, squinting at me from under a lock of chestnut hair. "Hopefully nothing by the end of the night."

I slapped him on his bare chest. The park was empty apart from a few moms and their children on the playground, but they were far away and preoccupied.

"I don't want to accidentally match like we did last time," I insisted. "They still haven't let us hear the end of it."

Nate tossed the soccer ball in the air and caught it again, thinking. "You should wear that dress I like. The one with the sleeves?"

I laughed, hitting the ball out from under his arm. "I have lots of dresses with sleeves, Nathaniel."

Nate rolled his eyes. I was the only one allowed to use his full name. "I mean the one with*out* the sleeves."

He took off after the ball, jogging a few yards away. His calf muscles bulged as he ran, reminding me just how much effort he'd put into the sport over the last few years. He could get into any college he chose with his talent, but he wanted to stay by me in New Haven. I was a very lucky girl.

Nate bent down to gather the black-and-white ball. When he stood, he was suddenly over half a foot taller. His teenage body morphed into that of a man's. Pectorals and biceps grew before my eyes. Ink blossomed on his right arm, intricate lines and plumes of smoke starting at his deltoid and trailing their way to his middle finger. His shaggy hair darkened, shortening into thick curls. His round, boyish face sharpened, stubble piercing through his skin. The mighty band of muscle along his abdomen tapered into the waistline of his jeans.

It was Jack O'Connell.

I wanted to run but stood rooted to the ground. Something about the way he was looking at me was paralyzing. Warmth spread outward from the pit of my stomach, making me lazy and suggestible.

Jack neared, his stare locked on mine. His expression was one of innate hunger, almost animal-like. As he stalked closer, I found it more and more difficult to fill my lungs. Like the mere proximity of him, the raw power he commanded, was taking over every element of the atmosphere.

When he reached me, I was transfixed. But there was something off about the way his eyes glowed. Not with anger or lust, but wickedness.

His irises were made up of thousands of minuscule shamrocks, twirling and twisting around, pulling me in like a vortex.

Chapter Ten

Emma

It was Sunday morning and I was coming to the conclusion that I wouldn't be getting answers any time soon, if at all.

Shannon hadn't picked up her phone, although I'd called her six times the day before. I would've gone to her apartment, but I didn't know where she lived. I even checked Roisin's Saturday night under the pretenses of looking at the schedule, but she wasn't there. Which was odd because weekends were always busy. I knew in my gut that she was avoiding me.

Jack's number was programmed into my phone, but I didn't bother calling it. I had a feeling he wouldn't answer either. Even if he did, I wasn't sure I'd like what he had to say. A part of me wondered if I shouldn't be avoiding *him*. Jack might not have had anything to do with what happened to me over summer, but he knew who did, and he had realized that on Friday night. It was the only plausible explanation.

Frustrated that I couldn't force myself to sleep in, I went for a run through Central Park. It was nearing seven and the city had awakened for the day. Steam rose along the pathways, bodega attendants bundled up and looking grumpy as they mulled about their stations, serving piping hot coffee to early risers. Pet owners took advantage of the waking hour to let their dogs run free before the tourists descended.

I delved deeper into the park, trying to avoid any signs of humanity, but there always seemed to be at least one other jogger in my line of sight. When I came across an adult soccer league, I tripped over my own feet. It was a normal thing to see at a park, but the visual caught me off guard. Perhaps last night's dream was at the forefront of my mind. Either way, my memory was triggered and I slipped back in time.

"It's our senior year, Em." Nate slung his soccer bag over a shoulder. A few students passed us in the hall, nodding in our direction. "You don't need to study so hard. You're a shoo-in for Yale."

I stood on tiptoe to peck his cheek. "Would I be Emma Marshall if I didn't have my nose in a book?"

Nate walked backward, still facing me. "I'll see you after practice?"

"The field is that way." I pointed to our right, wondering why he was heading toward the main doors.

"I have to jog home. I left my cleats on the stairs."

My house was less than a mile from Stonerose High. Nate and his parents lived across the street, so he'd be able to run home and back in under fifteen minutes. We made plans to meet at the diner when he finished training, then said our goodbyes.

An hour after the final bell, I was in my happy place – the library. It was our first day of school, so I had the room to myself. Apart from the rustle of papers on my desk, the space was quiet, soothing. I highlighted a section of my notes, getting lost in the AP Physics syllabus.

A hand settled on my shoulder. "Emma."

I jumped, shocked to see my father standing behind my chair. "Dad! What are you doing here?"

He held a finger to his lips, his face grave. Chills erupted along my spine as I gathered my things and followed him out of the library. Something was off. My dad should have been working in Hartford right now. The firm usually didn't let him leave before five unless he closed a big case.

"What's wrong?" I asked once we were in the empty hallway. My shaky voice echoed off the walls, which were decorated in colorful posters reminding students to purchase tickets for Homecoming.

My dad winced, like he already regretted what he had to tell me. "Something terrible happened today."

"Is Mom okay?" I asked, a wave of nausea roiling my stomach. "Is it Ella?"

He shook his head, downcast. "It's Maria Ranucci, Em."

I stared. "I don't understand. What happened?"

"Sheriff Donahue just called. He thought it would be best if I got to you before rumors spread. Maria was found dead in their home thirty minutes ago. Her neck was broken." He ground his jaw, struggling to get the words out. "The police suspect foul play."

Numbness spread from the top of my skull to the soles of my feet. "Nate…"

I didn't realize I was running until my dad grabbed me. "Emma, wait!"

"Nate went home after school!" I screamed, struggling against him. "He forgot his cleats!"

"You're confused, Emma." He tried to placate me, but I was yanking on my own arm to break free. "Nate is at practice. The police are picking him up now to take him to the station. He doesn't know yet."

I hesitated, shaking my head as the fight left my body. "He told me he forgot his cleats. He was going home…"

My dad pulled me toward his chest, wrapping his arms around my shoulders. My legs gave out, sorrow rocking me to my core. Maria… It wasn't possible. Nate's mom couldn't be dead. Someone had made a mistake.

"I'm so sorry, baby girl," Dad whispered, carrying my weight as I sobbed into his dress shirt.

"Walk now."

The automated voice at the crosswalk of Columbus Circle jarred me out of the memory. Commuters brushed by, bumping into my shoulders in their haste. I blinked a few times, struggling to return to the present.

Therapy had taught me some useful tools to extricate myself from a dissociative state. Deep breaths, counting backward, identifying three sounds in my reality. *Pigeons fighting over a mangled hot dog, a jackhammer from a nearby construction site and a Harley Quinn cosplayer popping her gum in my ear.* The coping mechanisms didn't always work. Fortunately, they did today.

When I rounded the block of my building, I remembered it was Halloween. Harley Quinn had thrown me off, but when I stumbled on a woman dressed like a slice of pizza, I checked the date on my phone. By the time I reached an Incredible Hulk, I felt like slapping my hand to my head.

I decided to stay in for the day. My professors were cramming as much as they could down our throats before Thanksgiving and I was falling behind. *You never had this issue before Jack O'Connell waltzed into your life,* I scolded. *Or did you waltz into his?*

After taking a scalding shower and throwing on an old pair of sweats, I dove headfirst into ancient history. It wasn't until my stomach rumbled around three in the afternoon that I resurfaced. My bed was covered in five different textbooks, corresponding notebooks for each and enough writing utensils to annotate the Bible. There were upwards of eleven tabs open on my computer and two research papers, which I was happy to say were complete.

As I rose from my bed, stretching to work out the kink in my neck, Ava popped her head in.

"Hey, Emma," she said, stepping out from behind the doorframe like I'd spontaneously combust if she made any sudden movements. This was a perfect example of why I couldn't wait to leave my hometown. I had been tired of people tiptoeing around and talking in hushed voices whenever I walked by.

I smiled, taking in her appearance. Black tights, a matching leotard I assumed was recycled from the bottom of her drawer and a set of striped cat ears. Her hair was natural, reminding me of how she'd kept it when we were younger. It worked well with the wild headband.

"Last-minute costume," she joked. I chuckled for her benefit. We might've started to talk more over the past month, but it was still awkward. Especially since we both knew she was playing spy for my mom but shied away from the confrontation. "I'm going to a party in Brooklyn tonight, so I won't be home until late."

"Have fun!" My voice was a little too cheerful.

"You too," she replied automatically before realizing her mistake and escaping down the hall. I looked at my bed, covered in academia, and laughed to myself. *So fun*. But, if I were being honest, there was nowhere else I'd rather be than home with the apartment to myself for the night.

I made a glamorous dinner of canned vegetable soup with a side of toast and ate it in front of the TV while watching an episode of *Seinfeld*. Since I was home alone, I indulged in some good old-fashioned self-pampering.

By eight o'clock, I'd taken a bubble bath, given myself a green tea facial, deep-conditioned my hair, mani-pedi'd my nails and even done some yoga. Feeling a little fancy, I slipped into a set of pale pink pajamas – a silk tank top and matching shorts – that I'd never worn. I was a sweatpants girl, but I figured *why not* for one night. Halloween was a good day to pretend. I was padding toward the kitchen for some strawberry ice cream when a firm knock reverberated off the front door.

Shit. I didn't have any candy.

Rummaging through the kitchen drawers for something – anything – that resembled candy, I tried to remember if we'd ever had kids at our door for Halloween. For the life of me, I couldn't recall.

A moment later, I swung the door open, holding half a bag of stale mints and hoping I wouldn't get egged.

"Trick or treat?"

I was too stunned to respond. Jack was standing in the hallway. *My* hallway. Outside the door. *My* door. Looking like a million dollars. He'd shaved and smelled warm and earthy, like a campfire during a rainstorm. The cut above his eye had already healed.

He wore black jeans, a matching thermal, Converse and a long wool coat. Mercy, why did he always have to look so appetizing?

I opened my mouth to try again, but nothing came out.

"I'd settle for either, to be honest." He looked me up and down in a way that made my skin sizzle. "Can I come in?"

My brain came flying back to me. "No."

He licked his bottom lip, his gaze melting into mine. My legs started to go, but I held my ground. His sexual weaponry wasn't going to work on me tonight.

He lifted a brow, challenging. "Are you sure?"

"Where did you go?" I asked, trying to put some emphasis behind my words. I hoped I sounded as angry as I felt. "You know the person that attacked me, don't you? Why do you have the same tattoo as him? Why did you go to Boston Friday night? And why the hell haven't you called me?"

I was breathless by the end of my inquisition, but I kept my hand on the door, ready to block him from entering if need be. As if I could. He was twice my size and the Mace was in my bedroom.

"I'll tell you everything if you let me in," he bargained. When he saw my hesitation, he explained further. "It's not the kind of conversation you have in a hallway, dove."

Fuck it. I let Jack O'Connell into my apartment.

"My roommate is studying." I locked the door behind him, deciding spur-of-the-moment to add a failsafe. "So we'll have to be quiet."

"No, she's not. She left your building four hours ago dressed like some sort of tiger and hasn't been back since."

I froze. Jack stood in the center of my living room, looking around my apartment with obvious interest.

"You…you've been following me?"

He pivoted toward me, his expression unreadable. "Not exactly."

I thought about his words for a few seconds and tried again. "You've been having me followed."

"I needed to make sure you were safe." He strode forward with purpose, but I stepped back, keeping the same distance between us. He looked at my pastel-pink toenails, then into my eyes, waiting.

"Why wouldn't I be safe?" I was trying to stay calm and determined, but I couldn't help swallowing the dryness in my throat. He noticed, his loaded gaze flicking to my neck.

"Does the name Nicoletti mean anything to you?" Jack narrowed his eyes, ready to evaluate my response.

"You didn't answer my question."

He sighed, running his hand through his hair impatiently. "I need you to answer mine first."

"No. I don't know that name."

"What about Luca? Luca Nicoletti."

I could hear the man's raspy voice in my ear. *Luca sends his best.*

"The man… That night…" I took a deep breath. It appeared as though Jack wanted to step closer, but I was happy he stayed put. "He said that name right before he let me go."

"What exactly did he say?"

"'Luca sends his best'," I whispered.

"And why would Luca Nicoletti want to scare you, Emma?"

I didn't like the way Jack was looking at me. Almost like he was...frightened? Of me? Of what I would say? It didn't make any sense.

"I don't know!" I yelled, frustrated and panicked. "I don't know who Luca Nicoletti is! I don't know why I was attacked!" Wetness pooled in my eyes. The rollercoaster of emotions I'd been trying to avoid over the weekend came crashing down. "I was just walking home from work and he came out of nowh—"

My voice broke and the tears fell.

Jack closed the gap between us, wrapping his arms around me before my legs had a chance to give out. With my hands pinned against him, he picked me up and set me on the couch, never once letting go. I cried for a while longer with my face against his chest, soaking the thick fabric there. Thoughts and feelings were running through me at speeds I couldn't catch. I grabbed the biggest one—curiosity—and latched on, willing it to pull me through.

"Who is Luca Nicoletti?" I asked, sitting up and wiping at my tears with the back of my hand.

"He's the don of the New York Mafia." Concern was etched on Jack's face. I blinked a few times. He caught a tear I had missed with the pad of his thumb.

"Why would the...don?" He nodded once, encouraging. "Of the New York Mafia want to hurt me?"

"He wasn't the one who hurt you. That was a man named Ghost. He's a friend of my father's."

I processed each tidbit of information as fast as I could, hoping to keep him talking. "Why does this friend of your father's want to hurt me? I didn't even know you back then."

"It has nothing to do with knowing me." Jack shook his head, taking a deep breath. "Nicoletti hired Ghost to scare you. He said… The don said you taunted him."

My lips parted in disbelief. "I…don't…*what*?"

Relief washed over Jack's features. He hugged me tightly, his nose in my hair. He sighed, the warmth of it heating my neck. I retreated from the emotional ledge. His proximity alone had a calming effect on me.

"I knew you would have no idea what he was talking about." He tickled a line from my collarbone to my jaw with his lips. I shivered, fighting the urge to melt into him. I was still confused. More so than before.

I pushed him away, keeping my fingers splayed on his chest to prevent further distractions. He looked down at my hand and raised his eyebrows.

"You promised to answer all of my questions," I reminded him, matching his expression.

He looked at the ceiling as if exasperated. He spent a moment removing his coat, then tossed it onto the coffee table before settling back in. "One at a time this go-around, if you don't mind."

I ignored the attitude. "Did you find this Ghost person?"

"Yes," he answered, his eyes hardening.

"And?"

"He won't be bothering you again."

I pursed my lips, choosing not to follow that line of questioning. "Why do you have the same tattoo as him?"

"My father, Frank, forced me to get it when I was twelve. He did the same to my brothers. Said it was time we hit the streets and started pulling our weight."

Twelve? I cataloged that away to examine later and refocused. "And Ghost? Did your father… Did Frank force him to get one as well?"

Jack shook his head. "Ghost did so willingly as a sign of allegiance to Frank. All of his men have it."

"His men?" I narrowed my eyes at the word.

"Men…allies…mob…"

"Mob." I hadn't asked it as a question. I'd heard what he had said. Jack's intense stare was laser-focused on me, once again waiting for my reaction. "And are you…" I paused, trying to form the sentence correctly. "Are you still part of this…mob?"

His breath came in and out a little faster, but his eyes stayed locked on mine, unblinking. "I run it."

My mind clicked everything together faster than I thought possible. It all made sense. Of course he was in the Irish mob. Jack and his brothers were incredibly wealthy. They owned more buildings in Manhattan than I knew was possible for anyone not named Rockefeller. He was into underground street fighting, illegal gambling and God knew what else. He was having me followed. He had gotten to the bottom of my attack and found the man responsible within a matter of hours. He'd spent the entire weekend making sure I was safe.

"What are you thinking?" he pleaded, removing my hand from his chest to cradle it in both of his. They were so warm that they drew me out of my own circuitous thoughts.

"I…" I wasn't sure what to say. Jack O'Connell was a mobster. I should be throwing him out, screaming at him to never contact me again, slamming the door in his face. As if in response to that idea, his palms heated even more. That invisible line tethering me to him tightened, tugging my chest in his direction. If Jack was such a terrible man, why did everything about him feel so right?

"You should be kicking my ass to the curb," he whispered, like he knew what was going on in my head.

Surprising both him and myself, I leaned forward onto my knees, pressing my lips to his before I had the chance to doubt my decision. God, his *mouth.* I hooked my arms around his neck, pulling him as close as I could. I ran my fingers through his thick curls. An animalistic groan ripped from Jack's throat as he grabbed my waist and lifted me off the couch. I wrapped my legs around him, locking my ankles behind his back. My nipples pebbled, rubbing against his chest. He was walking, but I couldn't say in which direction.

Every cell in my body was magnetized, drawing me closer to him. Instead of gravity holding me to the ground, it was Jack and Jack alone keeping me from drifting off into space. Thoughts of the Mafia and Irish mobs flew from my head. In fact, all cognitive function stopped. My brain misfired, neurons spinning to accommodate this new pleasure. Finally, being able to run my fingers through his hair. At last, his tongue in my mouth, studying it like his eyes so often studied my face. He licked and sucked, his teeth brushing against my lips like he wanted to bite them.

My head hit the pillow, breaking our contact. He sent my textbooks tumbling to the floor, then came down on top of me. His thick arousal was evident through his clothing. I tilted my hips, massaging him with my pelvis. He cursed, his tongue tickling my lips for reentry. I obliged. He tasted like warm caramel.

He peeled his shirt off, taking a moment to examine my body pinned underneath, eyes hooded and filled with utter satisfaction. His gaze lit a fire inside me, my thighs clenching together to quell the ache. I reached up and traced my hand along his forearm, following the smoky lines of ink there before interlocking my fingers with his. Jack watched avidly as I took my other hand and trailed it along his sculpted abdomen, curling my finger behind the button of his jeans. His erection strained against the denim fabric, so hard it looked painful. My own desire was liquid heat in my veins.

I was about to pull him toward me but hesitated.

"Wait," I whispered.

Jack didn't hear. He bent over me, holding our intertwined hands on either side of my head. I tried to ignore the voice telling me to stop. His lips were back on mine. I sighed into him, wanting this so badly it was agonizing. Everything was telling me to keep going, apart from that stupid little voice at the back of my head. *Not yet.*

"Hold on," I said, clearer this time.

Jack pulled his face a few inches away, his eyes searching mine. They were dilated and hazy with lust. Lord, he was so beautiful. How could I deny him?

His voice was gravelly, almost drunk. "Dove?"

I bit my lip to hold back tears of frustration. "I can't. Not yet."

I turned my head, staring at the bare wall of my bedroom. I was ashamed to admit it aloud. To acknowledge that my past still had a hold on me, no matter how long it'd been.

Jack untangled his legs from mine and laid himself on the pillow next to me. He wrapped his arms around my body and pulled me to him, my cheek resting against the solid expanse of his chest.

"It's okay, Emma," he soothed, but I knew he was disappointed as well. He was just hiding it better. Tears fell from my eyes as I listened to his steady heartbeat. "We can lie here forever if you want. I'm already the luckiest bastard alive."

"How so?"

"I don't deserve to touch you," he answered with blatant honesty, kissing the crown of my head. "And yet, I still have you in my arms."

I tucked my face into him and closed my eyes.

Chapter Eleven

Jack

I dreamed the sweetest dream I'd ever had.

Emma was in her cute little shorts and top, her nipples beaded under the silk, her ivory skin so smooth and inviting. The way her long, dark hair curled in tendrils, teasing and drawing my eyes down her backside. It smelled of apples and lavender. Her full lips moved in tandem with my own. Her tongue, small and sweet, playing in my mouth. Those willowy curves rocked into my body, driving me insane. But when she slid her finger behind the button of my jeans, she stopped. She looked off to the side like someone had called her name, her features marred with a wince.

I awoke hard and even more sexually frustrated than the night before. I'd finally given into my temptation and now *she* was the one saying no. I rolled onto my stomach, groaning into a pillow, before remembering where I was. The smell of ripe green apples guided me back to reality.

Emma was nowhere to be seen. A few of the books I'd pushed off her bed the night before were missing. The others were stacked on her bedside table. The thick spine of *East of Eden* glared at me from the top of the pile. My jacket was hanging on one of the white bedposts, and my sneakers sat beneath it. I had been sleeping so sound, I hadn't heard her tidy up. That wasn't like me.

A minute later, I slid into my shoes and coat, searching the pocket for my phone. There was a text from Emma.

Didn't want to wake you. Early class. Ava is home.

She didn't want her roommate to see me. I smiled at that. Usually, I was the one to slink out of a woman's bedroom. I'd bailed on the morning after more often than I cared to admit, so I was rather good at it.

As I checked the time on my phone – seven-thirty – I thought of how the tables had turned. Emma leaving before me was new. And I'd spent the night with a woman without having sex with her. That was also a first.

Shutting her door, I turned around to find someone standing in the hallway with me. She was dark-skinned, fit and wore a strange expression of disbelief and shock.

"Who the hell are you?" the short girl asked, her hands tucked into a large puffer coat that went down to her ankles. Clearly, it was her one line of defense against the autumn cold. She wore nothing underneath apart from a thin workout jumper and boots, a pair of satin ballet slippers hanging from her bag.

Ava Davis was easily recognizable from my research. While Emma had no social media presence whatsoever, her roommate was on all the major sites and she kept her profiles public. Photos of her out on the town with friends, pictures of food, artistic renditions of her dancing. There were even a few blurbs about her in some small papers. Juilliard accepted just twenty female students into its dance program each year. I knew nothing about ballet but, apparently, she was talented.

"I'm…" I hesitated. Emma wasn't very close to her roommate if she wanted me to avoid her. Well, too late for that. "A friend of Emma's."

"Oh." Her eyebrows skyrocketed as realization dawned. "*Oh*! Emma has an early class on Mondays."

"Figured."

Ava passed me, bag slung high over her shoulder, and I winced. She was heading out the door as well. We would have to take the elevator down together.

The living room looked the same as it had last night, albeit the couch cushions were rumpled and an Afghan blanket was tossed on the coffee table. Had Emma slept there? I hadn't stirred all night, but I was sure I would've woken if she were gone for that long. So maybe Ava had crashed there?

"I didn't hear you come in," I prodded the roommate while she locked the front door behind us. "Sorry if I startled you."

"I got home a few hours ago." Her expression was inscrutable as we made our way to the elevator bank. "Emma was still asleep on the couch."

I nodded for Ava's benefit as the doors slid open. So Emma *had* slept on the couch. I must've fallen asleep before her. She was so warm and small in my arms. I hadn't known I could be so comfortable. It felt...right.

"How long have you known Emma?" I asked, pushing the button for the lobby.

I was digging and not ashamed to admit it. There was something wrong with Emma and it had nothing to do with me or the attack by Ghost. I could see it in her eyes when she'd stopped me last night. The look on her face made my heart ache, like someone was squeezing it in their hand. Something—or someone—had hurt her. And it wasn't recent. That kind of trauma ran deep. I knew from personal experience.

"Since third grade." Ava fiddled with the strap on her bag. I got the feeling she knew where I was going with this. "But we were never that close. Different circles and all."

The elevator was descending too fast. I bit the bullet and went for it.

"Did something happen to her before she came to New York?" Ava's eyes widened. I had my answer, but I wanted more. "Something... Did someone hurt her?"

Her features hardened and she took her time answering.

"Look, you seem"—she eyed me up and down, searching for a suitable adjective—"nice. And Emma's been doing better the past couple months. I don't know if that has anything to do with you or not, but don't ever bring that up again. If Emma wants to tell you what happened, she will. Don't *ever* ask her about it. She's been through enough."

With that, the elevator dinged and Ava stalked off, leaving me in utter silence with Emma's battered copy of *East of Eden* clutched under my arm.

* * * *

Emma

To say it was difficult to focus in class that day would have been a vast understatement. I would've heard what my professors said just as well if I'd stayed home.

Of course, Jack was at the forefront of my mind. I replayed our long, feverish kiss—and how close we had come to something more—over and over in my head to avoid thinking about the more menacing things I'd learned last night.

A man—not just a man, but the leader of the Italian Mafia—had asked Jack's father to employ one of his mobsters to scare me. I didn't know what I'd done to taunt this so-called don, but his message was clear. I was scared.

"Luca sends his best."

Who was Luca Nicoletti to me? Better yet, who was I to him? Since moving to Manhattan, I hadn't made many connections. Hardly anyone in my classes knew my name. My coworkers at the Drop had been just that—coworkers. We clocked in, exchanged a few tired grunts then entered robot mode. Never once did I come across the name Luca Nicoletti. It was unique enough that I would remember.

The summer had been uneventful, aside from Ghost choking me, and apart from the manila envelope that'd been slipped into my mailbox by an anonymous sender.

You know what I did
Please know I'm sorry

That damn envelope had led me to the Booker Hotel. It was a week after that when Ghost attacked me. Did they have something to do with one another? Had Ghost delivered the photo of Maria Ranucci to me? Had Luca Nicoletti? I'd thought it was some sick prank, but now I wasn't so sure.

I considered returning to the Booker and asking the concierge if the photo had been left in lost-and-found, but that was a shot in the dark. The cleaning women would've thrown it out without looking twice at it. And the accompanying message was long gone, probably buried in a landfill in Jersey.

But what could Maria Ranucci's death have to do with the Mafia? The murderer had been caught and it was impossible for him to be orchestrating anything from prison because he was dead.

After eight hours of back-to-back lectures, I was spent. I'd gleaned nothing from my lessons. I had to ask my neighbor—I now knew his name was Jamie Carlyle—to send me his notes again. We took most of the same classes and he was more than happy to help.

Before braving the streets of New York, I buttoned my coat up to my throat. My hair whipped around my face as I battled with Manhattanites for a piece of the sidewalk. On the subway back to my apartment, my mom called. She sounded overly chipper and got through the pleasantries faster than normal.

"Your father and I will be in the city this weekend," she informed me. "For the Policeman's Ball."

"Oh," I replied, my attention span dwindling. My bed was calling to me. It would be an early night.

"We included your name on the invitation." The subway lurched and I became hyperaware of the words coming through the phone. "We'll meet you at the Met around five on Saturday, okay?"

"W-w-wait," I stammered, pulling myself out of my exhausted haze. No, not okay. The Policeman's Ball? Where the hell had this come from? "You've never asked me to attend this *ball* before."

My mom sighed. "Well, you know your father and I go every year. And we've just been missing you so much."

"So we'll go out to dinner when you're in town. Or a baseball game!" I was grasping at straws. I did not want to go to a *ball*. Anything—literally *anything*—but a huge, high-society event.

"Oh, that won't be as fun!"

I fumbled with my coat buttons, sweat beginning to trail down my back. "But you've never asked me to come to this thing before."

"I didn't think you'd have as much fun if you couldn't at least have some champagne, sweetheart."

I groaned, rubbing at the tension in the inner corners of my eyes. "No amount of alcohol could make this thing fun."

"Oh, don't be so negative, Emma." She laughed, but it sounded rehearsed. "Bring a date!"

Click.

No. There was no way she could know about...

Before I could finish that thought, I was dialing another number. My clammy palm slipped along the handrail as I waited for him to answer. He picked up after the first ring.

"So, she knows how to use a phone," Jack said by way of greeting. My lips twitched in a smile upon hearing his voice, but I was too determined to discover whether my hunch was correct.

"Did you see Ava this morning?" I demanded.

I almost hear his wince over the phone. "It was by accident, I promise."

I swore. A few of my fellow passengers turned their heads in my direction before going back to their own business. That wasn't the worst thing they'd hear on the train today.

"Jesus, Ivy League, I didn't know you had such a dirty mouth."

"I don't know if you can hear, but I'm not in much of a joking mood at the moment."

"Is everything all right?" His voice was serious now. "Are you okay?"

The subway came to a halt at Columbus Circle. I sighed. "Physically, yes. My mental state? Not so much."

"Come over."

"To where?" I paused, stepping onto the platform. A group of people also getting off swarmed around me, bumping my shoulders in a hurry to get to their respective destinations.

"My place."

My heart quickened, but not so much that I forgot about my mother. She knew I had a man in my bedroom last night. Ava had told her. If I wasn't so anxious about this Policeman's Ball, I would be angry.

"I don't know where you live," I reminded Jack, wondering if I should stay in the station. Could I walk to him or did I need to wait for another line?

"Eoghan will show you," he answered.

"Who the hell is Eoghan?" I asked.

"He's standing right next to you, dove." Another *click* and he'd hung up on me as well.

I turned to my right. One person remained in the station apart from myself. A tall young man dressed in street clothes leaned against one of the blue steel support beams. He had unruly, dirty-blond hair covered by a Yankees ballcap. I narrowed my eyes, vaguely recognizing him from that night in Soho. He'd driven me home, but I had been a little buzzed at the time and my mind had been elsewhere. He hadn't given me a name.

I approached him, sticking my hand out. "I'm guessing you're Eoghan."

He looked up at me from under the brim of his hat. I was surprised to discover he was close to my age and still had that boyish charm. He utilized it, hazel eyes glinting, smile lopsided. He reached out and took my hand, chuckling as he shook it.

* * * *

"Didn't want to spring for the penthouse?"

Jack smirked as I entered his apartment. He was wearing his signature T-shirt and fitted jeans, his feet bare. The stubble along his jaw had yet to come back, making him appear younger than usual. His building, it turned out, was just two blocks from mine. It had an unobstructed view of Central Park and was a much nicer—and pricier—piece of real estate.

"I like to be unpredictable," he replied, removing my coat and hanging it inside one of the closets in the foyer. "And it was a bit more inconspicuous."

Walking farther into the apartment, I noted it was anything but inconspicuous. Vaulted ceilings, dark furniture, brass accents, warm lighting—it was dominant and masculine, just like the man who called it home. The kitchen, as large and ominous as the living area, would've made Gordon Ramsay salivate. There were two wide hallways leading to the left and right on either side of the room. The entire back wall was made of double-paned glass. The sky was dark, but the lights of the city were familiar and welcoming.

I trailed my finger along the sofas and side tables, Jack following in my wake. He watched intently while I studied my surroundings, his expression unreadable.

"Inconspicuous," I murmured, smiling to myself. His apartment was twice the size of my parent's house in Connecticut. "Right."

Jack wrapped his fingers around my wrist, turning me away from the dizzying view. Music filtered throughout the room. I recognized the song as *Devil Like Me* by Rainbow Kitten Surprise. Jack tilted my chin with his knuckles. When he leaned in, his lips met mine in a slow kiss. My muscles melted on contact, warm honey seeping into my veins in response to his touch.

"Make yourself at home," he whispered against my mouth. "I'm cooking dinner."

He showed me into the dining room off the kitchen. Remembering why I was here in the first place, I opened my mouth to tell him about the conversation with my mom but stopped. Looking around at the beautiful place settings and the monochrome modern art adorning the walls, I decided I needed a break from thinking about family and Mafias and Irish mobs. From the moment I'd woken up, my mind had been devoted to the latter two.

Jack retreated into the kitchen, refusing my offer to help with a sexy wink. Stomach fluttering, I decided to review my notes—or Jamie's, specifically—from the day in an attempt to learn what I'd missed. More importantly, to abstain from falling down a rabbit hole of worry.

Chapter Twelve

Jack

While I cooked dinner, it was hard to keep myself from peering in at Emma. Every time I checked, I was sure she'd be gone. Just a figment of my imagination, or a very good dream.

Alas, she was there, in her little skirt and collared blouse, black glasses framing her eyes, long hair tied into a loose bun at the nape of her neck. One knee was tucked against her chest as she nibbled on her thumb, scrolling through something on her laptop. Her concentration rivaled my own when I was on the job. She never once looked up, which I was grateful for. I felt privileged to not only have her in my home, but to see her in her natural element. Because, if it hadn't been before, it was now obvious to me that Emma took her education seriously. She was first and foremost a scholar. The fact that she could focus on her schoolwork after all I'd revealed to her the night before was astounding.

I'd admitted to her that I was the head of an international criminal organization. Instead of telling me to never speak to her again, she'd kissed me and let me sleep in her bedroom. Now, she was in my home, voluntarily having dinner with a mobster. I wasn't complaining, but perhaps the girl should have her brain examined.

As I was finishing up, I called Mick and told him I was going dark for the evening. All my communication would be forwarded to him. He sounded surprised, as I never took time off from work, but was more than willing to hold the reins. I didn't want anything distracting me from Emma.

Her head snapped up when I placed a hot plate of teriyaki-glazed salmon on the table beside her. She seemed lost for a moment, as if returning from a faraway place, but her features lit when she saw me.

"What are you studying this evening, Miss Marshall?" I asked, sitting across from her. She was impossibly beautiful and I felt the need to keep her in my line of sight, to reassure myself she was real.

She slid her glasses from her nose, closed her laptop and pushed it to the side. "Stone composition and degradation in the Grecian aqueduct system."

I clamped my lips between my teeth, trying to hide a grimace. "Sounds…interesting."

"It's tedious." She rolled her eyes and took a bite of salmon.

"If anyone could keep my attention on the subject, it would be you." I paused, watching her blush. "Although I don't think I'd hear a word of it."

Her cheeks darkened further and she cleared her throat, taking a sip of the wine I'd set out. I was beginning to understand her ins and outs. If I had to bet on it, she was taking the time to think of a way to deflect the conversation from herself.

"This is amazing." She pointed to her plate, pulling her teeth along a pod of spicy edamame. "I didn't know you could cook."

I smirked. I was right. "I like to keep you on your toes, dove."

She giggled…literally *giggled*. It was the sweetest sound I'd ever heard. When she first walked through the door, I had planned on asking if she wanted to talk through what was upsetting her, but I kept putting it off. For now, I just wanted to keep her smiling. All night if I could.

"I didn't know you wore glasses."

"They're just for reading." She shrugged. "The words get all fuzzy if I stare at the page for too long."

"I think that means you read too much."

"There could be no such thing."

We chuckled, turning back to our dinner. Cooking was a way for me to get out of my own dark mind. Other options included breaking a jaw or a quick lay, but searing a steak was a bit cleaner. I had taught myself after realizing I had enough money to afford the type of food I'd only ever dreamed of eating. Growing up, my brothers and I had struggled to keep the cupboards full and the furnace on. Sometimes we had to decide between the two. In the dead of Boston's winter, the heat came first.

"Do you cook?" I asked, swallowing a forkful of rice.

"Not unless you count instant ramen as a meal."

I hated the image of Emma, tiny and alone in her apartment, heating up stale noodles in the microwave before drowning herself in books. "Come over for dinner any time."

"As if you're not busy with..." She trailed off, trying to find the right words. "Whatever it is you do."

"I'd drop anything to have dinner with you." And I knew it was true. I realized then and there that I would bend over backward just to spend a few moments with the woman sitting across the table. And that terrified me. I'd never felt that way for anyone before, not even my own family.

Emma was quiet, resting her cheek in her hand to hide the color rising there. A wavy strand of hair came loose and dangled in front of her face, teasing me. I wished I could be that close to her. My cock twitched. I wanted to shove the plates off the table and fuck her hard, but I fought to exhibit a modicum of self-control. She needed me to move slow. It was something I'd never done before, but I was willing to try anything for her. I would wait as long as it took. I would savor the little moments like this one. *You don't know when she'll run.* Deep down, I knew it was inevitable. Why she hadn't already was beyond comprehension.

Emma tilted her head, listening to the music. "I wouldn't have pegged you as an indie love song kind of guy."

I tuned in to the melody spilling from the surround sound. "I listen to a lot of stuff. Depends on my mood."

She met my eyes, curving her lips into a smile. Something funny happened in my chest and I had to remind myself to breathe. "You're a bit of a romantic, aren't you, Jack?"

I laughed at that. "That's the first time I've been called it."

Her expression turned curious. She thought for a moment before speaking again. "Have you been with many women?"

Fuck. I took a sip of wine and wondered how best to approach that one. "A few."

The way she lifted an eyebrow told me she knew I was being cagey.

"What about you?" I challenged.

"I've never been with a woman."

I leaned back in my seat, tongue pressed to the inside of my cheek. She was avoiding the question as well. "You know what I mean."

The conflict flitted across her face so fast I nearly missed it. Regret, guilt, shame. "One," she answered in a small voice. "But it was a long time ago."

Meaning she had been with one man before me. Technically, I hadn't even been with her, yet. I wanted to know everything about the guy. Not just out of jealousy, but because I knew she'd been hurt. Was this the source of her trauma? Had he done something to her? Something that made her face fall like it just had when she thought of him?

"Don't ever *ask her about it."*

Ava's voice swirled around my head like a red flag, but this was a conversation that needed to be had. If she'd been hurt in the way I was dreading, I would have to be even gentler with her.

"She's been through enough."

"About last night," I started, keeping my eyes glued to her for any discernible reaction. "I apologize if that was too soon. I didn't mean to frighten you."

She set her fork down, swallowing with effort. "It wasn't you. I…I think I frightened myself. Sometimes I get stuck in my head."

"That makes two of us," I replied. "Either way, I think we'd both benefit from a safe word. I've never felt the need for one, but it might be crucial in this situation."

While I spoke, she didn't break my gaze. She did, however, reach for her wine glass and take a long swig. She set it down with purpose, clearing her throat.

"It goes without saying that I'm a little inexperienced with this stuff," she said after a moment. "But when you say 'safe word,' I picture getting chained to a metal bed and whipped with a riding crop."

"Christ Almighty, lass!" I cursed, pushing my empty plate away. "Where the hell do you come up with this shit?"

She gave a laugh of relief, holding her hand to her chest. "I'm studying history, Jack. I learn about all types of things. I took an elective last spring called Sexuality Through the Ages. Nothing like holding a twenty-eight-thousand-year-old dildo in your hands."

I interlaced my fingers behind my head. "You just keep surprising me."

"I like to keep you on your toes," she replied evenly. "So, why the need for a safe word?"

"Listen, I'm not going to sugar-coat it for you." I took a deep breath. It was now or never. "I'm a bit of an asshole, I'll be the first to admit that. My work is unpredictable, which breeds a need for control. I've gotten used to people obeying my every command. You were right when you assumed I use street fighting as a means to blow off steam. The same goes for sex, but it's never at the risk of losing that control. Do you remember what I told you on the rooftop?"

She thought for a moment, eyes wide. "That I make you want to lose control?"

"Yes, and that's what has me worried, dove. If I push you too far, if things get to be too much… I'd never forgive myself if I hurt you. Especially if you've been hurt before. I know this is an uncomfortable subject for you, but I wouldn't be asking unless it was necessary." I put my hands underneath the table, clenching them into fists. "Were you – ?"

"I wasn't raped." She spoke over me, her voice clear and concise.

I let out the breath I'd been holding, dropping my face into my hands. I dug my elbows into the textured wood of the table, palms pressed into my eye sockets.

"Thank fuck," I said shakily. "Or I'd have to rearrange someone's face."

She was silent, but I couldn't look up at her. Not yet. I'd divulged more to her over the past twenty-four hours than most people could handle in a lifetime. She held the power now. The choice of whether to run or keep hashing it out.

"You, um…" She started and I listened with all ears, stars dancing behind my eyes from the pressure I was exerting on them. "You mentioned you're used to obedience. I'm guessing the reason we're having this conversation is because it extends to your sex life as well?"

I had to glance up to evaluate her reaction. "Again, you're correct."

She nodded, lips pursed in thought. "But no toys?"

"I don't need toys to make you obey, Emma." I was incapable of hiding the warning in my voice. No matter how hard I tried, I was always toeing a line with her.

"Then, what?" she asked, a mischievous glint in her eye. "Spankings?"

Lord, help me.

"I don't get off on hitting women. But if you want to spank me, feel free. Although I should warn you that my left ass cheek is a wee ticklish."

She tilted her head back, letting out a symphonic laugh. I smiled, biting my lip while she attempted to control herself. I hoped she never did. I could have sat there and listened to her giggle for an eternity.

She managed to wrangle her composure after some time. She shook her head at me, as if I was the tiring one. "I'll keep the spankings in mind, but what *does* happen if I disobey?"

"Then I stop," I said simply.

Her brow furrowed in disbelief. "Just like that?"

"I thought I made it clear that I don't want to hurt you, Emma." I locked her narrow-eyed gaze in mine. "Besides, pleasure, or lack thereof, can be painful in its own way."

By the look she gave me, she didn't understand what I meant. Just broaching this subject with her was sending my mind into fantasies, all of which involved Emma screaming my name, begging for my touch with her entire being. My palms itched with restlessness, wanting to *show* her.

I cleared my throat, shoving those images to the side. "Look, before we get to that, you need to pick a word. Something about you pushes my limits. If I'm not careful, I could wind up pushing yours as well."

"I don't know my limits. Can't I just say 'stop' or 'don't'?"

"No," I argued. "For instance, in the heat of the moment, if you were to beg me 'please, don't stop,' you can see where confusion might set in. Last night, I didn't hear you the first time. I need something that'll cut through. So pick—"

"Mercy."

The word froze me in my tracks. A chill went over my skin and my jaw tightened. My imagination brought me somewhere dark—a fleeting image of Emma running from me in terror. The walls of my stomach clenched in response, stirring up my dinner. Nodding, I let her know that would do. It was effective as hell, but I vowed not to give her a reason to use it. If I took it that far, she could very well leave. And she'd have every right to.

"I'll admit, I'm intrigued." She folded her hands on the table. The warmth returned to my body. "I think that's obvious, otherwise I wouldn't be here."

"Stay with me tonight," I demanded, my voice harsher than I intended. Now that we'd finished dinner, I didn't want her to leave so soon. I should've made multiple courses.

"I can't." She looked torn. "I don't have a change of clothes."

I smirked, the thought of her naked in my bed taking over my brain. I could think of a few activities that didn't require clothing. *Slow, Jackie.*

"You can borrow a shirt of mine. You'll drown in it, but at least it's something."

She smiled, her face a delicious shade of pink. "If I stay, will you be good?"

Don't tempt me, darling. "Will *you*?"

She gave that some serious thought. "I don't know…"

My mouth popped open in surprise, my mind flooding with the possibilities that little answer entailed.

"Yes," she stated.

"Come again?" I nearly laughed. *Poor choice of words.*

"Yes, I will stay tonight," she clarified, eyes narrowed. "But I need to shower. Long day."

Did she know what she was doing to me? Would I be able to control my most basic desires knowing Emma Marshall was naked in my apartment? *Yes,* I scolded myself. Emma had boundaries and they needed to be respected.

"I'll show you to it," I said, hoping I came off as somewhat aloof.

Leaving the dishes and her things in the dining room, I led her down the northern hallway, passing a few guest rooms as we went. At the very end, I opened the door and let her pass by into my bedroom.

I felt very exposed with her standing in there, her face exquisite and studious like it'd been earlier in the evening. No woman had ever stepped foot in my bedroom before. Hell, no woman apart from Shannon had even been in my *apartment.* So much had changed since the moment Emma had walked into my gym. The thick line I'd drawn between my personal and sexual life had been blurred beyond recognition. Was this what happened in a relationship? Was that what Emma and I were? In a relationship?

I'd lived my life closed off to the opposite sex. I was far from a monk, but I didn't like keeping anyone close for too long. It wasn't difficult and I felt in no way bereft. No one had caught my interest enough to make me want to stick around for breakfast the day after. Until now, that was. Emma was doing things to me and I wasn't completely comfortable with where my emotions were heading. I also wasn't sure how I'd be able to stop.

In simpler words, she was trouble.

My bedroom matched the rest of the apartment—a modern bedframe with a white comforter and dark furniture with copper accents. Like the entirety of my home, it held no personal effects. No photo frames or half-read books adorning the bedside tables—Emma's copy of *East of Eden* was tucked into one of the desk drawers in my home office. The glass wall held a view of the Upper East Side's twinkling skyline. Emma's gaze roamed, fascinated by something I couldn't see.

"Bathroom is through there." I pointed toward the far end of the room.

"Thanks," she said, but she didn't move.

"There aren't any monsters behind the door, dove," I teased. *Just one,* I thought. *But he's standing right beside you.*

She laughed, but it was shaky. She hadn't taken her eyes off the door to the bathroom and she was twisting her fingers into knots.

"Everything all right?" I asked, my concern growing the longer she stood there in silence.

It was then that she turned to face me, her brown eyes so deep I thought I might fall into them. "Join me."

Had I heard her right? Was this just another one of my fantasies? I was almost positive I'd dreamed something similar weeks ago. I sighed, looking up at the ceiling. "Emma, that conversation wasn't intended to make you feel pressured. I don't want to move forward at the risk of losing what we already have."

She gave me a quick kiss, but I was too stunned to process whether that was an answer. I kept my feet planted to the ground as Emma walked toward the bathroom, pausing to glance back at me. Her expression made me instantly hard, my dick fighting against the denim of my jeans. There wasn't a shred of doubt in that look.

"Give me five minutes." It was clear she wouldn't be entertaining an argument from me. "Then join me."

There hadn't been a longer five minutes in the history of mankind. I paced the room, listening as the shower turned on and the glass door shut. Four minutes. *Stupid fucking clock.* I sat down on my bed, legs jittery, watching the seconds tick by on my watch. Three minutes. *Jesus fucking Christ.* I leaned with both hands against the glass wall, the neon lights of the city flickering. Two minutes. *That'll have to do.*

My clothes couldn't come off faster.

Emma stood with her back to me, steam rising around her, water dripping off the glass that enclosed us. Still a few feet away, I paused to watch her rinse the suds from her long hair. I followed the trail of soap down her delicate spine, where it curved over her perfect, round ass and continued down her leg.

She turned to face me, her eyes even darker than before, and my knees weakened. Willowy curves, long legs, perky tits—she was fucking magnificent. I knelt before her, letting the water cascade around us. This woman was going to be my undoing. After all my talk about control and obedience, *I* was the one kneeling for *her*.

"Is this okay?" I asked roughly, holding her hips in my hands. I ran my thumbs along the decadent skin there, waiting for a solid answer. *Please say yes.* I might die if she stopped me again, but I didn't want to scare her. Her consent was a requirement.

"Yes," she acquiesced.

Thank fuck.

That was all I needed. I kissed my way from her belly-button down, lingering with each one, trying not to get greedy. As with the time spent together over dinner, I wanted to savor this. My dessert.

When my nose brushed her smooth mound, I glanced up to make sure she was still okay with what I was doing. Emma's eyes were closed, her head tilted back. Her erect nipples rose and fell with each breath. She was ready.

Hands on her hips, I gently pushed her against the marble wall of the shower. I followed, crawling. She snapped her eyes open when her skin hit the cool texture, but I couldn't pause again. Hiking her right leg over my shoulder, I balanced her there.

I reached my tongue out and sank into her folds with abandon. The skin over her hip bones formed goosebumps, her muscles trembling with arousal. I continued, circling my tongue around and around the sensitive pack of nerves, moving my hands to her backside to keep her from wiggling. She ran her fingers through my hair and pulled it. I groaned.

Yes, dove, show me what you want.

She was so damn wet. I craved to be inside her, but that wasn't what tonight was about. She hadn't yet run from me. The fact that she was letting me touch her anywhere was a miracle. For the second time in twenty-four hours, I was the luckiest man alive.

Feeling emboldened, I slipped a finger inside her channel. She was so tight, my cock ached with need. I moved through the silken tissue within, finding the spot I was looking for. She gasped, her back arching off the wall.

"So beautiful," I murmured, letting my breath travel across her sex. Her gasp turned into a low moan and she fruitlessly tried to churn her hips toward my mouth. "What do you want, dovey?"

She whimpered, tugging my hair in the direction of her greedy pussy. She tensed the leg that was draped over my shoulder, doing the same. I smirked, watching her features twist in frustration.

"You've had quite the education, Ivy League," I teased, licking my lips. "Use your words."

She opened those brown eyes, glaring down at me with unabashed lust. The sight of her dilated pupils almost had me blowing. "I want to come."

"As you wish, baby," I replied, my tongue returning to her clit. It was swollen, practically vibrating in my mouth. I pulled my finger out, diving back in over her G-spot. I tightened my grip on her, then loosened before I could leave marks. I wanted tonight to be as perfect as she was.

"Oh, God!" Her muscles contracted around my finger, her orgasm cresting. Sucking on her clit, I gave her ass a squeeze, letting her know it was okay. She didn't need more than that. She came, a sweet little moan rolling out of her throat. After her giggle, it was my new favorite sound.

Desperate, I lapped her up like a kitten. I swore I heard her whisper my name, but it was carried away by the echo of water hitting the marble tile. When the tension eased from her, I kissed her once more, tasting apples and lavender. *So fucking good.*

I didn't even need to see her face to know she was exhausted. Whatever emotional wall she'd just broken through, it was a tough one—a barrier keeping her from intimacy. Her eyes were half-lidded as I rose and turned off the rainfall faucet, one arm wrapped around her waist to keep her steady.

Her contented smile faltered for a moment and she mumbled her words. "But I didn't do you."

"Soon," I promised, carrying her into the bedroom. I set her down on the floor at my bedside. She looked dead on her feet as I dried her off with a heated towel, taking care to not scratch her skin. I was scared that if I took too long, she would collapse where we stood.

"I sleeped the moush," she slurred. I slipped one of my shirts over her. It hung loose down to her thighs.

"What was that?" I asked, smiling as her head popped through the collar.

"I have to sleep on the couch," she protested. I pushed her onto the bed. She sank into the lavish mattress and I pulled the comforter over her lethargic body.

"Shh." I brushed the wet hair from her forehead and she furrowed her brow, eyes fighting to stay open. She looked adorable, like a sleepy tiger cub. "I'll sleep out there."

I could tell she wanted to argue, but exhaustion took over. "G'night, Jack."

"Good night, dove." I kissed her cheek, so warm and inviting.

For a few moments, I considered crawling into bed beside her. She looked peaceful and innocent, not a worry written on her face. It had felt so good falling asleep with my arms around her the night before.

But I couldn't bring myself to do it. For whatever reason, Emma was frightened to share a bed with me and I had to respect that. I tried not to take it personally.

After learning who I was, she'd come back to me. Our relationship—*Yes, that's what this is*—had to be built on trust if there was any chance for it to survive in my world.

I would sleep on the bloody couch.

Chapter Thirteen

Emma

I was woken by the sizzling of something savory hitting a hot pan. I wouldn't have slept any better if I were dead. No nightmares, no waking up with a pounding heart. Jack's California king was so soft and cozy, the sheets like velvet against my skin, the pillows fluffy clouds. It put the rickety bed in my apartment to shame.

Oh shit. My apartment.

I grabbed my phone from the bedside table. I had a few messages from Ava. I sent a quick reply.

Sorry. Slept over at a friend's.

I hoped that would suffice, but I had a feeling my mom would be asking what I had been up to last night.

Double shit. My mom.

The stupid Policeman's Ball I was obligated to bring a date to. She knew someone—worse, a man—had slept over at my place.

No longer anywhere close to tired, I hopped out of bed and slid into my clothes from the previous evening. I tied Jack's shirt into a makeshift crop top so it wouldn't look like I was being devoured and pulled my tumbleweed of hair—the consequences of sleeping on it wet—into a messy bun. It would have to do.

Following the smell of breakfast, I made my way down the long hall and into the kitchen. It was even more impressive in the light of day. The rising sun glinted off the stainless-steel appliances and squeaky-clean surfaces, turning Jack's figure into a resplendent silhouette.

"Hungry?" he asked, his back to me as he slid food onto plates. He wore nothing but a pair of black training sweats, which sat low on his narrow hips.

Now I am. Images of our shower together floated to mind. How was it possible for someone to look that flawless? There was no other word for it. And even that didn't do him justice.

I cleared my throat, glad he was facing away so he couldn't see me blush. "Starving."

Jack set the plates on the island bar and I hopped onto the stool beside him. An array of food filled the dish before me—a vegetable omelet, bacon, toast, fruit and potatoes. Jack had two plates in front of him, both filled to the edges.

"So that's how you do it," I mused as he shoved a forkful of eggs into his mouth.

"Hmm?" He raked his gaze over my appearance, pausing on the shirt of his I was wearing.

"Stay so…" I tried to think of a word that wouldn't embarrass me. "Fit."

He smiled, taking a few gulps of what I assumed was a protein shake. "I'm a growing boy."

"If you grow any more, you'll have to become a superhero."

He laughed darkly, shaking his head. "I'm no hero, dovey."

We continued our breakfast, the soft sounds of a piano playing from the hidden speakers. With him sitting so close, it was hard not to recall every euphoric detail of our night together. He'd kissed me somewhere I'd never been kissed. And it had felt amazing. He had cleared away any self-doubt I had about my readiness to move forward in that regard. We'd talked more about sex last night than I ever had in my life. The recollection alone was stimulating. I focused on chewing my food to quell the throb in my core, crossing my legs for good measure.

"No bacon for you, huh?" Jack asked, oblivious to what his mere existence was doing to me.

I shook my head. "I try to avoid eating anything with feet."

"More for me." He grinned, grabbing a piece of bacon from my plate. His two were already empty. I had to keep my eyes off his mouth as he bit into the juicy strip of meat.

Just then, something soft and furry bumped into my leg. I squealed, jumping from the stool.

Jack bent over, picking up a ball of hair. "Don't worry. It's just Fia."

"Fia?" I asked. The creature in Jack's arms was a cat—black with bright green eyes and tiny, sharp claws.

Jack scratched the cat on the back of its neck before setting it down on the marble floor. "Short for Fiagaí. It's Irish for hunter."

The cat circled my feet, pushing its body against my legs. I smiled, kneeling to tickle its chin. "Girl or boy?"

"He's a man," Jack clarified. Fia climbed onto my lap with a purr. "And he likes you."

"You sound shocked." I scoffed.

"He normally hides when I have company. Tears Kieran to shreds whenever he tries to pet him."

I peered up at Jack in admiration. "You just keep surprising me."

He furrowed his brow. "Why is that?"

"Irish mob boss cooks like a professional chef, listens to love songs and shares his enormously inconspicuous apartment with a tiny kitty."

Fia hopped off my lap and sauntered across the living room to rest in front of the unlit fireplace.

"He's not a kitty." Jack grinned, his hand outstretched. I took it, letting him pull me to stand. "He's a house panther."

I giggled, his grin contagious. "A *thousand* apologies."

Jack kissed me slow and sweet, making my heart race. "What time does class start?" he asked, turning to clear the island.

I shifted gears, giving myself something to do other than ogle. "Eight o'clock."

Jack checked his Rolex. "It's nine."

I shrugged, placing a plate in the dishwasher. "I know."

He threw a dishtowel over his shoulder and leaned against the counter, his ankles crossed, one over the other, in front of him. "My, my, Miss Marshall. Am I being a bad influence on you?"

"I think you are."

From the flush heating my cheeks, he understood the double meaning in my words all too well. Before he could act on wherever his deviant thoughts had taken him, I blurted out the first—well, second—thing on my mind.

"Will you go to the Policeman's Ball with me Saturday night?"

That stopped him in his tracks. "Pardon?"

I set a clean pan on the counter, wiping my hands on the pleats of my skirt. "Forget it. It was a stupid idea."

"Woah, woah, slow down, dove." He took the pan and placed it high in a cabinet before holding my hands in his. I was forced to look at him. "What police ball?"

I tried to turn, but he held me in place. Begrudgingly, I explained.

"Ava spies on me for my mom. She told her about seeing you in our apartment yesterday morning and now my mom wants me to go to a ridiculous ball and—get this—I have to bring a date." I sighed, frustrated with the whole situation, but mostly with myself for not having the courage to confront either of them. "My mom is trying to be discreet, but I know what she's doing. She wants to meet the man who was in my bedroom."

Jack appeared concerned. Maybe even a little irritated. "Your roommate spies on you for your mom?"

I turned and Jack let me go this time. "It's a long story."

Understanding clouded Jack's expression. Before I could read too much into it, I grabbed my book bag off the counter and slung it over my shoulder.

"I'll go to this thing with you." He bit the corner of his lip in thought.

"You can't. It's a *police* ball, Jack."

His smile was mischievous. "Best place to hide out is under someone's nose."

An image of Jack getting arrested had my stomach in a pitfall. "You can't be serious."

"I am."

I could see that his decision was made. Why had I even mentioned this to him? Why had I gone and blabbed about it without thinking it through? If I caused him to get caught for anything he'd done, I would never forgive myself. *But what* has *he done?*

"Fine," I consented, angry. I might not have known Jack for long, but I'd already deduced there was no point in arguing with him.

I've gotten used to people obeying. His words floated to mind, eliciting another dose of belly-tingling shivers. Why did I immediately want to disobey when he said that? To knock the alpha male down a peg?

I swiped my laptop from the entranceway table and shoved it into my bag with force, a thought popping into my head. *Obedient, my ass.* "And stop having me tailed."

"No." I was surprised to hear his voice so close. He'd followed me to the elevator door, as silent as a ghost.

"It's bad enough I get spied on at home." I pressed the button for the lobby, turning around to find his face inches from mine. "Now everywhere I go, I'll be looking over my shoulder."

His eyes softened. "Stop using the subway. Eoghan will drive you wherever you need. Then I'll tell my men to back off."

This was Manhattan. The subway was the quickest way to get from point A to point B, but I had a feeling this would be my one counteroffer. Although poking the bear seemed thrilling, I wasn't sure I was ready for the consequences. At least not yet.

I nodded once. Jack smirked, proud of his victory. He pulled me in for another mind-numbing kiss and I forgot where I was. The Policeman's Ball, Ava, my mom, our compromise...all disappeared into clouds of insignificance.

"Go learn about your aqueducts, Ivy League," he murmured, his lips brushing the frantic pulse at my neck.

As if.

* * * *

With a smidgen of my sexual frustration eased, I was able to listen during the two lectures on schedule for the day. Jamie—my sidekick, so to speak—offered to send me his notes after class, but I politely declined. His notes had gotten me through on a few lessons, but they weren't as detailed as mine. That I might have to rely on them for a few sections of the finals made me nervous.

Around three o'clock, I grabbed a few vegetarian tacos from a food truck on campus, planting myself at a stone picnic table. I ate the first one, relishing as the salt and fat hit my stomach. Jack's cooking had been beyond delicious, but I was a junk food girl through and through. I survived on caffeine and carbs.

My attention was snagged when a nearby taxi cut in front of a city bus. The giant, blue-and-white passenger vehicle blared its horn, but that wasn't what made me flinch. On the side of the bus was an advertisement for the new *Alien Warfare* video game. My heart jolted in my chest. I tried to stay present, but my mind drifted, the tide of time dragging me far from shore.

Life didn't go back to normal after Maria's murderer was caught. Everything looked the same, felt the same, smelled the same – but there was something off that I couldn't identify. The world felt disingenuous, like if I breathed too hard, I might send everything spiraling out of orbit. My relationship with Nate felt hollow, artificial. Like he wasn't really there. He was drifting away and I didn't know how to make it stop.

When my dad told me the newest information on Maria's case, I was out of the door, sprinting across the street to Nate's house. I found him sitting in a red beanbag on the floor of his room, controller in hand, staring at the television.

"Hey," he muttered, not taking his eyes off the glowing screen.

It wasn't like him not to at least smile upon my entry, but this was post-murder Nate. I had to come to terms with his new personality, whether I liked it or not.

"I have news," I said, taking a seat beside him.

"Another acceptance letter?" Nate asked, his jaw slack as he shot an alien on the screen. Green blood squirted everywhere.

I analyzed Nate for his reaction. "About Jeremiah Murray."

His fingers, once dancing over the buttons, froze. He closed his mouth, his face draining of color. Finally, he looked at me.

"I don't want to know," he replied, his voice stiff and detached.

"But it's good news, Nate."

He ignored me, turning back to his video game. His character had died and he was forced to restart the mission. I continued talking. If there was any chance this would give Nate a sense of justice, I had to tell him.

"Jeremiah Murray was murdered in prison," I stated. "My dad just told me. It was another inmate."

Nate froze again, his bottom lip quivering. "What?"

"Dead," I repeated.

Panic flashed through Nate's eyes. "But he wasn't convicted yet. He was still awaiting trial."

"I thought you'd be relieved."

He jumped up, his controller landing on the hardwood floor with a clatter. "Relieved? Emma, a man is dead."

I stood alongside him, confused. "He killed your mom, Nate. Why do you care what happens to him?"

He raked his hands through his hair, pacing toward the window. "I have to talk to my dad."

"I don't underst – "

Nate whirled past, leaving me dumbstruck. I felt like I'd made a terrible mistake. I thought this would help him move on, but he was more distraught than ever. The news didn't have the result I was looking for. I was hoping it would bring the old Nate back.

Somehow, I'd made things worse.

My ringtone blared. My eyes were burning as I struggled to focus on my phone screen. *Three things I can hear in my reality. Bells from a cathedral up the block, water rushing in the gutters, a woman arguing with her boyfriend.* I took a shaky breath, then answered the call.

"Emma, Emma, Emma." Shannon tutted. My heart thumped, my brain catching up to the implication in her tone. Did she know Jack and I had spent the past two nights together? He didn't seem like the type to kiss and tell. From what I could gather, he was a private person. "What did you get up to last night?"

"Why?" I hedged, thankful she couldn't see the flush crawling its way up my chest. Maybe Jack had told his brothers.

"Connor said Jack went dark." *Went dark? What the hell did that mean?* "I can only hope you had something to do with it."

An idea popped into my head. If I was going to a ball at the Met, I needed to enlist some serious help. There was one person I knew with exceptional fashion sense, and she had fiery red hair and lips. Besides, I could use the distraction.

"I'm glad you called. I need your help," I countered, changing the subject. "I'm going to a fancy ball with Jack this weekend and I need a gown."

"What ball? Connor didn't tell me about any ball!"

"My parents invited us," I clarified before I got her husband in trouble. "It's the Policeman's Ball at the Met."

She was silent for a beat.

"Jack is going to the *Policeman's* Ball. At the Met. With you. And your parents." I didn't know how to answer that, but she whistled before I could think of something to say. "You have that boy *wrapped* around your sexy little finger, Ivy League."

My flush intensified. I picked at the frayed denim of my jean jacket. I'd gone home to change before heading to campus, tucking Jack's T-shirt in my dresser for safekeeping. *Was* Jack wrapped around my finger? I doubted that.

"But wait." Shannon's voice returned to its normal symphonic quality. "Did you say you needed a *gown*?"

I cringed. "Unfortunately."

"Oh, my God, a thousand percent *yes*! Meet me at the corner of Madison and Sixty-Ninth in an hour. It's already Tuesday, so we'll *pray* they have time to make alterations if you need them."

That had me confused. Alterations? I wasn't getting married.

"I was kind of hoping to just grab one off the rack. Quick and simple, you know?"

"Oh, Emma…" She laughed. "You don't just grab a Valentino off the *rack*."

A little over an hour later, I stood in a private Valentino fitting room, waiting for the sales associate to return with a dress for me to try on. Shannon sat cross-legged on one of the faux-fur cushions, gushing over having a chance to shop with another woman other than her Aunt Faye.

"What about your mom?" I asked, sliding my jean jacket off and throwing it into a corner.

She studied her manicured nails, which were done in a bloodred coffin style. "My parents died when I was nine. Car crash. So my Aunt Faye raised me, but she wasn't home much. I spent most of high school sneaking around with Connor. Not that we had to sneak around with Faye gone and Frank hammered day in and day out."

How had I forgotten that Shannon had known the O'Connell boys and their father for years? She had known them before they moved to Manhattan and she was married to Connor, which meant she more than likely knew everything there was to know about the mob.

"I'm sorry about your parents," I empathized. She flicked her wrist, unbothered. "That's cool you were so close with the O'Connells growing up, though."

I hoped my attempt at snooping wasn't transparent.

"Oh, my God. I gave those boys hell back then." She giggled, leaning back on her hands. "Still do."

Okay, maybe I'd been too subtle.

"So you…" I couldn't think of what to ask first. There was so much I wanted to know. First, about Frank O'Connell forcing his sons to get a tattoo so young, a tattoo that banded them together and ultimately sealed their fate in the Irish mob. Second, about what Jack had been like back then and about his past relationships. Something told me I wouldn't like what I found if I dug there. "So you know…about everything, right?"

Shannon's smile dissipated, teeth sinking into her signature red lip. She stood and walked toward me, taking my hand in hers and giving it a squeeze.

"The thing about living in their world," she started, her expression stern but her eyes warm, "is, first and foremost, knowing when to talk…" She tipped her head toward the curtain of the dressing room. Employees were chatting on the other side. "And when to just smile."

I nodded.

"Later," she whispered, retreating to the fluffy cushions as the sales associate came into view.

She pushed a clothing rack with six floor-length gowns dangling from it. I stifled a groan. I didn't want to try on one dress, let alone half a dozen. Grabbing the first one off the rack, I undressed and slid into it, careful not to pull too hard on any seams. The clean, white fabric clung to my modest curves. It was backless and the neckline plunged, meaning I couldn't wear a bra with it, which wouldn't be a problem for my B-cups. The thin straps were studded with tiny diamonds.

There was a slit in the side that traveled to the top of my thigh.

I'd already decided I would settle on the first gown. The more time afterward to talk with Shannon, the better. But I was surprised—and somewhat embarrassed—by how sexy I felt while looking at my reflection in the mirrors.

"Holy shit," Shannon swore, making her way to my side. "This looks amazing on you!"

"How much is it?" I asked, lifting my arm to locate the price tag.

She ignored me. "Matching shoes, necklace and long diamond earrings, please."

The saleswoman nodded and turned to leave.

"Actually, ixnay on the necklace."

"But how much is it?" I asked again, moving the slit at my thigh and finding nothing but my own skin. Where the hell was the price tag?

"Oh, thank you so much!" Shannon gushed when the woman jogged back with the items she'd requested. I assumed they already had accessories set aside to go with this particular gown.

"You like the dress?" the sales associate asked, excited.

"It's beautiful," I answered. "How much is it?"

"Mr. O'Connell said to charge his card when you chose a dress," she said. "I'll go charge the card now."

"Wait. What?"

"Add these too, please." Shannon handed the small woman the shoe and jewelry boxes, disregarding my protests.

"How the hell did Jack already give them his card information?" I asked her, outraged and slightly impressed.

Shannon shrugged. "I might've mentioned we were going shopping."

"Whatever." I rolled my eyes. "I'll pay him back. How much is the dress?"

Shannon scrolled through her smartphone, but the screen was black. Snatching the phone from her grasp, I held it over my head and out of reach. I had a few inches on her.

"Tell me how much this dress is or I'm throwing it in the fountain outside."

"Okay, okay! *Relax*." She groaned. "It's, like, twenty grand or something." She reached up, dragged my arm down and took her cell phone.

"That's not possible." I shook my head, jaw landing on the floor. "For a *dress*?"

"Yeah, you're lucky it fits you like a glove." She dropped her phone into her Chloé bag. "Otherwise, alterations would cost more. Leave it to Emma Marshall to be able to just *grab* a Valentino off the rack."

"All done!" The sales associate returned with a large bag in hand. "I'll bag the gown whenever you're ready, Miss Marshall."

"This so-called *gown* could feed a small country. This gown could buy school supplies for God knows how many children. This *gown* could…" I stopped, a hand on my stomach. "I think I'm gonna be sick."

Both women sprang into action. "Not on the dress, for Christ's sake!"

* * * *

With my stomach still churning, Shannon and I hopped into the back of a black SUV driven by Eoghan. I disliked using him as a chauffeur—I was sure he had more important things to be doing—but felt better about it with Shannon in the car.

I didn't throw up in the store, but Shannon insisted on carrying the bags just in case. Dollar signs danced in front of my eyes like a cartoon character. *Who spends this much money on a single article of clothing? Jack O'Connell, that's who.*

Despite never having to worry about finances growing up, my parents had taught me to be conservative, to give back wherever and whenever possible. There were too many people suffering in the world to be selfish. Sure, we splurged on occasion, the rest of my family more so than me. I had a large trust fund sitting in the bank, untouched. I never factored it into my income. What did I need it for? My parents paid for my school and housing. I made enough money at work to afford everything else I could need. Maybe I would have to dip into it to pay Mr. Money Bags back.

"Look." Shannon startled me. We were hurtling across West Fifty-Seventh, which was busy at this time of day. Eoghan had incredible luck in traffic. "I know you have a million questions, but I can't tell you anything."

Eoghan's hazel eyes caught mine in the rearview mirror.

I looked down at my lap, avoiding his stare. "Why not?"

"Jack hasn't told any of us how much you know. He's a very private person." She paused, sighing. "I didn't even know what was going on between you two until today. I'm *still* not sure I grasp what it is the two of you have."

"I think we're together on that one." I smiled sadly. What was I to Jack? A new challenge? As much as I hoped to be something more, was that just wishful thinking?

"Jack is…a tough person to know. He doesn't let anyone get too close. Frank was harder on him than the rest of the boys." She gave my shoulder a reassuring squeeze, then glanced out of the window. I wondered what memories were playing through her head. "Jack bottles up a lot of anger, but he's been changing since he met you. You focus him. We've all noticed. Unfortunately, that's all I can tell you for now."

"I understand." I nodded, unbuckling my seatbelt and reaching for the bags. "And it's enough…for now."

Chapter Fourteen

Jack

"Put this lot in bay nineteen," I told a Willie, pointing at a military-grade crate filled with an assortment of automatic weapons. "They're shipping to Tokyo on Thursday."

The Willie nodded, his reflective vest shining in the fog lights, and got to work preparing the shipment.

The breeze from the Hudson was relentless, and cold enough to make me wonder where my little brother was. He'd been scheduled to relieve me at nine but was notorious for being late. Frustrated, I fastened another button on my wool coat.

"Those go to Eoghan in Soho." I nodded toward a few containers of tech equipment that another Willie was loading onto the dock. He stopped, his body language conveying some serious attitude, before turning around to carry the equipment off the dock. He wouldn't be moving up in the ranks any time soon.

The pocket of my coat began to vibrate. I retrieved my phone, smiling at the caller ID. *Wings*. Eoghan had coined the nickname.

"How was your day, dove?" I asked, my mood instantly brightening.

"Expensive."

Oh, she's angry. This'll be fun.

"Did you find a pretty dress?" I teased, flipping through an inventory log.

"Yes," she admitted. "But I'm going to pawn it after the ball."

I chuckled, handing the log to one of my men. "And why is that?"

"And I'm going to use the money to donate to a charity in your name," she continued, ignoring my question.

I prevented a new recruit from opening a container filled with explosives, motioning for him to move onto the next one. Where the fuck was Kieran?

"What charity would that be?"

"I haven't decided yet." I imagined she had her arms crossed, her foot tapping on the floor. *Stubborn girl.*

"I'm sure you'll choose a good one."

My brother walked onto the pier, looking hungover. I flipped him off. He returned the favor, motioning for me to hang up the phone. I shook my head and he grinned.

"Emma?" he mouthed, wiggling his hips.

Fucking hell. From the river, a ship blew its foghorn.

"Where are you?" Emma asked, the noise loud enough for her to hear.

"Our pier." I shoved my brother farther down the dock. "Get to work," I mouthed at him.

"You own a pier?" she asked, incredulous.

"We own a few piers. And a hangar at La Guardia, in case you were curious."

"Jesus Christ."

My chest ached from missing her. I wanted to be by her side, to see her expressions shift, to watch her pretty lips as they swore.

"What are you doing tonight?" It was a little past nine. I could get to her in thirty minutes if I took the Sheene.

"I have to study."

"Are you *sure* there's not anything else you'd like to do?" I countered, adopting my most persuasive tone. There was definitely something—or someone—I would have loved to be doing right now.

She remained contemplative as I neared my bike. "I can't."

Damn her self-control.

I wanted to ask if she was available tomorrow but didn't feel like pushing my luck. I'd never once worried about smothering a woman, but I did with Emma. I couldn't figure out if she was as attracted to me as I was to her. Just when I felt like I was getting to know her, she went and did something I never expected. That fire I'd seen in her eyes liked to flare up at the strangest times.

There was also the trauma I had yet to uncover. She'd said she wasn't raped, but it was killing me not to know what happened to her. Did justice still need to be dealt? My knuckles itched in anticipation.

I'd never felt this possessive over anyone. Sure, I was protective of my family and my crew. The mob was an extension of my blood. But Emma? The idea of her even talking to another man—past or present—was enough to drive me insane. I needed to rein it in.

Revving the engine, I swerved my bike onto the congested street, allowing the call to transfer to my helmet. A frustrated sigh made its way over the line. I smiled in response. Every little noise she made was darling as hell. Right now, it sounded like she was rummaging through a drawer.

"You okay, Em?" I asked, unable to keep the amusement from bleeding into my voice.

She made that cute groan again. "I can't find my book, which is ridiculous because it's huge."

I bit my lip, throwing on my indicator as I headed uptown. "Another text detailing the excavation of forgotten lives?"

"No." Her rummaging grew more frantic. She cursed under her breath, then the background noise stopped. "It doesn't matter. I've read it three times. It'll turn up eventually."

I grinned like a fool. *"A kind of light spread out from her. And everything changed color. And the world opened out. And a day was good to awaken to."*

She gasped. I revved the engine once more, hoping the purr would drown out my chuckle. "You stole my book!"

"Sleep well, dove," I murmured, licking my lips with satisfaction.

* * * *

Connor decided last-minute to take Shannon on a short vacation to Charleston, which left me to step up to the plate in his stead. I had meetings all over the city and a few off the island as well. "Meetings" was a loose term. Instead of just talking business, I was forced to sit at the dining table and schmooze for hours. By the end of each day, I was filled with more than enough potatoes and red meat to feed half of Ireland.

The Murrays were still locked down, their war with the Nicolettis growing vicious. On Thursday morning, I convened with them at the East Village safe house, dressed in dark clothing so as to not be seen. It wouldn't look good if anyone knew we were on speaking terms, but I took the risk anyway. I needed information on Luca Nicoletti's movements, but even they hadn't heard anything about where the mysterious man was hiding or what he had planned. With the Murrays playing a solid defense, it was safe to assume Don Luca was up to his neck in pesky Irishmen. Which meant—and I hoped—Emma was far from his mind. Although it still more than bothered me not knowing why he felt Emma had taunted him.

The McKenzies, on the other hand, were frenzied. My meeting with them was supposed to be about a shipment of arms they'd lost in the Mojave, but I soon realized it would not be discussed. Two of their men had washed up in the Hudson that morning, their throats slit and nearly all the blood drained from their bodies. The men had been expected upstate when their bodies were discovered. I was able to excuse myself early while they went over the men's last movements, trying to find footage of who might've murdered them.

By that evening, I'd had enough. Bearing the weight of our family name was taxing. How Connor didn't drink himself to death was beyond me. But my brother had always been better with people—and much more responsible. Kieran, young as he was, wasn't much help. He rarely completed his work, opting to stay out late clubbing and fucking anything that moved. As a result, he was given the easier tasks, ones that wouldn't make a difference if they had to be pushed back a few days.

At six o'clock on Friday, I finally had a chance to call Emma. Eoghan had informed me she was sticking to our driving agreement, but I was desperate to hear her voice. I couldn't imagine the thoughts that were circling their way around that powerful brain of hers. I hoped she was going easy on me, although I didn't deserve her grace. She was pawning her dress to give to charity. She always bought coffee for the homeless and she never used plastic straws, according to Eoghan's reports. *Fuck me.* The more she found out about what I did, the harder it would be to hold on to her.

"Jack."

The flood of relief at the sound of my name spilling from her lips was crippling. I sat on a metal bench in the hallway of the Emerald, pinching the bridge of my nose.

"I'm sorry I haven't called." I forced my breathing to return to normal.

She's still taking my calls. She hasn't decided to run yet.

"It's okay." Her voice was sweet in its forgiveness, but I selfishly hoped she missed me as much as I missed her. "I know you're busy with Connor gone."

Shannon must've mentioned they were going out of town. I couldn't help but consider what else Shannon might've told her.

"Everything good?" I prodded, hoping Shannon hadn't said something that would frighten Emma. I was trying to keep my world from overwhelming her.

"I just miss you," she answered. That strange feeling stirred in my chest again—and a much more familiar one in my jeans.

"Where are you?" I asked, my voice gravelly.

"Eoghan is driving me to work. Shannon asked if I could help tonight and maybe process the liquor order."

"Bail," I demanded, but knew better. Emma was responsible. Reliable. It wasn't in her character to skip out on a friend. Still, Eoghan was on my payroll. I could order him to change direction, to bring her here. Would Emma be averse to kidnapping? *Yes.*

"I wish, but I promised Shannon."

That meddlesome sister of mine. She'd gone out of her way to force Emma and I together, despite my wishes, and now she was unknowingly keeping us apart.

"So tomorrow it is, then?" I asked, attempting to hide my disappointment. I needed Emma like a crack addict needed a hit, and that was frightening.

She sighed. "Tomorrow it is."

I couldn't help but think she felt a little put out as well.

Chapter Fifteen

Emma

Saturday came too quickly, but the week stretched on forever. Jack was busy doing whatever it was Jack did and I was hammered with schoolwork. Most days, I didn't crawl into bed until well after midnight. Friday was even worse.

Roisin's had been packed and what was supposed to be a quick favor had turned into an eight-hour shift. The one good thing it did was help me forget how much I missed Jack. It seemed a little unhealthy to feel so attached to someone after just two nights together. But our time spent apart solidified my feelings for him.

When I awoke Saturday morning, I was a medley of emotions, all of which combined to form a knot in my stomach. I was dreading the ball but couldn't wait to see Jack. I was excited to see my parents, but the thought of them meeting Jack made me want to regurgitate my cereal. He was older than me, beautiful, intense and his arm was covered in tattoos. I could imagine my parents—my father, in particular—were already rehearsing questions to pester him with.

While I got ready, I considered calling Jack to give him some warning. Maybe he should fabricate a convincing story for how he made his money. But I didn't want him to worry. This was a Policeman's Ball he was attending at my behest. He had enough on his mind without having to fret about my parents.

By four o'clock, I was dressed in the Valentino gown and a long, white cloak. My makeup was simple—mascara, winged eyeliner, blush and a bloodred lip inspired by Shannon. When I'd texted her yesterday to ask for a brand recommendation, she replied with a photo of a luxurious tube of lipstick and a suggestive message.

It won't wear off.

Ava did my hair, which she was exceptional at from years as a dancer. She teased, curled and braided for hours before revealing the final product—voluminous curls and tiny braids combined in a Viking style. I thanked her profusely. She pushed me out of our apartment with an excited wink.

Eoghan held open the door to the SUV as I left the building. He whistled low, respectfully eyeing my ensemble. In the past few days, he'd never once made me feel uncomfortable. He was so quiet I tended to forget he was there apart from the important fact that he was driving the car.

"You try'na kill the boss, are you?" He offered a roguish grin as I slid into the back seat. "I think his heart might stop when he sees you."

Given my apprehension, Eoghan's compliment was well-timed.

An hour later, we pulled to the curb outside the Met. There were dozens of people gathered on the steps. Most of the men were either in suits or formal police uniforms. The women, on the other hand, looked just as done up as me.

I breathed a sigh of relief, knowing I would fit right in, and took Eoghan's hand as he helped me from the vehicle. My phone and keys clashed with my outfit, so I left them behind and ascended the steps of the Met, losing myself in the throng of Manhattan's high society.

When I entered, a waiter approached. He checked my name and took my cloak before handing me a glass of champagne. Resisting the urge to chug it, I scanned the ballroom, unsure whether I was looking for Jack or my parents. I was nervous for either, but a buoyancy lifted my chest at the thought of seeing Jack again, which made me feel horrible because it had been much longer since I'd seen my family.

As I walked farther into the room, a warm sensation trickled down my spine. I knew he was there before I turned. How was it that I could *feel* his eyes on me?

Jack was dressed in all black. Tailored three-piece suit, shoes, pocket square—everything. He was all blurred edges, a shadow. He wore no tie, the top two buttons of his dress shirt undone, a subtle "fuck your standards" if I'd ever seen one. His dark hair had been styled in a way that looked effortless, his hands tucked casually in his pockets. The stubble along his jaw had returned, but it was clean and purposeful. His expression was unreadable, but his green eyes glowed in contrast with his clothing.

Good Lord, the man knows how to wear a suit.

"You look..." He trailed off, his gaze undressing me where I stood. Time froze. My skin prickled with awareness, the thin hair on my arms rising. The crowd was unimportant in comparison to the man in front of me. We were in our own little realm. "You look like an angel."

"And you look like the Emerald Devil," I replied. The colors we'd chosen to wear tonight were starkly opposite from one another. It was poetic, in a way.

He approached with confidence, brushing his fingers along the exposed skin at my thigh. I flushed, glancing around to make sure no one was watching.

"I can't wait to get this thing off," I divulged. I was more self-assured than before, but glitz and glamor weren't my thing.

"Neither can I," Jack murmured, leaning down until our noses were inches apart. "With my teeth, if I must."

You walked right into that one, Em.

The time we'd spent apart was more pregnant as his lips met mine. Had it only been four days? Being deprived of water for that long would've been easier. Our kiss was rejuvenating. My skin burst to life when he placed his hand at the base of my spine, teasing the fabric that hung low there. I cupped his face, gluing him to me, running my thumbs over the hair on his jawline. With a low growl, he leaned in farther, pressing his hard body into mine. My lips parted with a contented sigh.

"Emma!"

We broke away like we'd been electrocuted. Jack grabbed my hand before I could step too far from him. Scalding heat made its way up my chest, past my cheeks and to my forehead as my parents came into view. I felt like I'd been caught doing something worse.

It was just a kiss, but also so much more. A reunion, of sorts.

"Oh, you look beautiful!" my mother gushed, holding my face in both of her hands. She wore a golden gown, her hair in a loose updo. Her tan skin made the natural blonde stand out.

"And you must be Emma's date," my father said while my mom embraced me. I eyed my dad from over her shoulder. I hadn't seen him since Easter, but he looked the same. His consistency was comforting. Formal suit, thinning brown hair, his face hardened from years as a defense attorney at a high-volume firm.

It was obvious he'd seen Jack and me kissing. I could read his polite expression like an open book. As my mother held me at arm's length, he was examining Jack's right hand—the one with Roman numerals trailing down it.

"Jack O'Connell." Jack held his tattooed hand out to shake my father's. He seemed at ease and I wished I could say the same for myself.

"Well, I can see why Emma likes you." My mom smiled at Jack, intertwining her arm with my father's.

"Was the drive okay?" I asked, trying to steer the conversation toward small talk. If I got my mom going on the topic of traffic, she wouldn't stop.

"What is it you do, Jack?" my dad queried, ignoring my poor attempt. He was in interrogation mode—with cause. Jack was a walking, talking, giant "No" in Dad world.

"Trade," Jack answered, glancing toward me to make sure I was okay. I tried to give an encouraging smile, but it faltered.

"Wall Street?" my dad asked, impressed.

"Not exactly."

"Where did you graduate from?"

Oh, God…

"A high school in Boston."

From the look on my dad's face, I felt the need to cut in.

"College isn't for everyone, Dad."

"Just curious." My father shrugged. "Most people who don't go to college can't afford a suit like that."

Jack grinned, but it was forced. "I've been fortunate in my endeavors."

"Okay!" I announced, tugging on Jack's sleeve. "Enough with the inquisition. We'll meet up with you guys later."

"Oh, but, Emma—" my mother began, but I was already dragging Jack away. Whether to save him or myself, I didn't know.

"I am so sorry," I apologized once we were a solid twenty-five yards across the ballroom. "My dad can be—"

"Protective," Jack finished for me. He didn't seem upset. If anything, he appeared as confident as before. "It's a good thing."

"You just look dangerous is all," I continued, making excuses for my father's rude behavior. And he did look dangerous—dark and deadly, as always. Whether he was in sweats, a T-shirt and jeans or a suit, his cataclysmic energy was palpable.

The corner of Jack's mouth twitched upward. "Dangerous, eh?"

I smiled shyly, looking down at the way my dress pooled on the ballroom floor. "Maybe a little unapproachable."

Jack took my hand in his, pulling me into his arms with force. "I seem to remember a woman in a skimpy sports bra who was more than happy to…*approach* me in September."

I jerked my head up, my jaw on the floor. He was talking about our embarrassing first kiss. When I had all but attacked him at the Emerald.

"Don't ever mention that again!" I shoved his shoulder playfully, but he was solid.

"How can I not?" His fiery gaze melted me on the spot. "I dream about it every night."

"God, I missed you," I murmured, inhaling the earthy, smoky smell of him.

He smiled into my hair. "Let's dance, dovey."

Chapter Sixteen

Jack

I pulled Emma close, placing my hand at the small of her back. The dress, or lack thereof, was slaying me. The amount of skin she was showing should have been illegal for someone like her. I didn't care for the stares from other men, peacekeepers or not. One particular copper was eyeing her like she was a piece of meat. With Emma wrapped in my arms, I kissed her neck nice and slow, making it clear that she was taken.

To me, jealousy was an unfamiliar emotion. I'd been *envious* of others throughout most of my childhood—people with more money, kids who didn't have to fall asleep with empty stomachs—but I'd never wanted to pluck a man's eyes from his skull for simply looking at a woman I considered mine. Hell, I'd never even *wanted* to consider a woman mine until now.

"Where did you learn to dance?" Emma leaned back a few inches so she could see my face, oblivious to the attention she drew. Throughout the ballroom, a song by Ariana Grande was playing. It was an unorthodox choice, but the tempo matched a waltz.

"My mum," I replied, planting a chaste kiss on her lips. It was all I could do to keep my arousal at bay. *You're in the middle of Manhattan surrounded by the entire police force. Calm the fuck down.*

We glided across the floor with the rest of the couples. She was an impressive dancer as well, but I could've assumed that. Emma and I had grown up very differently. Based on the appearance of her parents, their blood was as blue as it came. My evaluation of her on our first meeting was correct. I had no doubt her childhood was riddled with some form of cotillion.

Rare as it was, she'd managed to remain down to earth. On the legitimate business side of my work, I often ran into people who had no idea what it was like to survive without a safety net. I rarely took risks with capital. I'd clawed my way to the top with blood, sweat and terror. And I had every intention of staying there.

As we transitioned into the next song, Emma moved seamlessly with me. I wondered if she might want to meet up with her parents, but her grip on my hand and shoulder told me otherwise. Her ivory cheeks pinkened and the mass of people disappeared as I focused on her.

"You're blushing," I pointed out. "What are you thinking about?"

She smiled crookedly. "Besides how yummy you look in that suit?"

That made my heart beat a little faster. What was I, twelve? "Yeah, besides that."

She bit her lip, the blush deepening. I leaned in so that my mouth was at her ear, watching with satisfaction as goosebumps rose along the column of her neck.

"Now I really want to know."

She sighed. "It's embarrassing. And petty."

That had me confused. Emma was a lot of things I had yet to discover, but petty wasn't one of them. "Dove..." I warned, my voice low.

"I'm guessing you've been with a lot of women." She spoke fast, her breath warming the exposed skin at my collar. "I mean, you're older than me and you clearly know what you're doing in that regard. I'm just wondering about your past relationships. Were they all...experienced?"

"I've been with my fair share of women, yes, but I wouldn't call any of those interactions a relationship."

She hung on to my every word, her brow furrowing in confusion. She wasn't getting it.

"They've all been pretty quick meetings, Em. There one day, gone the next."

At that, her dark red lips twitched with satisfaction.

I swallowed, catching the gleam in her eye. "Does that make you happy?"

Her smile widened. "A bit. You may hold the upper hand with sex, but I know more about how dating works."

I trailed my mouth along her jawline. "I have a feeling this relationship is going to require a learning curve for both of us, sweetheart."

Before I had a chance to pull back, she leaned the length of her body against mine and kissed me. She skated her tongue across my bottom lip, tickling it. She smelled so sweet. I ached to taste her, to bury my face between her legs. *Fuck.*

"You'll be the death of me," I rasped, sending her out into a delicate twirl. If she kissed me like that again, I was going to be arrested for public indecency.

When she spun back into me, her attitude had changed. "Have you ever killed anyone?" she asked with indifference, like she didn't care whether I said yes.

She had my mind jumbled between reality and fantasy. I chose to answer honestly. "Yes."

Emma's grip on my hand loosened, but her feet didn't skip a step. I held her at arm's length, dying to see her reaction. Her brown eyes were wide and glistening, the chandeliers dancing in their reflection.

"So have I," she whispered.

I didn't have time to process what she said. At that very moment, a conversation was occurring a few yards away.

A sergeant in a formal uniform adorned with three stripes stood not far from us. He was being introduced to a man with a dark mustache, an expensive suit and an air of righteousness about him. He shook hands with the sergeant, introducing himself in return.

It was impossible to hear what the foreign-looking man said over the music, but it didn't matter. I'd seen photos of him before. I knew what the don of the New York Mafia looked like.

My hold on Emma tightened so much that she noticed. Her eyes, once clear and truthful, clouded with concern.

"Go to the bathroom," I commanded through a clenched jaw. Had Don Luca seen her? I didn't think so. Regardless, I had to get her out of here. Now. If he felt threatened by Emma without her even knowing why, I would hate to see what he thought of her now.

"Why?" she asked, hurt. She thought I was reacting badly to her confession, but I didn't care. The one thing that mattered was getting her away from Luca Nicoletti, the man responsible for not only her attack but countless murders across Manhattan.

"Go," was my answer. Her wounded expression burned a hole in the side of my face, but I kept my eyes on Don Luca. His back was to us. "*Now,* Emma."

She turned and ran in the opposite direction, slipping through a crowd of dancers. It wasn't until the white of her dress could no longer be seen that I chanced another look at Don Luca. He was speaking with the sergeant, oblivious.

If he happened to glance my way, he wouldn't recognize me. Even at a young age, Frank had been a paranoid bastard. He had kept my role in his criminal activity a secret. As an adult, I'd yet to shake the habit. I preferred to stay in the shadows, letting Connor take the brunt of any media our last name garnered.

We didn't make deals in the city that weren't with an established Irish family. The bulk of our income came from foreign countries. After high school, Connor and I had decided it would be best if I traveled overseas. I had spent a few years building contacts on the black market. Our biggest partners didn't operate close to home. We didn't shit where we ate.

As a result, I clung to my anonymity like a lifeline. Oftentimes, it was the only thing that kept me above ground. *You can't kill what you can't identify.*

Once I'd given Emma ample time to reach the bathroom, I took off after her, trying not to bump into anyone along the way. A few policemen and women looked suspiciously in my direction, forcing me to slow my gait. *This was a bad idea*. However, if I hadn't come with Emma tonight, Don Luca might've run into or seen her. Either way, I wouldn't let myself imagine the outcome.

As I approached the door to the northern wing, I shot a text to Eoghan.

Looking cloudy. Check for rain.

He confirmed immediately—it was his job to stay connected—and I pushed the door open, shoving my phone into my suit pocket.

"Emma?" I called, my voice echoing off the marble walls. My heart started thrashing. There was no one in this wing. Where the fuck was she?

"Are you going to follow me into the bathroom, too?"

Her voice came from a doorway to my left. I followed it.

"This is a coat closet, dove."

She was standing in a long, dimly lit room lined with racks of winter coats. While I shut the door behind us, she crossed her arms and gave me a stern "don't piss me off even more" glare. I neared her with caution. This was the first time she was perturbed with me. How I handled it was paramount.

"Why did you tell me to go to the bathroom?" she asked.

I couldn't tell her I'd seen Luca Nicoletti. That would just scare her and that was the last thing I wanted to do.

"You've never killed anyone," I stated, attempting to finish our conversation where we'd left it. I'd only just realized what she had said. There was no way Emma was a murderer. The idea was laughable.

She kept her arms crossed in defiance. "Why would I confess to something I've never done?"

Antsy, I raked my fingers through my hair. I had to stall her here, away from Don Luca, to give Eoghan time to case the block.

"Emma, I know killers." I held my hands to my chest. "I'm one of them. Trust me, you've never killed anyone."

Her tone was accusatory, her chin lifting a notch. "How can you be sure?"

"Because you're a fucking *angel*."

And she was, in her long white dress, the neckline ending somewhere above her navel. The maddening gap that went up her thigh, exposing inch after inch of seductive skin. She was my own personal angel, designed exquisitely by God with my every desire—every need—in mind.

Emma licked her lips in thought. As I watched her tongue dance along her bottom lip, I lost it. I couldn't hold back my attraction to her any longer. The night in the shower felt like weeks ago, not days. And what better excuse to buy us time than Emma herself?

"There's no lock on this door," I said, my voice raspy with want. "You feelin' dangerous, killer?"

"Dangerous?" Emma challenged, raising an eyebrow. "I'm feeling deadly."

I had her pinned against the wall within a second, my mouth everywhere on her, my bones rattling with the raw, primal need to fuck this woman. To make her mine. Hot blood rushed south, tightening the fabric of my slacks. I needed to be inside her. Right. Now.

Emma wrapped her legs around my torso, my erection pressing against her sex. She moaned, pushing my jacket off. I slid my hand up her smooth leg, reaching under to where the slit in her dress ended. Her panties were soaking. I ripped them off with a snarl, stuffing them in my pocket.

"Condom?" I hadn't expected to get lucky with her so soon, but I'd brought a few just in case.

"Birth control." She ran her fingers through my hair, lifting her hips.

I hesitated. "I'm clean."

I never went without protection, but I didn't want another barrier between me and Emma. We had enough hurdles as it was. I wanted to feel her everywhere.

Her eyes met mine and, just like before, I saw no sign of doubt in them. "I trust you."

There was no explaining the way my heart swelled at those words. Her meaning was clear. She trusted me, not just with her health, but to take her to a place she hadn't been in a long time.

I couldn't get my fly down quick enough.

"Fuck," I cursed, sinking into her inch by excruciating inch.

She was so damn tight. She wrapped her arms around me, holding me close. I braced her neck with one hand, sliding the other down her exposed back and resting it on her ass. Eyes locked, we paused to catch our breath. I was a little above average and wanted to give her the opportunity to accommodate my size.

It wasn't long until the muscles inside of her started to clench. She whimpered, wanting friction. I skimmed my lips along the delicate skin at the base of her throat, her pulse racing underneath them like a bird flapping its wings.

"Jack!" she begged.

"Shh, dove, I got you."

I scooped her wrists, lifting her arms above her head, marveling at the way her nipples bulleted through her satin dress. I wanted our first time to be longer, but someone could walk in at any second. The idea both horrified and enthralled me. Even if we were found, I wouldn't be able to stop. No one could stop me from claiming this woman. I'd waited long enough, but this was worth it. *She* was worth it.

When I flexed my hips, my cock hummed with delight. I couldn't slow down and, by the symphony of moans she was orchestrating, she didn't want me to. She dragged her fingernails across the fabric on my upper back, desperate for something to hold onto. I pounded into her over and over, pushing her flush with the wall. Her channel began to pulse, massaging my dick from the inside. Every cell in my body contracted with impending release.

"What do you need, Emmy?" I asked, my breathing hitched.

Her hold on me tightened as she threaded her fingers in my hair. When she spoke, she sounded just as mind-blown as I did. "Just you, Jack. Please don't stop!"

Never.

Moving my hand to the small of her back, I arched her farther into my thrusts. She went slick around me, moaning wildly, sinking her teeth into the muscle between my neck and shoulder. The sound and feel of the orgasm ripping through her pushed me over the edge, my knees almost buckling.

Her pussy clamped onto my cock, milking me. I burst with a thick groan, white heat blurring my vision. My heart ricocheted inside my chest, threatening to shatter my rib cage. Her name ripped through my throat like it was the only word I knew. With my eyes squeezed shut and lungs burning, I clung to her as if there was nothing else keeping me rooted to the ground.

Let me live here, I prayed.

She had the power to make me forget who I was. All the things I'd done were inconsequential with her in my arms. It was like holding heaven and, in that moment, she was my salvation.

* * * *

Emma's cloak, brilliant and bright, was easy to find amidst the sea of dark clothing. There was a silly smile on her face as I slid it over her shoulders. Her hazy eyes told me her thoughts hadn't yet returned to her body. I wanted to relish and relive the moment as well, but she wasn't safe yet. I had to get us out of here.

"We're leaving." I grabbed her hand, guiding her toward the door. "I'd like to do that again somewhere a little more private."

I wasn't lying. I'd never come so hard in my life.

"My parents will wonder where we went."

I handed her my phone. "Call them."

She sighed as she dialed, but I could tell she didn't want to be here anymore than I did. "Mom?" She turned her back to me and I took the opportunity to check the hallway, finding it empty.

Emma continued her conversation while I fought to stay present. Half of my mind was still reeling from being inside Emma. The other half was in escape mode. Don Luca was somewhere in the building. Unaware, yes. And I needed to keep it that way.

Emma returned, passing me the smartphone. She was grinning ear to ear. I raised my eyebrows in question.

"Ella has perfect timing," she explained, slipping her hand into mine.

"Ella?" I asked, masking my growing anxiety.

Emma giggled. "My little sister. The sheriff called to say it looks like she's throwing a kegger at our house in Connecticut. My mom and dad just left."

Well, that worked out. Although even if Emma had insisted on staying to mollify her parents, I would've slung her over my shoulder and carried her away from the Met. Her anger would abate eventually.

"Where are we going?" she asked as we made our way farther down the hall, our shoes clicking on the stone floor.

"Staff entrance."

I opened another door, all but pushing Emma into the next wing. There were catering waiters and attendants in this room. A few of them eyed us with suspicion before returning to their conversations. They didn't get paid enough to care.

Once outside, I called Eoghan and told him to meet us down the block. I didn't want Don Luca or any of the Nicolettis mistaking him for a Murray.

"What's the rush?" Emma inquired as I ushered her toward the SUV.

Now that she was safe, there was one thing left on my mind. "I think you know."

A blush crept up her skin as I buckled her in.

Chapter Seventeen

Emma

Jack and I went back to his apartment and ordered Thai. We ate it on the kitchen floor as Fia milled about, hunting for food.

While Jack devoured a few courses, I nibbled at a spring roll, too nervous to eat much of anything. He had his sleeves rolled up, exposing iron-like forearms, his black diamond cufflinks glinting on the marble countertop. I swallowed hard every time he looked at me, a glint in his eye that indicated I would be his next meal.

I'd just had sex.

For the first time in a long while.

That fact was baffling.

Jack had moved quickly, like he couldn't stand not being with me any longer. I was grateful he hadn't given me a chance to overthink it, to second-guess myself. But I was sure now more than ever. I was ready.

I'd been ready for Jack from the moment I had laid eyes on him. As he moved within me, deeper than I'd ever felt anyone before, he seemed to be staking his territory, all but clearing out the signs that Nate had been there. Surprisingly, I didn't feel any guilt.

Something was bothering me, though. Jack admitted to being with other women—many other women—but he'd never been in a relationship. By the sound of it, they were all one-night stands. What would that make us?

Jack sighed, pulling me from my thoughts. "You're killing me, dove."

I glanced up at him from my position on the floor. He had finished eating and was watching as I pushed a single grain of rice around my plate.

"You've barely eaten anything," he continued, concerned and somewhat upset. "I can see your head spinning in circles."

I grimaced at his accuracy, dropping my chopsticks with finality. "I've been thinking about something."

"Obviously."

"It's about…" I looked at my hands, refusing to meet his gaze. I felt childish for bringing up his sexual history again. "I don't know if I want to have sex on your bed yet… Not if I'm just going to be another notch on it."

Jack was on his knees in a flash, cupping my face in his hands. He kissed me, putting a stop to the whirring in my brain. He tugged at my lip with his teeth, almost scolding.

"Don't ever talk about yourself like that, Emma." His tone was sharp with authority. "Trust me when I say, you aren't just a notch on my bedpost. If it makes you feel any better, I've never had a woman in my apartment."

"Then where have you... Where did you?"

"I have other apartments around the city. They're usually used for meetings and such. I don't like anyone to know where I live, apart from a few trusted individuals. Not even my mum sends her care packages here."

"Then why bring *me* here?"

"Have I not given you enough hints?" Jack kissed the tip of my nose. "You're different. You make me feel...different."

I bit my lip to hide a smile, warmth spread through my limbs. "You make me feel different too."

As my words hit him, Jack's smile dissipated. The lines of his face hardened and his pupils dilated, eyes black with lust. He stood, holding his hand out for me. The heat in my belly turned to chaotic butterflies. This was it. He was going to take me again. Something about this time felt different. Now, I was in his domain, under his discretion and entirely at his disposal.

"Will you..." I cleared my throat, keeping my gaze on his outstretched fingers. "Will you go easy on me?"

"Is that what you want?"

"No," I answered, surprising myself.

"Mmm." Jack groaned. He was swelling in his dress pants. "Good answer."

He grabbed my hand, lifting me up and over his shoulder with ease.

"You know I can walk, right?"

He set his palm on my backside, holding me in place as he strode toward his bedroom. He was so damn tall, it was like riding a horse—upside down. "Those heels may do wonders for my spank bank, but they look painful. Why walk when I can carry you?"

Spank bank?

He deposited me on the floor at the foot of his gigantic bed, then began unbuttoning his shirt. *Oh, okay. We're just going right into this.* I bent to unlatch my heel.

"Heels on."

I peered up at Jack, hands frozen at my ankle. His shirt was on the floor, his buckle undone. Jesus, his body was unfair. Broad shoulders, biceps with that sexy, bulging vein, a delicious V disappearing into his pants. He smirked, running a hand over his smooth chest, across his chiseled abdomen and down to his impressive erection. He palmed himself through his slacks, taunting me.

My knees turned to jelly, but I went with it. I'd never had a man in my mouth. If anyone deserved to be the first, it was him. I reached for his waistband, tugging at his zipper.

"Hey." Jack collected my wrists, pulling me to stand. He grabbed the back of my neck and kissed me. "If you wrap those pretty red lips around my cock, I'm going to blow in three seconds."

He flicked the diamond straps of my gown from my shoulders. It pooled at my feet like it was made to be taken off. Jack's heated gaze traveled the length of my body. I bit my lip, moving to cover myself. Again Jack stopped me, taking one of my breasts in his hand with reverence.

"Don't ever hide from me, dove," he murmured, dusting his thumb over the jagged peak of my nipple. His touch was a drug I wanted to overdose on. "I didn't tell you before, but your body is... Fuck's sake, I've never seen anything like it. You're so goddamn beautiful, Emma."

Jack lifted my chin, forcing me to look into his emerald eyes, which were hazy with want. "You'll believe me when I say that. I'm not a liar. Not with you."

He didn't wait for a response before diving in to steal my breath. Gripping my hair in his fist, he angled my head to his liking, his teeth trailing across my bottom lip. He gave it a sharp bite, then licked the sting away. When his tongue hit mine, pinpricks of light danced behind my eyes. My skin flushed, the apples of my cheeks fiery with arousal. I couldn't help but smile at the sensation.

"What?" Jack whispered.

"Nothing," I answered, not wanting him to stop. "It's super cringey."

He widened the distance between our faces. "Say it."

"When you kiss me…" I paused to clear the dryness in my throat. His stare made me feel like I was being dissected in the best way. "When you kiss me, I see stars."

"Fuck," Jack cursed, emphasizing the *F*. "I'm gonna help you map the galaxy, darling."

He pushed me backward onto the bed, his weight coming down on top of me. It was welcome. Having his body in close proximity made me feel safe. My legs parted on instinct, his groin coming to rest against mine. Jack ground himself into me, his zipper teasing my clitoris. He hissed, trailing wet kisses down the length of my torso. When he slipped his thumb inside me, I lifted my hips toward his beautiful face.

Eyes on me, he proceeded to feast on my pussy like a king after the hunt. He spread my lips with two fingers, exposing the sensitive flesh between my legs. He widened my entrance with his thumb, pressing upward into my G-spot. Mother of God, he knew what he was doing. Wetness dripped down my behind, my sex throbbing uncontrollably.

"Holy fuck," I whimpered, wriggling beneath his ministrations.

Jack chuckled, his breath skating across my molten core. "There's nothing holy about me, darling. Least of all the way I fuck."

My eyes rolled, hips riding his face like a madwoman. He gripped my thighs, pinning them to the mattress as I came into his sinful mouth. That had to be a record. I hardly had time to recover before Jack was above me, his cock at my entrance. *When did he take his pants off?*

"Open up for me, baby," he whispered, balancing himself on one elbow.

I glanced down, eyes widening. *He wasn't that big in the coat closet, right?* His erection was long and thick, veiny and heavy. Not to mention hungry. If a penis could be hungry, his was starving. He wouldn't fit. No way.

"I-I can't take that," I insisted.

Jack gripped my jaw in his hand, catching my wild eyes. "You already have, sweetheart."

I nodded once.

Jack slammed into me, sheathing himself to the hilt. The sharp pain took me by surprise. I sank my teeth into his neck, biting hard. Jack's responding moan was low and drawn out, but he didn't move, letting me adjust to his intrusion. His mouth descended onto mine, his tongue insatiable.

Once I tasted myself on him, adrenaline spiked my system. I reached down and grabbed his ass, digging my nails into the hard muscle there.

Jack flinched, then pumped once, twice, three times. My jaw slackened. He took one of my legs, hiking it over his shoulder for leverage. *Thank God I practice yoga.* He stared down at where our bodies connected, watching himself disappear into me with awe.

"You take my cock so well, baby."

His voice was guttural, like he was struggling to restrain himself. I didn't want him to. Another orgasm was cresting. Tears pricked the backs of my eyes. The pleasure was almost too much to bear. The way he stretched me, the way he touched me, the way he looked at me like I hung the moon…

"Do you know how hard you make me? You're so fucking hot. Jesus! You're perfect, Emma."

He took one of my nipples into his mouth, twisting the other between his fingers. We were covered in a light mist of sweat, sliding against one another. I tucked my free leg around his waist, pulling him closer. It felt so right, like we were two puzzle pieces that finally found their match. He moved faster and faster, his powerful hips bucking. An uninhibited ache grew in the depths of my belly. When his teeth clamped down on my breast, sucking and nipping, I snapped.

"Oh, shit!" I moaned, thrashing beneath him.

Jack pulled out, flipping me onto my stomach like I was nothing more than a doll. "Get that ass up, dove."

I hesitated, panting heavily. "I'm…I'm saving that hole for my future husband."

"Noted." He chuckled, palming my butt cheeks in his hands. "I'm not going back there."

"Oh." I breathed a sigh of relief as I lifted my hips off the bed, digging my knees into the plush mattress. "Okay, cool."

Jack's entrance was easier this time but deeper. I gasped in tandem with his hiss. He was huge this way, taking up every bit of me he could. The head of his cock brushed something deep within me. My neck went limp and my head fell forward. The sound of our skin slapping reverberated off the walls. He held my hips steady as he moved, his fingers delving into my flesh. I knew I'd see the marks tomorrow, but I wanted him to leave his trace. Proof that he'd been there. Proof that Jack was real and not just a figment of my imagination.

"What are you doing to me?" he asked, his lips at the nape of my neck. It seemed as though he was speaking to himself. I shivered, pushing myself into him. "Don't ever doubt your power. You control me, not the other way around. Do you understand?"

"Yes."

It contradicted what he'd said at dinner the other night, but I understood. The hunger in his tone, the desire in his eyes—I put those there. He'd told me on multiple occasions that I made him want to lose control. He was letting go of his authority, giving it to me. Not in the way he commanded me, no. He could lead, but I had the real power. To do other things to him. To make him experience things he never had with any other woman.

He wrapped my hair around his fist like a leash, tugging my head back. It didn't hurt. If anything, it helped. I felt useless beneath him, but I knew I wasn't. His breathing grew labored as he moved in and out. Whatever I was doing, it was right.

"I need you to give me one more, angel," Jack demanded, picking up his speed. "Squeeze my dick as tight as you can."

My lungs burned with exertion. I was borderline paralyzed, arms limp at my sides. He couldn't be serious.

"Not again," I whimpered. "Please."

Jack paused, pulling my back to his front. He wrapped his forearms around my torso like a cage, his lips at my ear. "Do you want me to stop?"

"Please, no," I begged, failing to recognize my own voice. I was so far gone. He was screwing me into outer space, into oblivion. "Please don't stop."

He turned my head to the side, his hooded gaze skating across my face to make sure I wanted this. "Then do as I say."

I let my head fall backward into the hollow between his neck and shoulder. "I can't."

"You will," he argued, palming my breasts in his giant hands. Chills erupted across my skin as he started thrusting into me again, faster this time. When I felt the beginnings of another orgasm, I was in disbelief. He was good. Too good. Way better than I had ever thought possible. "I'm going to count down from three, then I'm going to fill this greedy little pussy with so much cum, it's going to drip down your thighs. And you're going to scream my fucking name. You're going to milk my cock and take everything I give you. Understand?"

He sucked on the thin skin at my throat, eliciting a whimper of consent from my lips.

"Out loud, Emma," he growled, giving my hip bone a warning squeeze.

"Mhmm," I moaned, hardly able to lift my eyelids.

"Three..."

He slid his fingers down my pelvis, sinking them into my soaked folds. A tangible current, warm and heady, ran through the center of my body, expanding outward to my fingertips.

"Two..."

He nipped at my earlobe, pulling the diamond earrings into his mouth. They clanked along his teeth, the sound borderline erotic.

"One..."

When he pinched my clit, I detonated.

"Oh, fuck...*Jack*!"

My vision went white. The entirety of the galaxy exploded against my retinas. Planets collided, supernovas erupted. My muscles tensed, then relaxed, then clenched again. My core squeezed his cock with vigor, my scream hoarse and primal.

"Fuck, yes!" Jack growled, filling me with his seed. His heart beat a wild rhythm into my back as he guided me down to the bed. "Good girl."

Words escaped me. I checked out before my head hit the pillow.

When I opened my eyes, I was shocked to see water falling in front of my face. I blinked a few times. How had I gotten in the shower? I smelled my silken hair. My braids had been undone. My skin felt smooth and clean. I touched my lips, surprised to find my makeup had been removed.

Jack rose in front of me, blocking the rainfall spray. He held a loofah in his hand, having just finished washing my feet. He smirked, eyes flicking back and forth between mine.

"Welcome back, dovey."

"W-What happened?" I asked, my voice weak.

He pressed his lips to my forehead. "You may've blacked out."

My mouth fell open. "What does that mean?"

Jack shrugged, tossing the loofah onto the marble bench. "Not sure. You were awake, but nothing was getting through here." He tapped my temple.

I rubbed my palms over my cheeks. "You washed my face?"

"Of course," he answered, tilting his head in curiosity. "I assume you don't sleep in your makeup."

"Thank you," I mumbled, running my hands up and down my arms to work the life back into them.

"You okay?" Jack tugged me close, his nose in my wet hair.

"I think so." I burrowed into his chest, drinking in his scent. My core twitched, primed for more. What the hell was happening to me? I was getting addicted. "Is it always like this?"

"No," Jack answered, his erection bobbing against my stomach. Did that thing ever go down? "We've got something special here. You see that, right?"

"Yeah." I stood on my toes to kiss him. "I just didn't know you did."

"If I was blind, I'd still see you." Jack trailed his lips down the column of my neck, his hand drifting to my backside. He pulled my body flush with his, sighing. "I'm enjoying every second with you, angel."

I furrowed my brow. He said that like he thought I was going somewhere. Like our relationship had an expiration date. Seeking to quash those wayward thoughts, I gripped his cock in my hand, sliding my fingers down the length of it. It was velvet wrapped around an iron bat. He flinched, grinding into my palm.

"I'm going to be sore tomorrow," I joked, licking the water droplets from his chest.

"Oh, sweetheart." He smirked, flashing me those devilish eyes. "You're going to be sore for a week."

Chapter Eighteen

Emma

After crashing on the couch, I was surprised to find Jack still asleep at nine o'clock the following morning. He lay on his back, his arms up by his head. His face was serene and unencumbered, eyes fluttering with a dream, lips parted, jaw slack for once. *Wow. Just wow.* I could have watched him doze forever.

I got the feeling he didn't sleep in often, so I decided to let him indulge. Finding a navy-blue sweater in his massive walk-in closet, I threw it on and made my way toward the hall to ring my mom.

She sounded exhausted. I figured it must have something to do with Ella and her party. She mentioned Thanksgiving, but I couldn't make out much apart from a long yawn. I said "Yeah," pretending I'd heard her, and she got off the phone after that.

Stomach rumbling, I traipsed into the living area to find something simple to eat, giving an expectant Fia a pat between the ears. The kitchen had three different pantries and two refrigerators, but I found a blueberry yogurt in under five minutes. While opening drawers at random to search for eating utensils, I froze.

In the drawer to the left of the five-range, a gun lay where I'd hoped to find a spoon. It was some sort of black pistol with an ominous silencer attached to the end.

Shocked, I shut the drawer and exited the kitchen, leaving my hunger and yogurt behind. *What did you expect? Of course Jack has a gun. He probably has multiple. He's a mobster, after all.* Apparently, I hadn't considered all that entailed. I'd been too caught up in Jack himself to assume he lived in a world where people kept guns with silencers at the ready in their kitchens.

Rounding the doorway into one of the many guest bathrooms, I realized that I *had* thought about it, at least for a moment. I'd asked Jack the night before if he'd ever killed anyone. He had said yes.

And it didn't scare me. If anything, I was relieved. Jack wasn't the perfect man I'd made him out to be in my head. Beautiful, strong and wealthy, yes. But he'd done bad things. Maybe that made him more attractive in my eyes. We were both good people who had done very bad things.

Flashing lights, white sheets, loose pills…

"Emma, let go!"

I splashed cold water on my face and pulled my hair into a braid. As I tied the plaits, I examined my reflection. I didn't look too different—still small and wide-eyed—but it felt as if I was a new person. I'd had sex four times and orgasmed six since I'd last looked in a mirror. I hadn't even known my body was capable of that, and in such a short amount of time.

With Nate, it had been fumbling hands and awkward discoveries. We were young. Our bodies hadn't been in sync with one another like Jack's was with mine. Sex was something I thought came with the territory of having a boyfriend. It felt good, but he had always finished before I could lose myself. I didn't mind. I was just happy I could bring him pleasure in that way.

I lifted the oversized sweater, discovering small pink bruises on my hip bones where Jack had gripped me. Love bites dotted my throat and the insides of my thighs. It made me smile.

For the past few years, everyone treated me like I had "handle with care" stamped across my forehead. Jack had prodded my packaging last night, discovering just how much pressure it would take to get me to break. Finally, someone wasn't treating me like I was made of glass.

Jack had both marked his territory on my body. My lips were red and puckered from his kisses. I ached, but in a euphoric way. The soreness reminded me of his absence.

Seeking to rectify that, I snuck into his bedroom and crawled under the covers, being careful not to bump his legs as I burrowed between them. I wrapped my hand around the hot, silken skin of his cock. He was already hard—I hoped he was dreaming of me—and I closed my lips around the velvety tip, praying I was doing it right. *What a thing to pray about.*

He woke up with a sharp intake of breath followed by a low moan, his hips stirring. I continued with renewed confidence, twirling my tongue around the crown before taking him deeper. He gave a sleepy groan as I licked my way up his shaft, trailing my tongue along the thick vein at the base. When he gripped my hair in his hands, I placed my own on his thighs, releasing him with a *pop*.

"Emma fucking Marshall," he cursed, that vein pulsating against my bottom lip. I squinted at the sudden intrusion of light.

Jack had removed the blanket from my head and was looking down at me, his eyelids heavy. His tongue was caught between his teeth, his fingers moving restlessly within the tresses of my braid. He raised an eyebrow, egging me on.

More than happy to oblige, I wrapped my lips around him again, keeping my eyes on his. When I hollowed my cheeks and sucked, his head fell back against the pillows.

"Christ, Em. Just like that."

Fingers splayed against my skull, hips flexing upward, he guided my progress. His breath became audible, enlisting a hot glow of internal pride. He made it sound like losing control was a bad thing, but I loved it. I'd never felt so powerful.

When his cock thickened, I knew he was close. With his next thrust, he hit the back of my throat and I opened myself to accommodate him. He began moving at a rapid pace, fucking my mouth like he owned it. He fisted his left hand in the sheets, the tendons in his forearm straining. I reached between his legs, twirling his balls.

"Mother of—"

That was the only warning he managed to get out before his hot cum filled my mouth. I swallowed, but he continued to unravel with a string of expletives, filling me once again. The man was virile. Even the act of pleasuring him made me slick, wetness coating my inner thighs. He groaned, emptying the last of himself into me.

He released his hold on my head, but I wasn't finished yet. I could feel those eyes on me, but I focused my attention on the job at hand. While his muscles relaxed in the aftermath, I lavished his cock, licking him clean. I released his balls, trailing slow kisses across the skin that was now dampened with sweat. From his pelvis to the hard ridges of his six-pack, to the fluttering pulse between his collarbones.

"Was that okay?" I asked, pulling away before reaching his lips. I wasn't sure if he'd want to kiss me after that. Maybe I needed to brush my teeth first?

His expression was lost somewhere between sleep and awe, like he couldn't discern whether he was dreaming. "You're kidding, right?"

I shrugged, biting the inside of my cheek. "I've never done it before."

He wrapped me in his arms and kissed me with reverence, gliding his tongue against mine. It pleased me, knowing he could taste himself in there. And he didn't seem to mind one bit. "You can practice on me anytime, dove."

Out of my peripheral vision, I saw a dark object blur through Jack's room and into his closet, reminding me of something. I grinned. "I think I know why I like your cat so much."

Jack tilted his head, listening as Fia played among the racks of clothing. "Why's that?"

"He's the feline version of you. You both wear all black and have green eyes. And you're both up to no good."

"I think we know why he's obsessed with you, then." Jack wiggled his eyebrows. I flushed, burying my face in his chest. He tugged at the sweater I was wearing, tracing the curve of my spine with his palm. "Can I ask you a question?"

"Mmm?"

"If you don't have sex, why are you waxed?"

"I don't like hair." I shook my head, leaning back so he could see my face. He widened his eyes. "Don't worry. You're well-manicured. Although, my only recent experience with male pubic regions is from watching *Game of Thrones*."

Jack tossed his head against the pillow, his chest rumbling with laughter. "You're fucking adorable."

I pursed my lips, my face falling. How long until he stopped finding my lack of expertise amusing? How long until he wanted something more? I worried I wouldn't be able to satisfy someone like him.

"You still don't believe me when I say things like that," Jack concluded, his jaw firm. "What's it going to take, Emma?"

His question hit me like a slap to the face. I was perturbed by how on-the-nose it was.

"I'm batting out of my league here," I fired back. "I mean, do you not know what you look like?"

"Do you not know what *you* look like?" His expression softened as he pulled me toward him. "'Out of my league.' Jesus Christ, Emma. You're the most precious creature I've ever laid eyes on. I had to hold you so tightly at the ball last night because I thought one of New York's finest would swoop in at any minute. How do you not notice the way men look at you?"

I didn't know how to answer that. I'd grown up in a small town. Everyone knew I was with Nate. And here, in Manhattan, I hadn't been paying attention to my surroundings. Until now.

He combed his fingers through my hair, wrapping a few loose tendrils around his knuckles. "Believe me, I'm the one batting out of my league. You're breathtaking, your innocence is a total turn-on, you're a *scholar*... You don't even eat meat, for Christ's sake!"

I looked at him, wanting to see the expressions pass over his face. Words were flying out of him so fast, and with such passion.

"You're an actual good fucking person and it kills me because I'm a monster. If I wasn't so selfish, I would've left you alone."

At that, I pressed my face into his, shutting him up with my mouth. I didn't want to hear any more. I didn't care about how he felt I was too good for him, didn't care about all the terrible things he'd done, didn't feel like telling him I wasn't the angel he thought I was. It was when he mentioned leaving that I started to panic.

"Don't leave me," I said, rolling so that my body covered his, as if I could pin him down. "Don't say that. Keep being selfish."

"Just try and stop me, dove." His tongue didn't even have to touch my lips before I opened, letting him in. He growled, spurring his hips into me. "You're going to have to learn how to take a compliment."

"Why is that?" I asked, breathless.

Jack's eyes gleamed devilishly. "Because I'm going to put you on a fucking pedestal, darling."

He lifted me until my legs straddled his. My veins pumped molten desire into my heart when I realized what he was doing. If we kept going at this pace, we'd complete the *Kama Sutra* by day's end.

"You being literal with that terminology, Jack?" I asked.

He still had my body in his powerful grip, forcing me to hover above his arousal. My clit was a live wire waiting for a spark. I was sore, but ready.

Jack laughed, but it was strained. "You've got banter, lass. I'll give you that."

"Care to give me something else?"

His grin snapped my heart in two. "You're an animal, you know that?"

An unintelligible swear flew off my tongue as he dropped me down onto him. I was more than willing to let Jack impale me as often as he liked. I gripped the hard flesh where his neck met his shoulders and he groaned, our mouths clashing.

We spent all of Sunday morning in bed continuing our exploration of each other. We moaned and cursed, laughed and played. It turned out Jack wasn't lying about his left butt cheek being sensitive. Tickling and wrestling and fucking all warped together in Jack's bedroom, while the rest of the city's inhabitants went about their day. It was like we were trying to recover lost time, although I didn't think any amount of time with this man would be enough for me.

As Jack made us a massive brunch, I sat on a bar stool at the island. Watching him cook while Mac Miller rapped about oblivion was entertainment enough. Chin resting on the heels of my hands, I couldn't wipe the smile from my face. My heart somersaulted every time he glanced over his shoulder, our eyes catching. I felt lucky just being there, in his apartment—his safe, private sanctuary. He was relaxed, his jaw getting relief from the near-constant grinding. With his flannel pajama bottoms and freshly fucked hair, he looked so domestic. Nothing like the man who admitted to being a murderer. A monster.

At that thought, my gaze flitted to the drawer next to the five-range, the one with the pistol in it. I bit my lip, torn.

On my first night here, Jack hadn't been shy in his pursuit of answers about my past. He'd been straightforward, making my small disclosures seem necessary. Which, I assumed, they were. He'd thought I'd been sexually violated. I had to assure him that wasn't the case without letting my mind stray to painful memories, recollections of what *had* happened.

Now, I had a few questions of my own, but I didn't want to ruin our day together. Who knew when we would have another one like it? Clearing my throat, I made my decision.

"What does an Irish mob boss do?" My voice was light and playful, but the muscles along his spine tensed. He put a more literal meaning into the term *beating eggs*.

I twisted my lips to the side, wondering if he would even answer. Should I ask again? I didn't want to push him, but this felt important. His work was a large part of who he was. He lived in a world I knew nothing about.

He sighed, turning to set his hands on the edge of the island that separated us. "Don't worry about it."

I put my own hands in my lap, preparing for a confrontation. "Why?"

"You don't need to know." His tone was clipped, but I couldn't stop myself. I'd opened this can of worms and I wanted to get to the bottom of it.

"Do you deal drugs?"

Jack rolled his eyes at the idea, as if it was insulting. "No."

"Arms?"

He pinched the bridge of his nose. "Emma…"

My name was a warning, but I trudged ahead. "Are you a hit man?"

He dropped his palm to the counter with an audible slap. "If you don't stop running that mouth, I'm going to fuck it. And I think you know by now that I fuck hard."

I snickered, only to realize he wasn't joking. He cast me a glare that sent goosebumps over my flesh. It ended any hope of discussing the matter further.

"Coffee?" he asked, flipping the switch on his mood like normal people did with lights. Lord, he was giving me emotional whiplash. Caffeine was just what I needed.

"Mhmm," I answered, my lips clamped shut.

He poured a cup from a fancy espresso machine, not bothering to hide his smirk. He wasn't lying when he said he was used to getting his way. He also wasn't kidding when he'd said this relationship would require a learning curve for both of us. But I was a good student. I could figure him out, even if he didn't give me the answers.

Over a delicious meal of sweet crepes and mimosas, Jack inquired about Columbia. He seemed captivated by anything I had to say, which was encouraging. We were both careful not to touch subjects that could blend into the danger zone. For him, that was the details of his work. For me, it was my past.

By the time the sun began to set, I left Jack's. He offered to let me stay over, but Ava would be wondering where I was. Not to mention, I needed some time alone to process everything.

When I got home, I showered and changed into an old pair of sweats. I was achy and deflated, like I'd crash-landed from cloud nine. My twenty-four hours with Jack might as well have been minutes. And the fact that I never knew when I would see him again made me anxious.

Chapter Nineteen

Emma

The insides of lecture halls and the glow of my laptop screen mashed up to form a long, frustrating November. If I'd thought my professors were being heavy-handed before, I owed them an apology. I couldn't recall ever feeling so overwhelmed with my studies.

Whenever I wasn't reviewing dates of famous archaeological digs or underwater expeditions in the Mediterranean, it was thoughts of Jack that clouded my mind. Not just thoughts—a physical *want*. Every so often I would start to feel antsy like a caged animal. Or an addict needing a fix.

We saw each other on numerous occasions, but never had time to talk. Or we didn't want to. We met in his office at the Emerald, the back of the SUV parked in an alley, even a locked bathroom on campus. The location didn't matter. Whenever we had an hour free at the same time, we dropped whatever we were doing and ran. We tore at each other's clothes. Scratching, grabbing, pulling hair, just trying to hold on to something tangible. Trying to get enough of each other to last until we found time to meet again.

Shannon, on the other hand, I saw too much of. Whether she was barking orders at Roisin's or showing up unannounced at my apartment, I got the feeling Connor was just as preoccupied as his brother. She mentioned something while we were out to breakfast about friends of the family being in over their heads, but I didn't get any details. She held her finger over her mouth, silencing me on the issue. She was almost as secretive as Jack. It was infuriating.

On a weekday near the end of the month, I was lying on the desk in Jack's home office, my thighs wrapped around his hips. He buried his face in my hair, his hands roaming my body as if he had more than two. I dragged my fingernails along his back, losing my bearings as he thrust, tipping me over the edge of sanity.

"Shit." He stopped moving, straightening abruptly. I reached for him, missing the pressure of his body against mine, but then he said something that brought me spinning back to earth. "It's your mum."

He held his cell phone in one hand, pinning me down beneath him with the other. Before I could react, he answered.

"Mrs. Marshall." His voice had returned to its normal baritone, but his chest rose and fell as he struggled to keep his breathing under control. We'd been going at it for a while.

"It's wonderful to hear from you too."

He withdrew from me, circling his modern office to pause in front of the window overlooking Central Park. Good thing we were fifty floors up. There would be a massive car crash if someone were to catch sight of a shameless, nude Jack staring into the late afternoon light. For God's sake, his cock was jutting out, glistening with my arousal.

Shaking my head, I hopped off the desk and started putting clothes on. Something about being naked while Jack talked to my mom felt wrong. But why was my mom calling him in the first place? And how did she get his number?

You called her from Jack's phone at the Policeman's Ball, idiot.

"Sounds great," he continued.

I gave him a questioning look, yanking my top on.

He winked at me. "See you then."

He hung up and I rounded on him.

"*See you then*?" I repeated, my voice a pitch I'd never heard before.

Jack smirked, watching me fumble with my boots. "Why are you getting dressed?"

"Tell me why my mom just called you! What did she say?"

He leaned against the side of his desk, amused by my reaction. "Apparently, we've been invited to your family home for Thanksgiving. We're expected there Wednesday at five."

"*What*?" My mind was reeling. "That's tomorrow! My mom never *once* asked me to come home for the holiday. Let alone bring you!"

He held both hands flat against his heart, his face a wounded façade. "Am I not the type of girl you take home to mum?"

A heavy knot twisted in the pit of my stomach. I recalled my mom mentioning something about Thanksgiving earlier in the month, but I'd only said yes because I hadn't heard her correctly. If I'd known she had wanted me to return to Stonerose, I would've conjured a way to get out of it. And she wanted Jack to come *too*? This was bad. Very bad. Timelines—hell, *worlds*—were about to collide and I had zero control over the matter.

"I'm going to ask you one more time, dove," Jack continued, his voice darkening as he pulled me to him, my wrists shackled in his hands. "Why are you getting dressed?"

"Forgive me if my mom inviting my boyfriend home for Thanksgiving took me out of the mood."

Jack raised his eyebrows. "Boyfriend, huh?"

I flushed, glancing down at our hands. We'd talked exclusivity, but never put a label on us. "I don't think I can introduce you to my little sister as my fuck buddy."

He lifted my chin, earnest. "Is that what you think we are? Fuck buddies?"

I forced a small smile. "Well, we *are* very good at it."

He studied my face, refusing to let me look away. "I'm sorry if I made you feel that way. It's just...hard for me to keep my hands off you. Especially when we see so little of one another."

"I know," I agreed. "I feel that way too."

"Do you want to talk now?"

I laughed. He was still butt naked, but Jack wasn't the type to feel self-conscious. He had no reason to be. "About what?"

He thought for a few moments, releasing my chin. "How about why you won't sleep in the same bed as me?"

I froze. So that's why we were so much better at fucking than talking. There were too many subjects that were off-limits for us. I hoped going home for the first time since I'd left for college didn't bring everything to the surface.

"On second thought," I said, slipping back out of my boots, "I think I'll take my clothes off."

"Yeah, that's what I thought." Jack chuckled, helping me with my shirt.

* * * *

Jack

Emma's family home looked just as I had imagined it would. New England style, colonial accents, located in a small neighborhood. Once we entered the town of Stonerose, we arrived at our destination quick. The place was tiny. All homegrown businesses and quaint, well-kept parks surrounded by dense maple trees. I'd heard of small-town America but had never seen it. I had spent almost my entire childhood in Boston then, after a few years abroad, had relocated to Manhattan.

Emma was nervous the entire drive. She fidgeted—knuckles white, hands clasped together—to mask her growing anxiety. I was learning her in the way she expressed emotion. She liked to hold things in, like me, but gave away small clues. I'd gleaned more over the past three months from watching her than I could say for anyone else in my life. All five-foot-four-inches of her fascinated me.

After parking the sleek, black Spyder in the rounded driveway, I reached over and squeezed Emma's hand. She gave me a small smile when I kissed her knuckles.

"Don't worry," I murmured against them. "I'll be good."

She glanced around the interior of the vehicle, brow furrowed. "How many cars do you own?"

I hadn't been expecting that question. "I'm not sure. One short of a fleet, I suppose. I usually just grab one and go."

She rolled her eyes and exited the vehicle. *Keep her smiling,* I reminded myself, following to help her with the bags.

Gregory and Katherine Marshall made their way across the pristine lawn dressed in the usual upper-class holiday attire. Lots of cotton blends, plaid undertones and Ralph Lauren logos.

When Emma had walked into my apartment that morning, I'd considered what she was wearing—an oversized cashmere sweater, dark jeans and boots—before dressing myself. Casual-formal attire was something I could wrap my head around. I'd been dreading having to spend the next few days in a suit, but I would've suffered it for Emma.

After a round of greetings, Katherine ushered us inside. It was near freezing temperatures in Connecticut and an eastern wind had picked up. I was used to steel buildings guarding me from the winter chill, but it hit me now to the bone.

"Make yourself at home, Jack," Katherine said with warmth, taking my coat. "You'll be sleeping in Emma's old bedroom."

I paused at that, as Emma and I had yet to share a bed together, but Gregory clarified.

"Emma prefers to sleep downstairs in the guest room." He'd donned a courteous expression, but his eyes told a different story. He was wary of me, with good reason.

"Emma and her little quirks," a blonde teenager joked as she bounded down the stairs, pulling Emma into a hug. She turned her doe-like brown eyes on me. "I'm Ella."

"Jack," I replied, attempting to hide a smile as Ella shook my hand. Her grip was strong, her face stern while she eyed me up and down in appraisal. It was difficult to tell what she made of me.

"Do you own a motorcycle, too?" she asked, arching her brow. I couldn't help but chuckle. She reminded me of Emma. *Eyes, sass.* How else were they similar?

"Ella!" Katherine scolded.

"It's okay," I assured their mother. "I own a bike."

"You do?" Emma parted her lips in surprise. I made a mental note to take her for a ride on the Sheene once the weather warmed, though that could be awhile.

"Jack, I hope you like chicken." Katherine broke the silence, changing the subject with ease. She turned toward the kitchen, giving her youngest daughter a meaningful look. "Dinner will be ready in an hour!"

"That's my cue to set the table." Ella groaned, exiting the room after her mother.

"Emma, why don't you get settled?" Gregory suggested, then addressed me. "I've got some vintage scotch in my office begging to be opened."

Gregory clapped my shoulder once and walked off down the hall, intending for me to follow.

"You don't have to—" Emma started, but I shut her mouth with mine. Her shoulders loosened as I ran my fingers through her long hair, still cold from being outdoors.

"I'll see you in a few," I promised, following Gregory Marshall's shrinking figure.

The Marshall house was modest. With how well it was furnished and the designer clothes they wore, I knew they could afford something larger. It seemed Emma had inherited her humility from Gregory and Katherine. They hadn't let their daughters grow up too spoiled.

As I walked down the hall, I studied a few large photographs hanging in ornate frames. They were professional and included the family of four in various poses. Even in black and white, Emma was luminous. She gave a coy smile to the camera, her hair curled into tight ringlets. Ella leaned against her, starkly opposite with a wide grin and flaxen mane.

If I hadn't before, I now understood why Gregory Marshall was so protective of his daughters. If I ever had children who looked like that, I'd break the jaw of anyone who so much as sneezed wrong in their direction.

The remainder of the wall was lined with candid shots of the family, but I found something odd. Both girls were present in every school photo, but Emma's last one was missing. There weren't any shots of her during what I assumed would be her senior year of high school. All the recent pictures were of Ella—baking with her mom, fishing with her father, poolside with friends.

The omission of the eldest Marshall daughter almost seemed intentional.

Chapter Twenty

Emma

"That boy sure is something." Ella smirked as I walked into the dining room. The sun was setting, rays of light piercing the veil of the bay window. The backyard was impeccable. Everything was as I remembered.

When I flushed, my not-so-little-anymore sister shook her head, handing me a stack of porcelain plates from the antique hutch.

"How's school?" I asked, hoping to guide the conversation away from Jack. I didn't want her picking apart my love life. *Love*. I'd been dancing around it for a while now. Was I in love with Jack O'Connell? The idea sent a tingle of hope through my fingertips and, right after, an icy wave of fear spliced my belly.

Ella shrugged, taking a station across the table from me. "School is school. You?"

I smiled, opting to bury my mixed emotions until I had more time to reflect. "Same."

As we folded the cloth napkins just how our mom liked them, I let the shock of being home settle in. I'd panicked during the entire ride over from the city, unsure whether I was ready. One look at my family and I knew I'd made the right decision. It was long overdue for me to face this house—this town—again.

The one thing that had me on edge was the idea of Jack being cornered in my father's office. What did my dad have to talk to him about? Something along the lines of "Don't hurt my daughter." Lord, if he knew what Jack did for a living, he'd never let me return to Manhattan. I'd be stuck here, finishing the semester remotely.

"You look..." Ella paused, straightening a salad fork. "You look good, sis."

"Thanks," I whispered, my throat thickening with unanticipated tears. I did feel better, more present than I had in years. With Jack at the forefront of my mind, it'd been a while since I had thought of anything else.

"I'm sorry, Ellie," I blurted, in a rush to get it out now that I had the opportunity. Now that I could grasp what I'd put her through. "For everything. You were only trying to help that night and I—"

"It's okay," Ella interrupted, giving me a reassuring smile. "It wasn't that big of a deal. For me, at least. I know you've been beating yourself up about it, but you don't need to. I'm just so happy to see you're doing better. You have no idea."

I laughed, letting go of the breath I was holding. I'd been wanting to apologize to my sister for a long time—I just couldn't find the right words.

"So," she sang, slapping her hand on the table. "Tell me about Jack."

Ugh. She'd gone from being sweet to getting right back under my skin. If anything, this was the sister I remembered. She'd matured in many ways but hadn't dropped the pestering.

"Oh, come on! You can't bring a man like that into this house and not expect an inquisition. Mom's description didn't do him justice. What bin did you fish him out of, and do they have more?"

I made sure the plates were centered between the silverware settings, hoping my dark hair hid me from Ella's scrutiny. "I met him at the gym."

"The one Dad made you go to for self-defense?" She snorted. "If he'd known *that* guy worked there, he would've thought twice."

I set the last dish down harder than necessary. "He doesn't *work* there. He owns it."

Ella's face lit up. She was loving this. "He owns a gym in Manhattan? Is he rich?"

I rolled my eyes, pushing past her to grab the wine glasses. "No."

"You're lying," she argued. "Besides, Mom already told me he was wearing a custom Prada suit when they met at the ball."

I saw my chance to veer her off course. "You mean the ball Mom and Dad had to leave early from because you decided to throw a kegger? How many beers deep were you before they got home and busted you?"

To my surprise, Ella was grinning like mad. She circled the table, placed her hands on my shoulders and looked me straight in the eye.

"It's good to have you back, Em."

But I knew she wasn't just talking about me being home.

* * * *

Jack

Gregory's office was situated at the northernmost part of the house. It was small but impressive. The walls were lined with thick leather-bound books and prestigious awards. A mahogany desk took up a portion of the floor and the smell of fresh apples hung in the air. I smiled, despite my predicament, and thought of Emma.

Gregory shut the wooden door, muttering something about "Kitty not condoning the harder stuff." I took the glass tumbler he handed me and sat in a leather chair across from him, his desk a barrier between us.

"I know who you are, Jack." Gregory sipped his scotch, his eyes on me. I twirled my glass between my fingertips, waiting for him to continue. "After we met, I made a call to a friend up in Boston. We graduated from Yale together. He works in the DA's office now."

Taking a large gulp of scotch, I looked Emma's father in the eye, attempting my most innocent and curious expression. But I knew where this was going.

"The name Frank O'Connell carries a lot of weight in Boston," Gregory prodded, prompting me to speak.

"It's a good thing I am not my father's son," I replied, my jaw twitching as I fought to keep my teeth from clenching.

I wasn't afraid of being called out. My record was clean. I had never been arrested for my crimes. I was smart and, when need be, fast. But I was terrified of losing Emma. If Gregory planned to put a stop to my relationship with his daughter, I hoped we could overcome it. I wasn't sure how much weight Emma put on her father's approval.

"But you *are* an O'Connell," Gregory challenged, his expression inscrutable. "You may've gotten out from under your father's thumb, but you haven't changed the way you make your money."

I didn't break his gaze. "No."

Gregory sighed and leaned back in his chair, causing it to creak with age. He rubbed his forehead with his fingers before draining the rest of his scotch. I did the same and he refilled our glasses. I hoped his goal wasn't a drunk confession from me. It would take ten men the likes of Gregory Marshall to drink me under the table. And I got the feeling there wasn't enough alcohol in this town to do it.

"Look at this picture, Jack."

Gregory turned one of the frames on his desk. I eyed it casually at first. It was another family picture, but this one was recent. A graduation photo.

There were Gregory and Katherine Marshall with Ella standing nearby. It was Emma standing in the front and center that had me straightening in my chair. I grabbed the frame from his desk, inspecting it closer.

It was definitely Emma in a red cap and gown, adorned with multiple sashes and ropes. But she was a ghost—pale and thinner than she was now, which I hadn't imagined possible. The girl in the photo wasn't healthy. That was obvious. The warm, brown eyes I'd come to adore were black and hollow. She stared into the camera, but she didn't see it. Her lips were white and thin, unsmiling.

My voice barely left my body. "What happ—"

"I dragged that picture out of storage a couple weeks ago," Gregory interrupted. He'd been watching my reaction. "After seeing Emma at the ball, I wanted to remind myself. To make sure I remembered it correctly. How terrible things were for her."

"Was she sick?" I stammered, still staring at the stranger in the photograph.

"Not physically." Gregory sipped his drink. Mine sat abandoned on the desk. "Emma suffered a lot during her senior year. Kitty and I could only hope she would make it out the other end. One of the few times she spoke was to tell us she wanted to go to Columbia in the fall. Not Yale, like she'd planned for years. And who were we to ignore her sole request?"

Gregory paused to make sure I was following. I set the photo down and gathered my drink, looking him in the eye so he would continue.

"But Kitty felt Emma wasn't ready to be on her own. She was getting lost on her way home from school. Losing track of time. On a few occasions, the local sheriff found her wandering around town like a zombie. The nights were hellish. She would wake up screaming. It was a horrifying sound to hear as a parent. We thought maybe she just needed someone to sleep with her. Ella volunteered, but that was a mistake. Emma attacked Ella during a nightmare. She was fine but covered in scratches and shaken up. Emma felt terrible. After that, she refused to let anyone near her while she slept.

"When an article was published in the local newspaper about Ava Davis getting into Juilliard, Kitty jumped on it. We had the perfect opportunity to keep an eye on Emma. We just wanted her to be safe. New York's a big city. A huge change for a young girl."

Gregory refilled his tumbler. I refused to interject what seemed to be a stream of consciousness, scared that I would derail him. This was what I'd been wanting for months. For someone to tell me something—*anything*—about what had happened to Emma.

"I took this photo out," he continued, gesturing with his drink, "to remind me. When I saw you and Emma at the ball, I felt like punching you in the face. Especially after I got a good look at you. Not that I would survive a hit back." Gregory nodded with regret. "But my daughter. She hasn't looked that...*alive* in years."

Something wet trickled down Gregory's clean-shaven cheek and he wiped it away. I pretended not to notice.

"Ava told Kitty she's been doing better for a while now, so I know it doesn't all have to do with you. But when she was attacked this summer, we worried it would break her again. Kitty thought we should bring her home, but I held off. Suggested self-defense. Did some research and found a good gym. Nice and private, which I knew would make it easier on Emma. And in walks you." His face was bitter, defeated. "I have no control over this situation, Jack. I see the way my daughter looks at you. All I can say is that if you hurt her..." His voice broke and he pointed to the photo again, his finger shaking. "If you do *that* to her..."

Going off instinct, I reached forward and took Gregory's hand, placing it against his chest. His shoulders shook and he dropped his head. He had nothing more to say.

My turn.

"I need you to look at me, Mr. Marshall," I said, my voice earnest in its command. Gregory gazed up, his brown eyes small and shiny. "I am in love with your daughter."

He opened his mouth to reply, but I continued.

"I haven't told her. Or admitted it to myself, for that matter, so I'd like if this stayed between us."

Gregory's lips twitched like he wanted to smile.

"I spend most of my days thinking about keeping Emma *out* of danger, not putting her in it."

He rose from the desk chair, rubbing his face with his palms. "Does she know? About your work?"

"She does," I answered. "But not the details."

"Good." He smoothed his hair, all evidence of his previous emotions vanishing. "Now, if you'll excuse me…"

He patted me on the shoulder twice and I left the room.

* * * *

Emma

"Who are these from?" I asked my mom, gesturing to the greeting cards lining the fireplace.

"They're from Ella's birthday," she replied, fluffing a pillow.

I winced. Shit. I'd forgotten my sister's eighteenth birthday.

"It's okay. You still have time to write me a check," Ella joked from her spot on the floor. She was scrolling through Instagram on her phone. I didn't even know she was paying attention.

"I'll get right on that," I said, plucking one of the cards from the mantel and opening it. Something about the writing caught my eye.

Upon realizing where I'd seen the distinctive scrawl, I almost dropped it into the roaring fire. I'd been so wrapped up in Jack the past few months, I'd forgotten about it, pushed it to the back of my mind where I hid all the other painful things. My heart raced, but I forced myself to act natural. My hand shook as I returned the card to where I'd found it.

"I'll be right back," I chimed, grabbing my coat from the arm of the sofa. "Left something in the car."

But I wasn't going to the car. I felt stupid for not putting it together. I knew that writing. The tiny, jagged letters with the elongated loops for the l's and y's.

You know what I did
Please know I'm sorry

It was a perfect match to the manila envelope I had received in August. The one with the photograph of Maria taken by a security camera. The one with the note attached leading me to the Booker Hotel.

I'd known the sender's identity all along.

Chapter Twenty-One

Jack

Despite the cold, I stood in the Marshalls' backyard, hoping to clear my head after my conversation with Gregory.

I still was no closer to uncovering what had happened to Emma. If anything, the urge to know was greater after hearing his story. At the ball, she'd admitted that she'd murdered someone, but that wasn't possible. Emma was the victim in this situation. The haunting image from her graduation was evidence enough. I just needed to know *what* the situation was. If she wasn't raped, what was it? My mind was spinning with possibilities, but they were endless.

"Couldn't handle my dad's scotch, huh?"

I turned to find Ella Marshall closing the sliding glass door to the deck. She wrapped her thick coat around her and stepped up to the wooden railing, leaning over it to look at the icy pond below.

"I can't stand the stuff," she continued.

I raised my brows at her.

"What? Isn't the drinking age in Ireland, like, twelve?"

I cracked a smile. "Last I checked, we aren't in Ireland."

"Last time I checked, you're my sister's *boyfriend.* You're supposed to be getting on my good side."

"Am I not?"

Ella was quick with the comebacks. "That remains to be seen."

"You remind me of my sister-in-law."

Ella flipped her long, blonde hair over her shoulder in a way that would make Shannon O'Connell proud. "Is she heartbreakingly beautiful?"

I laughed. "That she is."

Ella grinned and looked back out over the lawn, her eyes getting lost. Nightfall had descended, but the twinkling lights from the garden made it seem like fireflies were milling about. It could very well be the dead of summer if not for the frigid air. The pine trees marking the edge of their property line were thick. I tried to peer beyond them, but darkness made the forest impenetrable.

"Is anyone willing to talk about what happened to Emma?"

Ella bit her lip, hesitating a moment. "My parents always told me not to speak of it, but Emma is doing better now. She's different, but better."

I fought to control my growing rage. "Who hurt her?"

Ella sighed, resigning. "It was Nate. Her high school sweetheart."

"I'll kill him." I gripped the railing with force, my knuckles whitening. I didn't know where the bastard was or how I would do it, but I would find him. And it would be slow.

"You can't kill him," Ella said. "He's already dead."

I blinked a few times, the revelation hitting me with the force of a freight train. "Explain."

Ella glanced to where her mother was heating dinner in the kitchen. With the windows closed, we wouldn't be overheard. "It's a long story."

"Summarize," I demanded.

"Fine." She rolled her tongue over her teeth, cracking her neck like she was getting ready for a bout. She took a deep breath, then began. "The night of the incident, I went to bed angry. I was arguing with my mom about dating privileges. At the time, it didn't make sense that Emma was allowed to have her boyfriend sleep over, but I wasn't permitted to go to a movie with my crush."

Like my father, Ella Marshall preferred to take her time with a story. I clamped my jaw shut, biting back the urge to hurry her along.

"It was Emma and Nate's senior year. On the first day of school, Nate's mom, Maria, was murdered. Things like that don't happen here. Everyone in Stonerose was on edge. Nate became distant, but I suppose that's normal for someone who just lost a parent. I mean, Maria was killed in their home right across the street. It was gruesome."

Ella shuddered, shutting her eyes with a wince. I stared at her, rapt by the words falling from her mouth.

"Jeremiah Murray was caught soon after. He was shanked in prison while awaiting trial. The news of Jeremiah's death hit Nate hard, so my parents let him spend the night with Emma. The next morning, a noise woke me up. I banged on the wall connecting my bedroom with Emma's, but I heard it again." Ella ran a hand through her hair, taking a deep breath. "I'll never forget Emma's scream. My blood turned to ice and, I swear, my heart stopped beating for a few moments."

Goosebumps prickled the nape of my neck, my pulse thrumming in my ears. "Why was she screaming?"

"I was out of bed, racing down the hall toward Emma's room within seconds. I threw open the door but froze when I saw my sister." Ella's eyes clouded with tears. She wrinkled her nose, trying to quell them. "Emma was straddling Nate, clawing and yanking at his body, but he wasn't moving. Even from where I stood, I could see he was dead. His limbs were stiff, his fingers were blue. Thank God his eyes were closed.

"Emma was pleading with him, begging him to wake up. I couldn't have been standing there long before our parents got to us. Mom called an ambulance while Dad tried to get Emma off Nate. He kept telling her to let go, but she wasn't giving up the fight. He asked me to help so I..." Ella shuddered again, her shoulders hitched by her ears. "I pried Emma's fingers from Nate's face. Dad and Emma tumbled to the floor and then..."

"And then?" I asked, my voice cracking.

"Emma broke." She shrugged, wiping a stray tear from her cheek. "There's no other way to describe it. She curled into a ball, scratching at her own face, tearing her hair out. She was making these noises like a wounded animal. Her eyes were wide and panicked, but she wasn't present."

My chest ached for her. My brain felt fuzzy, struggling to process the information. "How did Nate die?"

"Suicide," Ella answered with a grimace. "He couldn't recover from his mom's murder, so he took his own life. Swallowed a bottle of pain pills that Emma was prescribed for a wisdom tooth removal. They went to bed together and, when Emma woke up, he was dead.

"There wasn't a single day in our lives that didn't include Nate Ranucci. When Mom was pregnant with Emma, she saw the same doctor as Maria. They had similar due dates, so they were inseparable. Nate was born two days after Emma. He lived right across the street. Emma and him shared the same playpen. They were best friends and, eventually, lovers. When Emma walked into a room, people looked over her shoulder, expecting Nate not far behind. Nate's death destroyed Emma, stole a piece of her soul."

I rubbed a hand over my face, covering my mouth. "Holy shit."

"Yeah." Ella laughed, but it wasn't a happy one. "Holy shit."

I was infuriated beyond measure. Nate was a fucking coward. Sure, he was hurting from his mother's death. But instead of crawling off into a ditch to die a solitary death, he'd done it in front of Emma, forcing her to sleep with a dead body before waking up cold and alone. Even I wasn't that selfish.

"Wait." I stopped Ella before she could turn around. "Did you say Maria was killed by Jeremiah *Murray*?"

Ella's eyes narrowed. "Yeah, why?"

"So that's why he was in prison," I muttered, recalling the fiasco in the Murray family back then. One of the Murray sons had been shanked in prison by a member of the Italian Mafia. It was what had kickstarted the war between the families. What was Jeremiah doing in this off-the-map town?

"Earth to Jack," Ella sang, waving her hand in front of my face.

"Dinner's ready!" Katherine called from inside the house, but my mind was far away.

"Where's Emma?" I asked Ella, my voice darkening. Something wasn't right. A chill went down my spine and it had nothing to do with the weather.

"She said she had to get something from the car." Ella paled at my change in attitude. "That was, like, twenty minutes ago."

I took off at a sprint—passing Katherine and Gregory as they moved about the kitchen, blowing through the living room and its roaring fire—and was out of the front door in seconds.

It wasn't fast enough. There was a loud *bang* and a flash lit up one of the windows in the house across the street.

* * * *

Emma

I crossed the street, my sights trained on the house I knew too well. The lampposts cast an orange glow on the sleepy neighborhood, but there were no lights shining in his home. I knew he was there, though. His vintage red Mustang was in the driveway, looking immaculate as ever.

When I knocked on the door, Mark Ranucci answered like he'd been waiting for me. He stepped aside and I entered the dim living area. Mark looked worse for wear. He had unruly facial hair, was thinner than I'd ever seen and smelled like he needed a hot shower. Or a tropical vacation. He shut the door behind me with trembling hands.

"I knew you'd come," he croaked, as if he was getting over a cold.

"Why did you send me that envelope?" I asked.

Mark circled me to stand in front of the lit fireplace. It was the one source of light in the room. The house looked exactly how I remembered it growing up, but now it felt empty, like no one had been living in it for years. A film of dust coated everything within sight. Mark clearly wasn't faring well with his wife and son gone. *Who would?*

"You're the one who sent the photo to me in the first place." Mark chewed at his thumbnail. "In July? It had your return address on it."

I shook my head, keeping my eyes on him. "I don't know what you're talking about."

"The photo of Maria at the Booker. I gave it back to you. With my note. Didn't want the memory of what I did sitting around."

"What you did?" I repeated.

"To Maria." Mark broke down, hands on his knees. "I didn't mean to! She was going to leave us. You have to know that!"

I was shocked into utter stillness, my jaw slack.

"That man was waiting to pick her up and take her back to the city with him."

I found my voice. "What man, Mark?"

"Jeremiah Murray!"

"The man who killed her?"

"Haven't you been listening?" he boomed, pushing my back against the brick fireplace. He gripped me so fierce that I was sure he'd leave bruises on my shoulders. "*I* killed her! I killed my own wife!"

His voice shattered on the last word. My palms burned from the closeness of the flames. I stayed as calm as possible, although adrenaline wreaked havoc on my body.

When Mark met my eyes, regret eclipsed his features. He dropped his head into his hands. I took the lapse in his concentration to walk away from the fire. I inched toward the front door, but it was still yards away. He could stop me from getting out if he wanted to.

I came to a realization that forced me to take pause. "Nate was here when it happened. He came home to get his cleats. He saw everything, didn't he?"

Mark's cry was that of a tortured man but a confirmation, nonetheless.

"How did Nate get back to the school so fast?" I asked, hoping to keep him talking so I could get closer to the door. I didn't like where this was heading. Mark was hysterical.

He sighed, removed his hands from his face and set his eyes back on mine. I couldn't escape with him watching.

"I told him to run back. Told him to pretend he was there the whole time. No one was supposed to find out what happened."

I nodded. "That was smart of you."

"But *you* found out. You ruined everything. And now he's coming for me."

I was about to deny knowing anything, but something he said made the hair on the back of my neck freeze. "Who's coming?"

"He's going to find me any minute." Mark glanced around frantically, pacing the living room. "He's going to kill me. Or worse."

"Mark…" I started, reaching out in an attempt to calm him, my hand trembling.

"Nate left you a letter," Mark said, stoic. The lines in his face evened out, his eyes growing wide. He stopped pacing. "I don't know where he hid it. He told me that if anything ever happened, you'd know where to find it."

"Who do you think is coming for you, Mark?" He wasn't making any sense. None of this made any sense.

"Luca Nicoletti. But I'm not going out like that." His words were emotionless, chilling me to the bone. He strode toward the fireplace, grabbing a shotgun from beside it that had been hidden in shadow. "I'm sorry, Emma. For everything."

And with that, Mark Ranucci aimed the shotgun under his chin and pulled the trigger.

Chapter Twenty-Two

Jack

I burst through the door, almost tearing it off its hinges.

The room was dark, but I found Emma immediately. I almost cried in relief when I saw she was standing. But she was frozen, her right hand held out in front of her. And she was covered head to toe in blood spatter.

"Emma!" I grabbed her by the shoulders, pulling her into me. She was unresponsive as I surveyed the scene. Shotgun. Man lying on the floor. His head was blown off. "Jesus Christ…"

I held her at arm's length, cupping her face in my hands. Her lips were parted, her blank eyes staring at the beheaded body. She was white as a sheet. Like the picture on her father's desk.

"Are you hurt?" I asked, wiping at the fresh blood on her cheek with my thumb. She was ice cold with shock. She probably didn't even register that I was here. "Dove, can you tell me what happened?"

She didn't answer.

I cursed, looking toward the man on the ground. My instincts were kicking in. Had she shot this person? If she did, I needed to clean the scene. Figure out how to get rid of the body. We were on a residential street, so it wouldn't be smart to move it until much later. But that'd give my men time to get to Connecticut.

Fuck, I left my phone at the Marshalls'.

I turned back to Emma, attempting to shift her focus. "Emmy, can you tell me what you touched? The doorknob, the gun? Did you touch anything else, baby?"

Her lower lip trembled, but that was it. *Screw it.* I would return later to clean everything. For now, I needed to get Emma as far from the scene as possible. I wouldn't let her go down for this. Hell, I'd take the fall if I had to. Lord knew I'd earned more than a few life sentences in my twenty-six years.

"I'm gonna get you out of here."

Her legs were locked to the ground, so I picked her up and cradled her against my chest. She was light as a dove and her body shook. It was the only evidence that she was in there. My heart thumped as I carried her out of the house.

"Drop the girl!"

The headlights of at least four police cruisers blinded me. Their sirens were off, but the blue-and-white on the hoods flashed ominously. I'd been too preoccupied with Emma to notice them through the windows of the house. *Damn small towns.* I'd grown up in a neighborhood where the police didn't bother responding to calls about shots being fired.

"Not until I know her father can take her," I yelled, holding Emma close.

"I'm here!" a familiar voice replied.

Gregory jogged into view. He was shivering in just his sweater but held his arms out. As I passed Emma to him, he cast me a worried look, but there was nothing I could say. Even I didn't know what had happened in that house.

Once Emma was clear, three policemen knocked me down onto the wet lawn. One of them knelt on my spine, pinning my hands behind my back. Emma stared straight at me, signs of life stirring in her eyes.

Much to my surprise, Gregory came to my defense. He addressed the man who was now cinching the handcuffs tight on my wrists. "What the fuck, Sheriff!"

"Relax, Greg," the sheriff said, his voice straining with exertion. "Dispatch got a call that there was a gunshot in my town for the first time in thirty-some-odd years. I'm just doing my job."

"Yeah, we all heard the shot, but this is insane. Jack's dating my daughter. You don't need to detain him."

"Look at your daughter, Greg. She's covered in bl—"

"Uh, Donahue?" a new voice interrupted. It came from somewhere near the entrance to the house. I wanted to turn my head, but the side of my face was pressed into the grass. "We got a body in here. Can't tell, but it looks like Mark Ranucci."

The sheriff's hold on me loosened as he rose. Another officer grabbed my biceps and hauled me to stand. Emma's eyes were locked on mine, but all I saw was my own terror reflected. I couldn't lose her. Fuck's sake, I'd only just found her.

"What do you mean you 'can't tell'?" the sheriff asked. "Is it him or not?"

I turned just in time to see a much younger police officer exiting the house, hand on his stomach, face pale. He leaned into the bushes, spewing vomit.

"You just have to see, Sheriff."

Sheriff Donahue looked exhausted as he crossed the lawn and entered the home. Did it belong to Mark Ranucci? If Emma had been avoiding her hometown for years after her ex's suicide, why seek his father out?

A headache formed behind my eyes. The lights of the cruisers were blinding against the dark suburban backdrop. I glanced up, stunned by how clear the sky was without New York's light pollution. I hadn't seen that many stars since the last time I'd visited my mum in Ireland.

"Set up a perimeter." Donahue was back, the command in his voice recognizable. It was the same tone I adopted when directing my own men. "Start interviewing neighbors. And call the medical examiner."

"Can you take the cuffs off Jack now?" Gregory asked, still holding Emma to his chest. "My daughter has been through enough tonight. I need to get her home."

"Sorry, Greg," Donahue replied, not sounding apologetic in the slightest. He clapped a heavy hand onto my shoulder. I bit the inside of my cheek to keep myself from throwing it off. "We're going to have to take him to the station. I've got a few questions for the kid. Bring Emma by as well so we can swab that blood."

Emma's face went from frozen in terror to wide-eyed in less than a few seconds. Her gaze shifted from me to the dark trees at the end of the street, as if someone had called her name. Before anyone apart from me noticed the change in her demeanor, she jumped from her father's arms and raced off.

"Emma!" I hollered—along with a few others—after her, but she was at a full sprint. I'd had no idea the tiny girl could run that fast. Her coat billowed behind her as the sheriff barked more orders, officers clambering into their vehicles. *I could catch her myself if they undid the damn cuffs.*

"Where's she going, Greg?" Donahue asked, giving Emma's father a stern look.

Gregory shook his head, panicked. "I have no idea."

I swallowed to clear the dryness in my throat. My worst nightmare had come to life. Emma was running. Not away from me, but the pain spearing my chest didn't seem to know the difference. I balled my hands into fists behind my back as I watched her disappear into the thick tree line.

* * * *

Sheriff Donahue pulled a metal chair from the table and sat backward on it, resting his arms casually.

I spat blood out of my mouth. It landed on the table, smack dab between us. "Is Emma safe?"

We were in one of the interrogation rooms at the unimpressive Stonerose police station. I'd managed to get my wrists chained to the table. After Emma had run off, I couldn't control my temper anymore. For me, fighting was a natural reaction to fear. It was my first response to any emotion.

When an officer had put his hand on my shoulder to usher me into a squad car, I'd lost it. Turning, I'd slammed my head against his. It was a stupid move, but I couldn't help myself. The man recovered, ramming his knuckles into the side of my mouth.

I licked the busted corner of my lip, waiting for the sheriff to answer me. Donahue was fit for his age and job title. Pushing sixty, gray mustache and a large ego. This was his third round of questioning. I didn't know how long I'd been in the room, but Emma had to have been found. She was one girl and the town was small.

Still, the forest surrounding it was what concerned me. Connecticut was fucking cold in November and the rugged terrain was unforgiving. She could be lost or hurt.

"Tell me what happened tonight, Jack," Donohue prodded, ignoring my query. "Why were you carrying Emma Marshall out of that house?"

I stared at the wall behind him, refusing to meet his eye. When would he realize I didn't have a damn thing to say?

"Who shot Ranucci?" Donahue pressed forward in his seat. "Was it you or Emma?"

"Where is she?" I asked, my voice low.

"You know, you've got some real anger, kid." Donahue stood, pacing the length of the interrogation room as he prepared a new tactic. I'd never been questioned by law enforcement, but I knew the drill, studied their handbooks. Emma looked guiltier than me. She had run from the cops and it didn't help that she was soaked in blood. Donahue was just trying to get under my skin. "You're really playing into that Irish stereotype."

I stayed quiet, waiting for him to finish with his power trip.

"Is that why you killed Ranucci?" he asked, turning on me. "Just couldn't control that anger?"

My jaw twitched, but I wouldn't take the bait.

"Or maybe the person you wanted to kill was Nathaniel. You know, for fucking your girl before you could get to her."

I yanked at my cuffs, managing to lift the table a few inches off the ground. My wrists began to smart from the pressure.

"Easy now," Donahue warned. When I sat back down, he continued. "But you couldn't kill him, so you went after his father, is that it? The next best thing?"

Again, I kept silent, seething inside. The fury was building, so much that it could very well rip me to shreds. My vision was darkening, black spots dancing behind my closed eyelids.

"Am I getting warmer, Jack?" Donahue's voice was a few feet from me. The other officer had probably warned him not to get too close. Still, I prayed he would throw caution to the wind. I wanted to sink my teeth into him. Maybe tear off his ear.

"Is Emma safe?" I bit out. Focusing on her was the one thing keeping the rage at bay. Her delicate face, something I'd memorized over the past few months, was holding me back. Keeping me sane.

"She's okay, Jack."

My eyes snapped open as Gregory Marshall entered the room. He looked exhausted but alert. He shoved a few sheets of paper into Donahue's hands, then motioned for someone in the hall to enter.

I straightened, but it was just another officer. He held a key in his hand, wary of me.

"I think that exonerates my client," Gregory said to the sheriff.

Donahue smiled, having read whatever was written on the first sheet of paper. "Maybe of murder. But he assaulted one of my officers."

"Read the next one, Sheriff." Gregory stepped closer, eyeing him with malice. "Charging Jack is the least of your worries. And if you want me to keep my mouth shut about obstruction of justice, you'll let Mr. O'Connell go immediately."

Donahue skimmed whatever was written on the thin paper. When he looked up, an odd tremor passed over his features.

"How did you find this?" he whispered, shaking the paper for good measure.

"It was left for my daughter. And that's just one of many copies, so don't get any ideas."

Donahue appeared conflicted for a few moments, then relented. "Let the fucker go."

The officer holding the key neared me, leaning across the table to unfasten the handcuffs. I stood and the young copper nearly ran from the room. Even Donahue retreated a few feet.

"You know better, boy," he warned, his hand on his belt, taser at the ready.

"Yeah, I know better," I mocked, swallowing a mouthful of blood. I would've preferred to spit it out again, but Gregory was here. His perception of me was tainted enough as it was.

I followed Emma's father out of the station, holding my tongue. A few uniforms glared in my direction, but I kept my head down. Once we were in the privacy of his truck, the question burst from my lips.

"Where is Emma?" I asked as he buckled himself into the driver's seat. I didn't bother. Seatbelt safety was the last thing on my mind.

"I made her stay put to warm up by the fire," Gregory answered. His calm tone put me at ease. If he said his daughter was safe, I trusted him. "Although, knowing her, she's probably pacing around waiting to see you."

"What the hell happened in that house?"

"That coward shot himself in front of my fucking daughter." Gregory grimaced, pulling the truck out of the station's lot. "After they found Emma, she knew better than to speak without representation. They interviewed her at home and took samples of Mark's blood as well as a gunshot residue panel. That's why I couldn't get to you sooner."

Realization flooded through me. *It's always the damn husband*. "Mark killed his wife."

"Yes," Gregory confirmed through gritted teeth.

"Did Emma know?" I prayed Emma wasn't naïve enough to confront a murderer in his own home.

"No." The streets were getting narrower. We were almost back to the house. "She went over to wish him a happy holiday. He must've thought she was going for a confession."

"And so he shot himself." Gregory was right. Mark Ranucci was a coward. *Like father, like son*. "What did you hand Donahue?"

"A few things." Gregory's voice was stern again. "One was an advance from the medical examiner confirming the suicide. The doc is a colleague and owes me a couple favors."

"And on the other?" I prodded.

"Nate's suicide note." Gregory threw his blinker on even though the roads were empty. "No one could find one after he killed himself. Apparently, he told Mark that if anything bad happened, he'd left a letter for Emma in a place only she could find."

"And?"

"She found the letter in a cave on the edge of town. Emma and Nate used to sneak out there every summer. That's where she disappeared to. She was hoping whatever it said would help you."

"How did you get Donahue to drop the assault charges? You said something about obstruction of justice."

Gregory nodded, pulling into the driveway beside my sports car. "When Mark was first questioned about Maria's murder, a bunch of men came forward to corroborate his alibi. Men that would have been paid off. Something Mark couldn't afford on his own. Most of his capital was tied up in his chop shop."

"So whoever wanted to frame Jeremiah Murray—"

"Also paid to get Mark off, I'm assuming. It would take little digging to realize the confessions were bogus. Time stamps on security feeds and such. Donahue would've known they were lying."

"He was paid to look the other way," I concluded.

Gregory put the truck in park. Before he could take the key out of the ignition, I was halfway to the front door. I would unpack what he'd said later. Right now, I had to see my girl.

Chapter Twenty-Three

Emma

"You're hurt!" I yelled once I got a good look at Jack.

He jogged across the living room, relief flooding his features, and enveloped me in his arms. I relented and returned his embrace, standing on my tiptoes to get closer. I ran my fingers through the soft curls that ended just above his collar. A sigh of contentment escaped at having him near again. I closed my eyes, relishing in his warmth. But he was injured.

"You need to see a doc—"

"I'm fine." His voice came out rugged and filled with emotion. I loosened my hold on him, but he didn't let up. "It's just a scratch."

"Jack—"

"I'm not letting you out of my sight ever again," he snapped, ending the argument.

I peered over his shoulder. My dad walked through the front door. He pointed upstairs, mouthing "Mom," then took them two at a time.

"You need a shower, dove," Jack muttered, brushing his thumb over my cheekbone. I was still covered in Mark's blood and God only knew what else. My mom had been trying to get me to bathe for the past hour, but had given up and retreated to her bedroom. I had refused to do anything but pace while I waited for Jack's return.

"So do you." A large cut on his forehead glistened with blood and his lower lip was busted.

He glanced upstairs to where my parents were undoubtedly talking over the events in their room. "Together?"

"I won't tell if you don't," Ella teased, startling us.

My little sister entered from the kitchen. She wore a pair of fuzzy pajamas with dancing reindeer on them, her hair tied into a loose braid. She swung a bottle of champagne from one hand, holding a flute in the other.

"Is that Mom's Cristal?" I asked.

She rolled her eyes, starting up the stairs. "What? This town is fucking crazy. I can't *wait* to graduate and get the hell out of here." She made her way to the top landing and shut her bedroom door, not once looking back.

Thirty minutes later, Jack and I were in the guest bathroom shower. I'd already scrubbed my own body and was working on his. I started with his hair, massaging the shampoo into his curls. He closed his eyes, humming in approval. I continued with the cut on his face, careful not to dislodge the clot forming over it.

"Do you still love him?" Jack asked as I wiped a few leftover suds from under his ribs. He was talking about Nate.

"Yes," I answered. "I'll always love him, in a way. But what Nate and I had was…a childhood. The way I feel when I'm with you…" I struggled to find the right words. "The feelings I have toward you are…in an entirely different realm. A realm I didn't even know existed until we met."

Jack smirked, my answer satisfying his ego. "You know you didn't kill him, right?"

"He was my best friend. I knew there was something wrong. I should've assumed the worst. Maybe I could've gotten him help."

Jack pulled me to stand. The water rebounded off his shoulder, spraying my eyes, but I forced myself to look at him.

"You were kids," he argued, but the edges of his green eyes were soft. "That wasn't your responsibility."

I glanced down at my hands. The skin of my fingertips was beginning to pucker. "They were my pills."

He held my chin between two fingers. "That he *chose* to take, Emma."

"I know." My throat tightened. Tears welled in the corners of my eyes, but I refused to let them fall. I'd spent more than enough time mourning Nathaniel Ranucci. I refused to devote any more of my future to his memory.

Nate's suicide note was addressed to me. He'd placed it in a Ziplock bag and tucked it into the wall of the cave we'd spent four summers making love in. He had laid everything out in the open. How losing his mother was hard enough, but the secret of what his father had done was eating away at him. When Jeremiah was falsely imprisoned for his father's crimes, Nate hoped they didn't have enough to pin it on him. The evidence was all circumstantial, but it didn't matter. He didn't live long enough to face a jury. Jeremiah's death was the last straw. Instead of betraying his father, Nate ended his own suffering.

Once I realized what Mark had said about Nate leaving something in a place only I could find, I knew where to go. I had made it to the cave in twenty-five minutes, grateful for my many runs through Central Park to aid in stamina. The pond was iced over, but I'd kept to the edges. It wasn't cold enough to be solid all the way through at this time of year. The cave was smaller than I had remembered, but so was I. It was too dark to read the note in the middle of the forest, but I wouldn't have done so even if I could. Jack had been waiting for me. Had needed me. And I could only hope Nate's note held answers.

"Are you still opposed to me sleeping in your bed?" Jack asked nonchalantly, but I knew he wanted to stay in the guest room with me.

He was looking better after our shower. We both did. I'd used butterfly bandages to close the wound above his eye.

"I'm sorry," I whispered, handing him an icepack for his head. We were standing in the dark kitchen. My mom had cleaned it vigorously and packed away the untouched dinner—her way of coping with the stress. Jack and I were each wrapped in plush, white towels. Despite everything that had happened tonight, it was still difficult to keep my eyes from roaming his exquisite body. "I don't think I can yet."

"I understand, dove." Jack leaned in, kissing my forehead. "Just know that I promise to never leave your side. I'm much too stubborn."

As it turned out, I didn't sleep well. I flipped and flopped in bed. I paced the room. I filled glass after glass of water from the tap in the ensuite bathroom, attempting to cure the scratch in my throat.

I hadn't told my dad—or, for that matter, the police—everything that Mark Ranucci had confessed. I was still having trouble putting the pieces together. It was the why that bothered me. Why had Luca Nicoletti gone to all that trouble just to frame Jeremiah Murray? If his goal was to get him imprisoned, why frame him for *this* murder? Why not one that took place in Manhattan, where both men lived? And speaking of Manhattan, why did Don Luca have me attacked? How the hell did I fit into this? Was it even connected?

My mind was plagued, bombarded with questions for hours on end. I let them flow through, hoping they'd keep the image of Mark's decapitated body from finding its way in. I feared the nightmares would return if I let myself sleep too sound. I was sure there were a few new ones I could add to the roster.

When the sun began to rise and I felt it was a respectable time to make coffee, I discovered just how honest Jack had been about his promise the night before. I almost stumbled over him as I opened the door. He was sitting upright against the wall in the hallway, his head lolling to one side as he slept.

He'd been outside the bedroom all night.

* * * *

Thanksgiving was unconventional. My mom, flustered by recent events, didn't feel up to cooking. Ella and I helped her reheat the chicken Alfredo from the previous night.

We gathered in the living room, drinking wine and eating pasta. The fire warmed our skin and the alcohol warmed our bellies. I was happy that my dad had accepted Jack, begrudgingly or not. Whether it was from the conversation over scotch the evening prior or the ride home from the station, I didn't care.

We all came to an agreement to not discuss anything related to the night before. Our family had spent the past few years suffering from the death of a Ranucci. We weren't going to continue the tradition.

"Oh, Emma!" my mom chirped, batting away Ella's hand before she could reach for my dad's wine glass. "I forgot to tell you! We're all moving to the city this summer."

I almost snorted wine out of my nose. Jack chuckled at me.

"You what?" I squeaked.

"I think it's about time we got out of this town," my dad added. "Manhattan can't be much worse. I'm transferring to my firm's offices in Midtown."

"You're burying the lead," Ella sang, turning to me. "I got into Tisch!"

"What?" I exclaimed, setting my glass on the hardwood floor. My mom snatched it away from her vintage rug. "So soon?"

"Early admission." Ella grinned. I pulled my not-so-little sister into a hug, congratulating her. "It's no Columbia," she joked, dragging out the university's name pompously. Jack laughed.

"NYU is an incredible school, El!" Releasing my sister, I turned and slapped Jack on the chest. He winked at me, unfazed.

"We're getting a place not far from yours," my mom continued. "And Ella can move in with you."

"What about Ava?" I was excited at the thought of living with my sister—it had been a while since we'd spent any length of time together—but I didn't want to turn Ava out.

My mom waved it off. "She told me she signed on with a ballet company in Milan. La Scala. Isn't that amazing?" Her face fell when she realized her slip.

"It's okay." I patted her hand. "I know you've been using Ava to spy on me. I'll make sure to congratulate her."

She opened her mouth to apologize, but Ella cut her off before she had the chance.

"Don't worry, Em. We don't have to tell Mom *anything* about our lives once I move in." The sentiment didn't seem to bring my parents much comfort, but Jack and Ella laughed.

We ate and drank our fill, then tag-teamed the cleanup process. With five people in the kitchen, it was crowded, but we finished easily. I got a sentimental feeling in my stomach, knowing I'd remember this moment for years to come.

With a dishtowel over his shoulder and suds on his hands, Jack fit in well with my little family. Ella was enamored. She teased him and he bit right back. It reminded me of his interactions with Shannon.

My mom and dad caught each other's eyes a few times, smiling lovingly, and a flush crept into my cheeks. I hadn't seen my family this happy in a long time. It was strange, given the circumstances. But maybe we were all learning to appreciate the small things. We were together, alive and healthy. That was what mattered.

An hour later, Jack and I sat on the guest room bed in our pajamas. Having him in my childhood home made our relationship even more real. I'd nearly convinced myself I was living in a fantasy with Jack. But he was here, solid and tangible. He made me feel safe and protected in a way I hadn't known I yearned for.

"Will you stay with me for a bit?" I asked, pulling my knees to my chest. I didn't want to be alone with my thoughts just yet.

Jack's smile was crooked, his hair still wet from a shower. It was beginning to curl, a dark strand or two falling across his forehead. "I'll stay as long as you'll keep me, Em."

My cheeks heated and I pressed my lips to my kneecap, hiding the silly smile on them.

"Do you want to talk about it yet?" he asked, resting his elbows on his crossed legs. His fingertips met each other, splayed out in his lap.

"Yes," I answered, surprising myself. After internalizing everything for so many years, the stories ached to leave my body. "Where should I start?"

"Your choice. I want to know everything there is to know about Emma Marshall."

I took a deep breath, pausing for a moment to collect myself. "Okay, so Nate and I were born two days apart..."

Once the words had started, I couldn't stop them. We talked for hours. I spoke emphatically, using my hands to express myself. Some topics were harder to relate than others, but I powered through. Each memory—the good and the bad—seemed to hold less power over me as I recounted them to Jack.

He was a good listener. He hung on to my every word, nodding when necessary. His gaze flitted over my face, studying it as I spoke. He interjected at all the right times, encouraging me to explain certain things further. With how possessive he was, I knew it would be hard to discuss my relationship with Nate, but he took it better than I thought. Perhaps he could tell I wasn't hung up on it anymore.

Nate's suicide was the hardest to speak about. I didn't remember much of it. He haunted my dreams at night, but I didn't know what was real and what were imagined horrors. I hadn't been able to sleep or talk, and eating had been out of the question. I'd learned to block out conversations at school after overhearing Nate's name one too many times. I couldn't even *think* his name in the beginning. Every time I did, a pain would sluice through my stomach and I'd double over, a panic attack ensuing.

Sorrow was my only consistency. I'd get lost and wander around town, forgetting where I was supposed to be. The ticking of the clock, in general, was cruel and unforgiving. One minute I was watching Nate's coffin get lowered into the ground, and the next I was standing in front of the mirror in my bedroom wearing a cap and gown—unable to recognize the girl staring back at me. I knew it was hard on my family, but I couldn't seem to get myself out of the black hole.

It wasn't until I'd left home and moved to Manhattan that I began to recover. The city beckoned me. I wanted to get lost in a sea of people who wouldn't constantly be looking over their shoulder in my direction. The streets of Stonerose—the halls of my high school—were lined with eyes that filled with pity when they met mine. I wanted anonymity and it was impossible so close to home.

"With therapy and a new environment, I got better." I tucked a strand of hair behind my ear. "Ghost threatened that. After he attacked me, the nightmares came back. I was terrified." Jack's face hardened, but I continued. "How was I going to find my way out of the darkness a second time? But I didn't have to. I met you and I kind of got…distracted."

"I'm glad you chose Columbia for entirely selfish reasons." Jack smirked, flipping through a photo album he'd asked me to retrieve from my old bedroom. "Although the circumstances that brought you into my gym were terrible, I thank my lucky stars every damn day that you did."

I smiled, nuzzling my face into his neck. He was so warm and smelled heavenly. He felt like…home. God, I couldn't let myself think that. It was too soon. I'd only known him since September. He just made it so easy.

Jack tapped on a picture, his finger disturbing the plastic cover. "I like this one."

Squinting at the image, I discovered yet another embarrassing photograph from my youth. Ella and I were posing in the living room, feathered boas around our necks, bright pink lipstick lining our mouths. It was the summer before seventh grade and our mom had just taken us shopping at the mall.

"Oh, God." I rubbed a hand over my face. Jack grinned at my obvious discomfort. "Every year after my mom took us clothes shopping for school, my sister and I would put on a fashion show for our parents. We decorated the living room like a runway and blasted pop music. Our parents would vote for which outfit they thought we should wear for the first day back. Mom always picked the pink dresses. Dad chose whichever ones covered the most skin."

Jack closed the album and set it beside him on the bed before cupping my jaw. He brushed his thumb over my bottom lip, his eyes hazy like a foggy marsh. We stayed silent for some time, the air thick with everything I'd divulged.

"Why do you look at me like that?" I asked, my voice a wisp.

Jack threaded his fingers in my hair, examining the strands wrapped around his knuckles with interest. "Like what?"

"Like I'm a riddle you're trying to solve."

"I've never taken the time to get to know anyone who wasn't already a part of my family—the blood or the extended one." He moved his hand to the base of my neck, tilting my head. "But you're fascinating. You grew up so different from me."

"How is that?"

"My brothers and I didn't put on fashion shows for Frank, that's for damn sure." Jack chuckled, but it was dry. He trailed his other hand down my ribcage, resting on my inner thigh. My heartbeat fluttered. By the way his pupils dilated, I knew he could feel the pulse in my throat. "I don't understand why you allow me to breathe the same air as you. Part of me wants to put you in a glass box, pure and untouched from my soiled hands."

He rubbed light circles into my thigh, watching my reaction as he drew closer to my sex. My core clenched, oxygen laboring in and out of my lungs. His gaze fell to my chest, a lethal smile twitching his lips.

"And the other part?" I rasped.

"I want to make you as dirty as me. Ruthless, with twisted morals." He tightened his grip on my neck, my hair straining in his fist. His fingers delved into my sleep shorts, brushing over my panties. He kept his mouth centimeters from mine but didn't close the meager distance. "I want to take my dark and your light, and mix it so there's no beginning or end to us. We'd be forever entwined, shrouded in gray."

Holy shit.

Jack crashed his lips to mine, his tongue demanding and rough in my mouth. Wetness soaked my underwear. Instead of addressing it, he just continued to play, refusing to apply more pressure. I whimpered, arching into him. He loosened his hold on my hair, tearing away from me.

"So far," he continued, catching his breath, "you've seen the best parts of me because that's what you deserve."

I was playing with fire, but arousal soothed the burn. "What if I want to see your worst?"

"Trust me, you don't. And you never will." Despite his clear warning, Jack's eyes were ardent. He placed a kiss to my temple, pausing to smell my hair, then rose from the bed. "Get some rest, dovey. I'll see you in a few."

I knew he wanted me to ask him to stay, but I just couldn't. Soon, maybe. Some wounds ran deeper than others. I didn't want to hurt him if I had a nightmare. Although the fear was irrational, I was horrified of waking up to find Jack dead.

Chapter Twenty-Four

Emma

After breakfast the next morning, we packed our bags and said our goodbyes. Hugs went around, cheeks were patted, jokes were made. We'd see each other for Christmas, but they'd have to come to Manhattan. Braving Stonerose once was enough. I'd more than proved that I could face my past. That it no longer had a hold over me.

Before we could leave, I had one more person to speak with. My roommate was in town visiting her parents, so I shot her a text asking to meet up. Jack drove us to Stonerose High and we walked hand-in-hand around the gloomy brickwork until we reached the athletic fields. He was still sticking to his word about not letting me out of his sight, but I made him stand in the endzone when my gaze lighted on Ava.

She was sitting on the bottom bleacher, leaning back on her hands and staring at the football field. She glanced up when I took a seat beside her, giving me a hesitant smile. By the look on her face, news had traveled. This was a small town, after all.

"I'm okay," I placated, patting her hand.

She breathed a sigh of relief, pulling me into a hug. "I am so sorry you had to go through this again, Emma. I can't believe Mark killed himself!"

I returned her embrace, feeling less awkward about the status of our relationship. It was strange to grow up with someone and never really be able to call them a friend. But I think we were on track to becoming just that.

"If you don't mind, I'd rather not talk about it. It's just that I had to tell my dad and the police and then Jack, of course. I've rehashed it a lot since it happened."

"I totally get it," she assured me, leaning forward to look at Jack. I turned my head. He was at the end of the field talking to someone on his cell phone. By the way he was pacing and moving his hands, I had no doubt he was ordering that person around. "He's like your guard dog."

I laughed. "Yes, he's very protective."

"Maybe that's what you need right now." She shrugged. "I mean, you don't have to deal with *everything* on your own. You know that, right? First Nate and now his dad…"

"Yeah, I know. It's kind of scary, though. Leaning on someone for support."

"It's a risk for sure. But what's life without a little risk? Honestly, I wasn't sure what I thought the first time I saw him. I think my brain stopped working. I hope you're not offended when I say your boyfriend is gorgeous."

I giggled, the sound drawing Jack's attention. He met my gaze and smirked, biting his lip before returning to his conversation.

"Jesus," Ava whispered, huddling close. "How the hell do you even form a sentence with him?"

"I usually just drool," I replied. "By the way, congratulations on La Scala. My mom told me."

Her amusement vanished. "I'm so sorry about telling your mom everything, Emma! I was eighteen when she approached me and naïve and she was offering a free room and—"

"It's *okay*, Ava," I interrupted before she could reach the end of her breath. "I understand. I put my family through hell. I would've done the same if I was in your shoes. People do much worse for free rent in Manhattan."

"Well, either way, I told her I'm not doing it anymore. I've been uncomfortable about it for a while. You're an adult. Your mom needs to cut the cord."

That had me smiling. *If only my mom could hear her little spy now...* "So Milan, huh? I'm sure your parents are proud."

"Well..." She winced. "They're a little bummed that I'm dropping out of Juilliard but being signed to a company was always the goal. I didn't know if La Scala's offer would still be on the table in a year, so I just went with it."

I winked. "What's life without a little risk?"

We laughed together and chatted about her plans for the fall semester. Come summer, she was leaving America and heading to Italy for her next adventure. Even though we'd just opened our line of communication, I would miss Ava. Spy or not, I had grown accustomed to having her in the apartment over the past three years. Switching to Ella as a roommate would be a huge adjustment, but I'd prepare myself for it, prying and all.

Before long, the cold began to eat away at our outer layers. The metal bleachers weren't helping in that regard. We rose and departed in opposite directions. Her parents lived on the western side of town.

As we wrapped up, Jack ended his phone call. He gave me a lazy smile, his ever-protective arm slung over my shoulders as we made our way back to the Audi.

The roads from Stonerose to Manhattan were flooded with holiday traffic, but Jack was an expert driver. He commanded the wheel like every other aspect of his life—with indifferent aggression. He liked to push the boundaries of the speed limit. Jesus, even watching him drive was sexy as hell. But it got me wondering just how far his need for control extended.

When we reached Bridgeport, Jack reached forward and shut off the music—some Irish rock band I didn't recognize. He glanced sideways at me, that maddening jaw working again.

"You've been very quiet," he said. "Your fingers are going to fall off if you keep twisting them like that. What's on your mind, dove?"

I relaxed my hands, stretching the sore digits out along the tops of my thighs. Although it was warm in the car, goosebumps pebbled my flesh. I was nervous but determined to not let it show. I'd told Jack everything there was to know about myself. It was time he returned the favor.

"Can I ask you something?" Once the words left my mouth, I cursed inwardly. Not two seconds in and I was already requesting his permission.

"Of course."

I cleared my throat. "Why are you so protective of me?"

"Really, Emma?" He scoffed. I looked over at him, but his concentration was on the road. "When I heard that gun go off, I thought you'd been shot. Then I was interrogated for four hours, all the while thinking you were lost or hurt in the woods and I couldn't get to you. Why do you think I'm protective?"

"But you were like this before," I reminded him, finding some backbone. "You forced me to take on Eoghan as a chauffeur."

He laughed, but there was no humor in it. "He's not your chauffeur, darling. He's your guardian. He's there to keep you safe when I'm not around. And don't think he's not fully equipped for the job, either."

I waited. He was dodging my inquiry, but I wouldn't retreat. Not this time. I needed answers. I felt I deserved as much.

He let out a long sigh, his grip on the steering wheel tightening. "Emma, what I do… What I've done…" He ran a hand through his hair with force. "I've made a lot of enemies. You need to follow my orders without question when it comes to your safety."

"You said you want my obedience during sex, but it obviously doesn't end there. You need it with everything else as well, don't you?"

He cursed, pulling out of traffic. He threw on the hazards and turned to face me. We were on the side of the Connecticut Turnpike now, on a stretch of asphalt lined with tall, barren trees and dilapidated warehouses. The outskirts of Bridgeport at its finest.

"Jesus, Emma," he hissed, pinning me with his molten stare. "That's the last time I let you stay silent for this long. How much shit goes flying through that head of yours on a daily basis?"

I clenched my jaw as he so often did. Already I was beginning to take my cues from him. Adopting his habits. "A lot. But you didn't answer my question. Having me followed, assigning me a *guardian*"—I made air quotes around the title—"That's a huge need for control, Jack."

He rolled his eyes, looking out through the windshield. It was beginning to pour, sheets of water pelting the top of the car while I did the same to him.

"It comes from my childhood, I guess. I didn't have much of a say in anything. Frank controlled my every move. Couldn't breathe unless he gave me permission to do so."

I licked my lips, excited that he was giving me something. "Your brothers, were they treated the same? Shannon told me you had it worse."

"Shannon doesn't know the half of it." A malicious smile thinned his lips. "But no, my brothers weren't treated the same. Doesn't mean they had it easy, though."

"Why did Frank single you out?"

"Christ, I don't know. He's a fucked-up piece of shit. I look more like him than Connor and Kieran. He'll never admit it, but he hates himself. We're a lot more alike than I care to admit."

Concern marred my brow. "But you don't hate yourself, right?"

He pinched the bridge of his nose, his eyes shut. "I don't want to talk about this."

"How could you not be proud of yourself, Jack?" I asked, leaning forward in my seat as he pushed back against his. "I know you don't always do legal things, but you and your brothers got away from Frank. You pulled yourself out of a toxic childhood. Most people can't say that."

He dropped his hand, giving me a hard glare. "We're not discussing this."

"Why?" I challenged, crossing my arms over my chest in defiance. "I told you about my childhood and what happened with Nate. It's not fair that I can't know anything about your past."

"It's different. I can't have you involved in that part of my world. It's dangerous. The less you know, the better."

The sound that left my mouth was nothing more than pure frustration. His stubbornness was infuriating. Was I just as bad?

"But I want to know everything about what makes you *you,*" I said, catching his hand in mine. His were hard and cold, unrelenting. "Don't you understand that?"

He sighed, snatching his hand away before placing it on the wheel. "I understand you want to know, Emma, but you can't even begin to comprehend the questions you're asking."

"So explain it to me! You said your father controlled every aspect of your life. What did you mean by that?"

His jaw clenched tighter than I'd ever seen it, the muscles there twitching. "Emma, I swear—"

"Please, just trust me. I can handle it."

My heart leapt into my throat when Jack's fist hit the center of the steering wheel. "Fuck, Emma! *Mercy*!"

He was out of the car before my jaw had time to drop. The door slammed shut and he walked in front of the dark hood, running his hands through his curls in aggravation.

My spine was pushed into the passenger door, lungs shaking with the adrenaline that word induced. *Mercy*. Our safe word. The one I told myself I'd never use. Instead, I had forced Jack to say it. Pushed him past a hard limit. Just how dark was his past? What had Frank forced him to do as a child?

The anger I felt toward a man I'd never met rattled me. Whatever he'd put his son through, it still affected him. Violently. Maybe I could handle hearing it, but Jack couldn't speak about it without reliving painful memories.

As Jack paced, the rain soaked his hair, turning it jet black. His T-shirt billowed in the harsh wind, sticking against the ridges of his torso. Every muscle in his body was clenched. His hands formed fists and he shook them out at his sides, like he was pumping himself up for a fight.

Should I go to him? He'd used the safe word. That meant stop everything. I wasn't sure my legs would work even if I wanted them to. The cars on the turnpike sped past, jostling our idle vehicle. It wasn't safe for him to be standing on the side of the road.

Before I could decide whether it was a good idea to approach him, he returned. As he settled into the seat, his signature smell overwhelmed the tiny space. The gloomy weather served to enhance that wonderful aroma. He was a storm in every way and I was caught in it, unable to move from my position. I was flush with the passenger door, angled toward him, waiting.

"Are you okay?" he asked, his voice hoarse.

I wasn't sure how to answer that. "Jack, what just happened? It looked like you went to hell and back."

He let out a quick breath, but it sounded like a laugh. "That's fitting. People seem to think I'm the devil."

The Emerald Devil. It wasn't just a moniker for fighting. He'd earned the title somehow.

"Are *you* okay?" I asked.

Jack turned toward me, regret marring his features when he saw my position. I was as far away from him as I could get within the confines of the car. It wasn't *him* I feared. Just his reaction. And that damn word.

"I'll be fine." He moved his hand like he wanted to reach for me, then pulled back. "Just please don't push me like that ever again. I've buried that part of my past for a reason and it has to stay that way. If we can't move through this… If you can't take me as I am and not constantly be wanting to know more…" He ran that hand through his hair again, shaking droplets loose. "Fuck, you're putting me in a horrible position here."

My heart fractured at what he was implying. If I couldn't be satisfied with what he could give, there would be no us. Not now, not ever.

"Jack, it's okay," I whispered, letting my own hesitation go. I leaned toward him, grabbing his hand in both of mine. "I'm so sorry I pushed you. I should've listened. I'm sorry. Please forgive me."

The nine circles of hell still raged within his wild eyes. "Are you going to leave? If I can't give you everything, will you leave me?"

He gripped my fingers tight, like he had no intention of giving me a choice. It didn't matter. My answer would always be the same.

"Of course not, Jack." A sharp pain lanced my chest at the mere idea. "I'll take every piece of you I can get my hands on."

He released the breath he'd been holding, the tendons in his neck relaxing. "I can't let you into that part of my world. My enemies are ruthless bastards.

People who would jump on any weakness if I gave them the chance. If they caught wind that I cared about you as much as I do…" He loosened his grasp, looking out into the rain. "The more you know, the more integrated you are, the bigger the risk. Tell me you understand, Emma."

"I do," I answered, a chill settling into my bones. "I understand. I promise."

He searched my face for any doubt. He wouldn't find any. I'd heard him crystal clear. "Are *we* okay?" he asked.

"We're okay."

Once we'd reassured each other, Jack rejoined the traffic on the turnpike. His movements were calm, but I could feel the agitation in the car like it was a third passenger. We'd just gone through something huge and I wasn't entirely sure what it was.

I relaxed into my bucket seat, tugging the eyelet lace of my dress toward my knees as I did so. It had ridden up during all my shifting and the length was making me feel vulnerable.

When I adjusted, Jack's attention snapped to my legs. The small giveaway was imperceptible, but it made me flush. The chill in my body was subsiding and all because he was checking me out. Thank God I hadn't managed to ruin the intense sexual chemistry between us. He still wanted me just as much after I'd mistakenly hurt him.

"It's too quiet," Jack said, his focus back on the road. "Can you pick something?"

It took me a moment to figure out what he was referring to. Jack listened to a ton of different music. He picked genres based on what he was feeling.

"What mood are you in?" I asked. Death metal? Screaming? Angry Eminem? *Sad* Eminem?

"I have no clue." He shook his head. "You've got me scattered, lass. You choose."

I thumbed through my options on the touch screen. Everything was at my fingertips, but an idea occurred to me. Music meant a lot to Jack. It was always playing in his cars, at the gym, in his apartment. Every time we got together, he was pulling AirPods out of his ears. If I couldn't find the words to tell him how I felt right this second, maybe someone else could.

My gaze lighted on a track. I pressed it, then settled into my seat as the soft chords to *Hostage* by Billie Eilish began. When her low vibrato echoed through the air, Jack's hold on the steering wheel tightened again. He worked on a swallow, casting me a look I couldn't fathom the meaning of.

Not a moment later, Jack slid his hand onto my lap. He played with the delicate lace at the end of my dress. I watched, enraptured. The back of his hand was misted with rain, the Roman numerals on his middle finger inkier than ever. He trailed his fingertips along the inside of my leg, pushing the fabric up as he went. A new kind of goosebump rose along my skin, aching for more of his touch.

When he reached my panties, he pressed two fingers along my sex. I bit my lip, looking toward the sunroof. The rain fell from the darkening sky, but the sound was hardly noticeable with the somber melody filling the moment. Jack split his attention between the road and what he was doing to me. What *was* he doing to me?

When the deep bass entered the song, Jack pushed my underwear aside and slipped a finger into my folds. I didn't know if my mind was ready for him, but my body was. And he'd sensed it. The vibration of the bass rattled the leather seat, heightening his ministrations.

Only Jack could turn me on at a time like this. He managed to make my clean-cut world blur into oblivion. The once-obvious differences between light and dark, black and white, were becoming harder to identify. What were opposites to me, Jack held hand-in-hand. Adrenaline and arousal, pain and pleasure, control and release, good and evil – the list was endless.

Was I doing the same to him? Did I *want* to? I had my hand on the lid of Pandora's box. Did I hold the power to open it? And if I did, what would come pouring out?

Jack increased the tempo, building something inside of me that I couldn't identify. I rocked my hips into the heel of his palm, the balls of my feet pressing into the floor. My toes curled within my boots, a soft whimper passing my lips. I gripped his biceps, digging my fingernails into the tattoos on his skin. I would leave my own mark on him – I was sure of it. My right hand ached with the pressure I was applying to the edge of my seat.

My heart was a tiny flutter under my ribs, seeming to grow in size. It pushed against the walls of my chest, threatening to burst through that barrier too. My lower lip trembled and I turned my head to the window as warm tears ran down my face.

Fuck.

Possession. That was the feeling I couldn't place. Jack O'Connell was possessing me in every way he could. His hands on me, his fingers inside, his smell filling my lungs, the carnal taste of him on my tongue, his command invading my mind.

The message was clear. He wouldn't—couldn't—give me everything, but I didn't have the luxury of holding back. He wanted all of me and he wanted it now. Was he doing this because I had made him use the safe word? Because I'd challenged his limits? Using pleasure as a form of punishment… What a mind-fuck.

With a clenched jaw, I rebelled, denying both of us the orgasm that was begging for release. It was the strangest fight I'd ever been in, one where sex was the weapon. I knew he would stop if I asked, but I couldn't speak through the constriction in my throat. Maybe I didn't want this to end. Maybe I wanted to dangle on the edge of this cliff for eternity, a form of insanity in and of itself.

"Emma, let go." Jack's voice cut through the music. It was hard and demanding, just like him. "I want to feel you get all tight around my finger. I want you to come apart in the palm of my hand."

I whimpered, shaking my head. My hair fell around my face, hiding the flush of my cheeks. "I can't. I don't want to fall…"

What didn't I want to fall into? In love? Was that what would greet me at the bottom of this cliff? I'd never felt it in this way before. I thought I'd been in love with Nate. Maybe I had, but this was unworldly, this new realm that Jack seemed to be dragging me into by his teeth. An internal war raged as he sucked me into his vortex. I struggled with my orgasm, but there was no point in holding it in any longer. Like a fish on a line, I was tiring.

I was in love with Jack O'Connell. Devil or not, he held my heart in his hands. What he would do with it was up to him.

"I feel it, too." The husk of his voice surprised me. I glanced over at him, but he was glaring at the road. His cock was hard as stone, straining against his jeans. The electricity sizzling across my skin was insurmountable, but I was scared to give into it. To give into him. Could I lose myself in the process? "It's okay. You can let go. I've got you, dove."

At his promise, I shattered. The burning in my skin skated along my nerves, wracking me with shudders. I squeezed my eyes shut, a sob escaping as I let the tears fall. I fell, too. My stomach dropped, but Jack's touch was there, guiding me through the confusing tunnel inside my mind.

When Jack removed his hand, he finally looked at me. He was so beautiful that I was devastated. He put his fingers in his mouth—one by one—licking them off like I was the best thing he'd ever tasted. I stared, transfixed with my eyes wide, jaw slack, heart racing.

He reached over, wiping a lone teardrop with his freshly cleaned finger. Then he licked that too. Was it sadness he consumed? No, it was unconditional love. My words rang true. I'd take any piece of him that he could offer. Just a slice of Jack would suffice. Maybe I'd feel different tomorrow, but it was more than enough for now.

"You're all mine, Emma Marshall," Jack murmured, placing both hands back on the wheel like he hadn't just ravished my soul.

I nodded, my brain skittering to a halt. I was emotionally raw. After returning to my hometown, witnessing Mark blow his head off, reading Nate's suicide note and now this, I couldn't take much more. I was one person. A tiny human in a savage sea of people.

When the Manhattan skyline came into view, my eyes almost rolled into the back of my head. Jack drove us into Lincoln Square. I was worried he'd want me to stay with him. He hadn't let me out of his sight for two days, but I needed some time alone to decompress.

"When does Ava get back?" he asked, expertly managing the change in traffic. NYC was a different playing field.

"Sunday," I replied, my voice weak.

I didn't have to look at him to know he was concerned. It was an expression I knew well. My family's eyes had held the same trepidation when we said our goodbyes this morning. They were all scared I would fall back into my depression.

I wouldn't. I knew myself better than anyone. I'd suffered far worse and come out the other side better for it. In the story of my life, I wasn't the damsel in distress. I was stronger than people gave me credit for, even if I didn't feel like it right now.

"I just need to get some sleep," I assured him, planting a kiss on his cheek as he pulled to the curb outside my building.

"Come here, baby." He caught my chin, tugging me back to his lips. He encompassed my jaw with his large hand, running his thumb along my cheekbone. "I'm sorry if I scared you. Do you trust me?"

"Yes," I whispered against his mouth.

Jack locked his eyes with mine, our faces inches apart. "Then believe me when I say that my past doesn't matter. It made me who I am and set me on the path to you, but that's it. From here on out, it's just you and me. It's all about us, dove."

I gave him a hopeful grin. "Okay."

Jack returned my smile, leaning in for another kiss. "If the nightmares come back, call me. Fuck, if you need me, call me, Emma."

I nodded, my forehead pressed against his. "I will."

Chapter Twenty-Five

Emma

On Saturday, I was awakened by a hard knock on the door.

I rubbed my eyes, trying to orient myself. My body felt like it'd been in a terrible car accident. Sore limbs, aching lungs. Getting out of bed hurt, but I dragged myself from my room nonetheless. As I walked toward the front door, my stomach rumbled. The last time I'd eaten was breakfast at my parents' house the day before. What time was it anyway? I'd have to go grocery shopping or get takeout. There was nothing in the apartment aside from that stupid bag of stale mints from Halloween.

"Delivery for Miss Marshall?"

I blinked a few times, clearing the sleep from my eyes. A short man stood on my doorstep. He was reading from a receipt, listing off food items that I couldn't understand.

"I didn't order anything," I stammered, clinging to the edge of the front door.

The young Asian man looked up at me, pushing the bags into my arms. "From a Mr. O'Connell, miss."

"Okay, thanks."

I set the food on the small dining table in the living room, unpacking it with shaky hands. Even apart, Jack was meeting my needs.

My heart warmed when I realized what he'd ordered for me. Along with an appetizer and a side of rice, it was legitimate Japanese ramen. With fish cakes and egg and scallion.

While I dug into the crispy vegetable gyoza, I scrolled through my phone. It was four o'clock in the afternoon and I had a missed call from my mom, but I needed to text Jack first to say thank you. His response was immediate.

I want a photo of the empty bowl within an hour.

It wasn't a difficult request to obey. I was starving and Jack had figured as much. I'd slept for the past twenty-four hours, fighting dreams. Visions of Mark, Nate and Jack had dominated my subconscious. My sleep was marred by violence, as was my past. Blood, gunshots and loose pills haunted me. Every so often, I'd wake up and shake my head to clear it like I was purging myself of everything. Everything apart from the one thing I couldn't and wouldn't let go of—Jack.

As I ate, I dialed my mom and set my phone on the table. We talked for a short time. I knew she was just checking on me. Making sure I hadn't retreated into the darkness.

What I'd gone through after Nate's suicide had changed me. When my best friend had died, a piece of me had gone with him into the grave. My innocence. The little girl who only saw good in the world had slipped away. And in her place, I'd curated armor.

But I didn't need to suffer in isolation this time. Like Ava had said, it was okay to rely on others. Even though I was alone physically, I could feel the support of the people in my corner. Those people now included Jack. And his shoulder was powerful in every meaning of the word.

Reminded of him, I sent the picture of my empty ramen bowl. He replied before I could even rise from the table.

Good girl.

* * * *

On Sunday afternoon, Ava got home. I hopped up from the couch and helped her with her bag. It was heavier than to be expected for a simple weekend trip. I had no doubt she'd spent a majority of her time training. There was a reason she was one of the best at what she did—it took a lot of practice. Even her bedroom furniture had been pushed aside to make room for a ballet barre and wooden dance mat.

We ordered a giant mushroom pizza from the Italian deli down the block and settled on the couch to watch the new Kevin Hart stand-up.

"Are you even allowed to eat this?" I joked, mouth full of grease and marinara. I was on my fourth piece and Ava was matching me with every bite.

"No one's lifting me until Friday." She shrugged. "Plenty of time to drop a pound of flesh."

I glanced sideways at her. She wore leggings and an elastic tank top, the thick line of muscle around her torso flexing as she grabbed another slice of pizza from the coffee table. The girl didn't have an ounce of flesh to lose.

We returned our attention to the television. The comedy was just what I needed. Something to remind me that not everything had to be taken so seriously. It was okay to laugh, even when things seemed dark.

By seven o'clock, I'd showered and thrown on a fresh pair of sweats. When I reached in my sock drawer, I found Jack's white T-shirt and slipped it on, obsessing over the smell of him. Fire and rain. It put me on edge. I couldn't help but look over my shoulder, hoping to discover him standing right behind me.

The sleep, food and laughter improved my mood. I dove back into schoolwork. I had a few research essays to review and I wanted to get ahead before winter break. The end of the semester was coming and I wasn't about to let it sneak up on me.

I was highlighting a section of my notes when there was a soft knock on my door. Ava popped her head in a moment later.

"A courier just dropped this off for you."

She set a small black gift box on my bed. It was tied with a matching silk bow. There was no tag attached, but I could assume who it was from.

"Thanks," I said as Ava left the room, shutting the door behind her.

I fumbled with the delicate wrapping, hoping to God it wasn't too expensive. By the size of the box, it was something small. Maybe that would factor into the price.

Above the tissue paper sat a black card with a message written in gold ink. The penmanship was masculine—block letters and quick lines. Even his script was straight to the point.

From your hostage – J

Inside was a small piece of solid gold jewelry. The chain was delicate and short, a choker. The clasp was made up of two handcuffs, which fastened together with a soft click. I swallowed, thinking of the cuffs Sheriff Donahue had put on Jack.

The back of the card had a few French words and a foreign address typed onto it. I grabbed my phone and typed them into the search bar.

L'Ange Défendu was a luxury jeweler in Paris. Their website was simple, but they didn't have any prices listed. All of their pieces were edgy and exquisitely feminine. I couldn't find any jewelry matching the one sitting on my bed, so I assumed it was a custom order. L'Ange Défendu, the forbidden angel.

Exiting the translator, I pulled up my message thread with Jack and shot a text off.

What are you doing?

Jack's reply was quick, a photo attached. I paused to study it, zooming in to glean any and all clues.

Been working with this ugly mug all day.

The picture was first and foremost of Kieran. He wore jeans and a button-down with the sleeves rolled up. Over that was a reflective orange vest. He was bent over a large crate that appeared to be military-grade, but there was no writing on the side. With one hand, he was flipping the camera—or, better yet, Jack—off, his finger partially covering his face.

They seemed to be in some sort of warehouse. The lighting was artificial and harsh on Kieran's soft, youthful features. Still, he looked handsome as usual. I assumed all the O'Connells were. And they liked to surround themselves with beautiful things—people included.

Your brother doesn't have an ugly "mug"

Jack's response was almost immediate.

Don't make me jealous, dove. I've grown very possessive of you.

You don't say… I grinned, rose to my knees and slipped the gold choker around my neck. Releasing my hair from its messy bun, I let the wet curls fall over my shoulders in waves. Giving the camera a small, mischievous smile, I sent him a selfie.

I don't know what's making me harder, seeing you in my shirt or the fact that you color-code your notes.

I giggled, checking the photo again. He had zoomed in on my background as well. My notebook was lying on the bed, a rainbow of thoughts. I thumbed the miniature handcuffs that rested where my collarbones met, a thought occurring to me.

Is it a collar?

I bit my lip, eyes unblinking as I waited for his reply. The little text bubble floated on my screen, letting me know he was typing.

You're not a dog, Emma. It's a necklace.

I could practically hear the bite in his voice. I tucked a strand of hair behind my ear, fingers flying across my keypad.

You got dinner plans tomorrow?

His response made my heart thump in anticipation.

I do now.

After I shut everything down for the night, I did some yoga on my bedroom floor. I focused on my breath, allowing my mind to settle. When I lay my head on the pillow, I replayed Eilish's song through my AirPods, willing myself to conjure every spectacular detail of Jack's face.

No more nightmares if I could help it. I wanted to dream of him, and only in the best possible way. Recollecting every facet of the body that loved to torture me. The way he caught his tongue between his teeth, the way he cursed when I was on my knees in front of him. And that unidentifiable look he'd given me in the car when I chose the song.

Was I his hostage, or was he mine?

Chapter Twenty-Six

Emma

Christmastime in Manhattan was especially brilliant this year. Maybe because it was the first season I had noticed it. Or maybe because Jack was in my life. Either way, the decorations adorning the streets and storefronts brought literal cheer to my days as I traipsed around the city. The month of December was filled with lectures and shifts at Roisin's, essays and end-of-semester finals. And Jack. Lots and lots of Jack.

After Thanksgiving and our fearsome exchange on the drive home, I was happy I'd spent the weekend in solitary confinement. By the time I met Jack for dinner at his apartment, I was starving for him. I had barely exited the elevator before he was on me, pinning me to the foyer wall, his erection against my hip.

I'd spent more than a few nights at his place over the course of the month, but we always parted ways at the end. Even if it was five in the morning when we tired, he let me go without a fight. I could see in his eyes that he was desperate for me to stay—to fall asleep in his arms—but I couldn't yet. I had to remind myself that he wasn't giving me everything either. Not being able to share a bed with Jack was okay. I'd shared damn near everything else with the man.

Our relationship had changed. The dynamics were the same but magnified. The feelings I harbored in my heart for him made every touch, every taste, that much sweeter. My education—something I'd always valued above everything—was becoming inconsequential. I was keeping up, but I didn't have the same tenacity as usual. Not when my heart and mind lay elsewhere. It was difficult to stay present while my professors droned on. My thoughts were always roaming, my cheeks heating, thighs rubbing together.

A week before the holiday, Jack informed me that his mother, Roisin, would be visiting from Ireland. I was excited to meet her, assuming she had a different parenting style than his father. Based on the stories Jack told, she certainly did. He didn't seem to mind talking about his life before they'd left Ireland. Whatever had occurred between him and Frank, it had taken place in Boston.

Before I could let myself get too sucked into the holiday season, there was something I had to do. There was one name that kept popping up in the worst places. My questions always led back to him. It was time I went searching for the man himself.

The sky was threatening snow but had yet to follow through on its promise. I hoped it would hold out as I made my way into the warm, stadium-seating classroom. Eoghan had dropped me off on campus. It was supposed to be one of my longer days. He wouldn't be back to pick me up for hours.

What Eoghan didn't know was that I'd gotten out of this final by acing my last three essays. I had a high enough percentage in class that the professor had let me and a few other similar students off the hook. And my next two lectures had been postponed. Thank God for the flu. I had the entire day free and no one expected me to be anywhere else.

I threw my hood on, wrapped my cashmere scarf over my face and exited the lecture hall. Checking in all directions to make sure I wasn't being tailed, I jogged to the nearest subway station. The promise I'd made Jack rang in my ears as I boarded the train. I had sworn to him that I wouldn't use the subway if he had his men stop following me. But I didn't plan on Jack ever finding out about this.

When the train reached Bowery Station thirty minutes later, I stepped off, anxiety growing in the pit of my stomach. The Booker Hotel loomed overhead as I neared its entrance.

"Room 1523, please," I told the concierge at the desk, handing him a wad of cash that I hoped would suffice.

He eyed me with curiosity. "That room is taken."

Shit. I wasn't expecting that. "Anything on that floor is fine, then. It's my lucky number."

The concierge gave me a strange look but rang it up anyway, handing me a dirty key card.

Once I was on the fifteenth floor, I steeled myself for what was to come. If my hunch was correct, I was walking into the lion's den. And I had no intention of becoming prey. I needed answers. I needed to close this chapter of my life for good. Then, I needed to get the hell out.

With that in mind, I knocked on the door to room 1523, eyeing the camera in the corner of the hall. Its red light blinked back at me, watching. There was a sudden silence on the other side of the door. I almost wished no one would open it, but that thought was crushed seconds later.

A skinny, dark-haired man held the door ajar, his mean glare roaming over my body. Behind him, from what I could see, stood two burlier men and one younger woman. She was tall and skeletal, her dark eyes boring into mine with unwarranted hate.

"Wrong room, *topolina,*" the skinny man said, pushing the door closed.

I took a deep breath and stuck my boot out, stopping him. "I need to speak with Don Luca." My voice was strong. I didn't know where it came from.

The skinny man's eyes widened. He glanced behind him. The rest of the crew joined him in laughter.

When he turned back to me, he was still grinning, but his black eyes flashed with a threat. "If you don't move your foot, I'll break it."

I kept my foot right where it was. "It's about Maria Ranucci."

They all quieted and, after a brief phone call, I was let into the room.

* * * *

An hour later, I was seated between two people in the backseat of a car. I couldn't see their faces or where we were going because a cloth bag had been placed over my head. My purse and phone had been left behind at the hotel. My wrists were wrapped together with zip ties, my hands useless in my lap.

"Good thing you guys keep this stuff on hand, right?" I deadpanned as the vehicle lurched through the streets of Manhattan. I was trying to hide my panic, but it kept rising like acid furrowing its way up my throat.

Someone chuckled. "She's funny."

A female voice hissed in Italian and no one spoke again for another forty-five minutes. At least, I thought it was forty-five minutes. I'd been counting the seconds in my head.

Finally, I was dragged from the vehicle. I didn't feel cold. My feet echoed on the ground. We were in some sort of garage. I'd kept track of the turns for a few minutes after we left the Booker, but it was impossible. Apart from being somewhere in the city, I had no idea where we were.

I was led into a warmer area, most likely indoors. A large hand fastened around my upper arm, tugging me up a flight of carpeted stairs and down what I assumed were hallways. The hand pulled back and I was forced to halt.

"Is this how we treat our guests, gentlemen?"

His voice was like warm chocolate. Slow and decadent with a foreign accent. I knew before the cloth was removed from my head that Luca Nicoletti would be standing in front of me.

A man cut the ties from my wrists as I appraised the don. He was shorter than I had imagined, but not small by any means. He was thin and fit, his sinewy muscles twitching as he twirled a pool cue between his fingers, studying me in return. He wore dark suit pants, a lightweight collared shirt and Italian loafers. He had a well-kept mustache and trimmed beard. His teeth glistened, his smile welcoming.

"Emma Marshall," he greeted, snapping at another man to take my coat. "Do you play pool?"

We were in an old-fashioned billiard room. The walls were made of dark wood with built-in bookshelves. A large velvet pool table inhabited the center of the floor. No windows, I noted. I wouldn't be able to narrow down my location. And I couldn't hear any traffic. Were we underground? Or was the room soundproof?

"I'm not any good," I replied.

Don Luca motioned for his men to leave the room. They obeyed without hesitation, closing the large oak door as they went. Once it had been shut, all noise was canceled out apart from soft opera music playing in the background. The room *was* soundproof.

"Entertain me." Don Luca's grin was congenial. He handed me a cue from a varnished rack on the wall.

"Why did you frame Jeremiah Murray for Maria Ranucci's murder?" I asked, not wanting to play at pleasantries.

Don Luca wagged his finger at me. "Show some manners, Emma."

I took the pool cue from him and his smile turned polite again. He racked the billiard balls, switching a few numbers around. I couldn't say whether it was correct. I knew nothing about pool.

He turned to me, stepping away from the table. "You break."

Fine. Nicoletti liked playing games. I could play games.

I stomped to the top of the table, lining my cue up with the white ball. I struck as hard as I could, hoping to at least scatter the cluster at the other end.

"See," Don Luca said from the corner of the room. "That wasn't so hard, was it?"

None of the balls had reached a pocket, but I wasn't paying attention to the game on the table. When I opened my mouth to repeat my question, Don Luca held his hand up, stopping me.

"I framed the Murray boy because I wanted him dead," he answered, aiming his shot and sinking a solid red.

"So you got him sent to prison," I continued. "So that you had easier access to him."

He nodded, striking another ball. "You are a very clever girl, Emma. But too trusting."

"And why is that?"

Don Luca chuckled. "You think it wise to come into the home of the don by yourself? Accusing him of such nasty things?"

"Not wise." I stuck my chin out. "Maybe a little brave." I felt nowhere near brave, but I was putting on a solid front.

"Bravery will get you killed in this world, Emma." He wagged his finger at me again. "Don't forget that."

"Mark received a photo of Maria taken at the Booker Hotel," I said, ignoring his advice. "It was addressed from me, but you sent it to him. Why?"

Don Luca's satisfied grin sent a chill down my spine. "There are many ways to kill someone. Guilt. Fear. It *eats* away at a man."

"You wanted Mark to kill himself." I was hoping he would confirm my theory, but he pointed to the table. It was my turn to play.

"Of course, I did," he answered once I took my shot and missed. He had to know I wasn't putting any effort into the game, but he didn't seem to mind.

"Why? If Jeremiah was your goal, why did you care what happened to Mark Ranucci?"

"Ah, but you don't know the whole story, little one." Don Luca analyzed the table, weighing his options. "I was the one who told Mark to kill his wife. He was in debt to me. Gambling is a terrible addiction." He sank another one. "But Mark was unraveling. Losing his nerve. I had to push him."

"So you fabricated her affair with Jeremiah to give him incentive?"

"No, her affair was real. Maria had been carrying on with that Irishman since childhood. It was a betrayal to our family name."

I was bent over, lining up my shot, when his words hit me. I stood straight as an arrow. "Wait. Maria was—"

"Maria *Nicoletti* was my daughter, yes." Don Luca nodded with obvious regret, chalking his cue. He looked remarkably young for his age. "My firstborn. But she stopped being anything to me decades ago."

"You ordered a hit on your own daughter?"

"Don't sound so surprised, Emma." He pointed, intending for me to continue the game. I did so, but refused to tear my eyes away from him as he spoke. "She betrayed me. Running off with that Irishman, then sleeping with that low-life Ranucci and getting herself pregnant. I gave her one last chance to make things right, but she ignored me and fled the city, taking my unborn grandson with her. Never once allowing me to see him."

"Nate..."

"Nathaniel was an innocent casualty," he said, appearing crestfallen. "My one regret from all of this was his suicide. It was never my intention to hurt him."

"And all of this…this violence…just to get back at Jeremiah for loving your daughter?"

"No, Emma. It was to get back at my daughter for betraying me." He moved around the table. "She took my only male heir and hid him from me for too long. I needed her out of the way if there was to be any hope of a relationship with Nathaniel. Framing Jeremiah for her murder was just convenience. Eight ball, corner pocket." A clatter echoed as he followed through.

"You're sick." I fought the bile rising in my esophagus. Don Luca might have had a thousand reasons for his actions, but the greatest motivator was to gain access to Nate, his only male descendant. Did that carry weight in the Italian Mafia? If Nate hadn't killed himself, would he have been sucked into this world? Would I have ended up in this same position? Either way, Don Luca's appearance in my life seemed like an inevitability.

"I didn't ask your opinion of me." His sharp tone cut through the air like glass. "But if we are exchanging impressions, I believe you are neither very brave nor very stupid. You wouldn't come here simply to ask for my candor. What is it you want, girl?"

"Amnesty," I answered, following him into his adjoining study. "In exchange for my silence."

Don Luca'd had my attack outsourced to the Irish mob, to Ghost. He hadn't wanted to involve his men. Mark Ranucci had been terrified that I'd discovered he killed his wife. He had said I had ruined everything. All of this was done under the hush-hush. There was no doubt in my mind that the rest of the Nicoletti family knew nothing about Don Luca's order to have Maria killed. They probably still thought Jeremiah was the murderer. Now that I knew the truth, it made sense.

Having his own daughter killed was something Don Luca would want to keep secret at all costs.

Don Luca lit a cigar and sat down on an antique stuffed chair behind his desk. "Amnesty for yourself?"

"No," I said, forcing myself to sit across from him. It would've been easier to sit in front of a dragon with a cough. "For Jack O'Connell."

"Ah." He sighed, bitter. "Another Irishman."

I ignored his comment. "I don't want him killed in the crossfire of whatever war you have going with the Murrays."

Don Luca eyed me for a few moments, puffing on his cigar. The smell of tobacco and vanilla filled the room. I fought the urge to shift in my seat. I didn't like the way he was scrutinizing me, like he was sizing me up.

"Jack O'Connell, was it?" he asked. Before I could reply, he continued. "I'm aware of the other two brothers. Jack is elusive. I've never had the pleasure of meeting with him. But there *are* rumors. People call him the devil."

"So I've heard," I replied, waiting for him to get to the point.

"Does he know you're here? I can't imagine he'd allow someone like you out of his sight for too long."

I didn't know what he meant, so I didn't answer. Someone like me? What was he referring to?

"Tell me, Emma." He flicked the ash from his cigar into an ornate crystal bowl. "Do you know why people call him the devil? It's because he has no soul. Only a few men have been lucky enough to escape his wrath and live to tell the tale. He is ruthless. A killer without conscience."

I bit back my retort. *Look who's talking*. I was sitting in front of a man who had murdered his daughter. Not by his own hand, but that didn't make him any better for it. He had some nerve trying to smear Jack when he'd done far worse.

"He doesn't deserve your heart, Emma. You shouldn't be asking me to grant amnesty to a monster. You should be running for the hills while you still can. He'll take what he wants and leave you with nothing."

"You said it yourself." I clenched my jaw to keep my teeth from chattering. "You don't know him."

"I know enough," he forewarned, leveling me with his glare. "He'll destroy you, little one. You won't survive him."

"You had me attacked in August," I reminded him. "Now, you care about what happens to me?"

Luca sat back in his chair, the leather giving a low squeak. "And what did your attacker say to you?"

"Luca sends his best." I didn't intend to whisper, but the memory of Ghost still elicited a chill.

"I wanted you to find me on your own," Don Luca continued, now smiling with pride. "I wanted you to put everything together. I just *had* to meet the person who knew my grandson best. The little girl who grew up by his side and loved him dearly."

My mouth popped open, aghast. "*That's* why you dragged me into this? Sending Mark the photo with my return address, having me attacked, it was all to meet me? Why not just ask me out for coffee?"

"Old habit." Don Luca set his cigar in the crystal ashtray, flexing his fingers as if to shake something off them. "Moreover, I've been keeping track of your progress since Nathaniel's suicide. You've impressed me. You are a stellar student, you work hard, you stay out of trouble. That is, until this Jack O'Connell managed to get his hands on you."

I shook my head, refusing to hear another slanderous word about Jack. I wasn't going to believe what anyone else told me about him. I'd get the truth from Jack himself. It might take a while, but we weren't short on time. I could be patient.

"Amnesty," I said, reminding both of us why I was here.

Don Luca sighed, running a hand along the nape of his neck. The gesture made him appear more human. "And what makes you think I owe you this? I could kill you and no one would know I ordered Maria's death. You're the last loose end."

"You won't kill me." I was bluffing, but I hoped to God he wouldn't call me on it. "You wouldn't go to all this trouble to get me here just to turn around and end my life. Besides, I'm not the last loose end."

Don Luca studied me, resting his index finger on his chin. Whatever he saw there, it wouldn't be weakness. I took a deep breath and forged ahead, willing my eyes to ring true.

"Mark told his son that someone paid for his alibi. And for the sheriff to look the other way. Nate left it all written down in a suicide note to me. Your entire war was fabricated. It won't be hard for someone to read it and put two and two together. And if it gets to your family, I'm guessing it won't be that big of a leap for them to realize you ordered Maria's death. Will that sit well with them? I don't think so. They'll turn on you. You'll lose your war with the Murrays."

My heart pounded as I watched Don Luca process my lie. Nate hadn't known his father's freedom was bought. He hadn't even known the name Nicoletti.

Maria had told Nate his grandparents were dead. Jack's safety—quite possibly his life—relied on Don Luca believing me.

"And you have this letter?" Don Luca asked, his eyes betraying the slightest shimmer of fear.

"You'll have to take my word for it," I said, brushing a piece of lint off my tights. If I faltered—if I portrayed a single shred of doubt—I was dead. If Don Luca had killed his own daughter for betraying him, he wouldn't blink an eye to do the same to me. "I've made dozens of copies. All safe. But someone will make them public if anything happens to me. Or Jack."

"It appears we should've been playing chess, little one. You have me checked." His tone darkened as he leaned across his desk. "For now, Mr. O'Connell and yourself are untouchable."

I stood to leave, but he stopped me.

"One more thing. How did you know the room at the Booker was a safe house?"

"You ordered my attack after I left the photograph there. I did some digging and found out you own the hotel. It was an educated guess."

He tapped his finger to his temple, grinning wickedly. "It goes without saying that if you feel the need to contact me again, that room is the best place to start." His men materialized around me, but I made sure not to show my unease. Everything about the way I conducted myself around this monster was a fabrication.

"Merry Christmas, Emma," Don Luca stated, then addressed his men as they put the cloth bag over my head. "See that Miss Marshall is safely returned to the Booker. And no need to tie her hands, gentlemen. They aren't what she chooses to do battle with."

Chapter Twenty-Seven

Emma

Shannon O'Connell put all other Christmas Eve hosts to shame.

We convened in the loft above the warehouse, the one where I'd seen Jack participate in the underground street fight, but that seemed like ages ago. And the loft, which I found out later belonged to Kieran, couldn't have looked any different than it had the night of the party.

A twenty-five-foot live fir scraped the makeshift ceiling. How Shannon had decorated it right to the tippy top was beyond me. Candles and icicles hung from the copper ventilation system. The glass wall separating the room from the outdoor area had been iced over. The balcony itself was getting snowed upon, although the weather hadn't yet done so over the rest of Manhattan. A few couches and loveseats had been relocated to make room for a long, solid oak dining table. And the table was packed with food, some of which Roisin gladly explained to me—roasted goose, Guinness mince pies, corned beef, sausages and black pudding. The empire waist of my dress was getting tighter just looking at it all.

Shannon and I had gone shopping a week earlier. Or rather, Shannon had shopped while I'd balked at the price tags of everything in the store. When my attention had homed in on the dark green minidress, I was reminded of Jack's eyes. Shannon, following my gaze, had grabbed the dress off the rack and didn't give me a choice in the matter. It shouldn't have come as a surprise that Jack had already provided his card number to the clerk. Eventually, I'd have to chat with Shannon regarding Jack's knowledge of our shopping sprees.

Kieran sidled up to where I stood by the dining table, giving me a mischievous wink. "It's like Harry Potter's wet dream," he whispered, dipping a finger in the mashed potatoes.

Roisin slapped his hand playfully, her cheeks rosy from whiskey eggnog. She deserved to relax. She'd traveled all this way and immediately sought out the kitchen to cook—with Shannon's help, of course. If I'd known Christmas was this extravagant in the O'Connell family, I would've offered my assistance as well. I wasn't much of a chef outside the realm of TV dinners, but I could follow directions.

It was my first time meeting Jack's mother. She'd landed the day before and was staying with Shannon and Connor in their penthouse. I hadn't met many Irish "mums," but she seemed to be as classic as they came with her round bottom, ruddy cheeks and flyaway red hair. It was obvious she missed her sons and cared deeply for them. For family, in general. It took all of thirty seconds for me to decide I liked her.

Now, I wiggled my nose at Kieran. "You're a Hufflepuff if I've ever seen one."

Kieran grinned, pulling me under his arm like he'd done to Shannon months ago. It warmed my heart that he felt comfortable enough to joke around with me. I hoped I was blending into Jack's family as well as he'd done with mine.

"Whatever, Ravenclaw." He planted a sloppy kiss on my cheek. Kieran was a lovey-dovey drunk, which I found adorable. It was impossible not to feel happy in this environment.

"Hands off my girlfriend, shrimp," Jack said, appearing out of nowhere. He grabbed my hand and tugged me into his side, giving Kieran a menacing glare.

Kieran and I snickered, looking at the dark and deadly O'Connell child. "Slytherin," we whispered in unison, breaking out into giggles.

When Kieran left to join Connor by the fire, Jack turned me to face him, his eyes narrowed. "There's a bit of a nerd in you, isn't there?"

"Took you this long to find out?" I challenged, raising a brow.

Jack licked his lips, towering over me. It was as if the rest of his family had disappeared. We were alone in the giant room, eyes roaming each other. *Heartless, my ass*. I could feel it now, the beats quickening under my hand in response to my touch.

Everyone—Jack included—might think he was a soulless devil, but I knew better. There was a soul in there. And I was discovering it, with or without his permission.

"Mmm." Jack made a contented noise at the back of his throat, biting the inside of his cheek. He was studying me with the same attentiveness that Don Luca had days ago, but my reaction couldn't be more disparate. A low fire burned at the base of my belly. I pressed onto my toes, planting a chaste kiss on his lips. When I broke it off, Jack met me once again, his lips parting mine with ease.

The tip of his tongue danced along mine, his hands on either side of my face, keeping me there. My arms were pinned against his hard chest. As the room began to spin, I forced myself to remember where we were—surrounded by Jack's family. They were all drinking and wouldn't notice or care, but still. The rhythmic throbbing in my clitoris was inappropriate with an audience of any kind.

"I've been fighting for years, dove," Jack whispered, moving his mouth to the sensitive skin behind my ear. "I've never lost, but I've never had an opponent like you."

"Does that mean I'm winning?" I asked, my voice breaking with the heat of the moment.

He pressed his lips to the wild pulse at my neck. "I think so."

"Jackie, ye can't keep the lass all to yerself!"

Jack stepped a foot away from me, cheeks reddening at the sight of his mother. I smiled shyly as Roisin approached and placed a warm hand on my face right where Jack's had been.

"Oh, I just can't get over how beautiful ye are," she gushed, running her thumb along my cheekbone.

"Emma doesn't like compliments, Mum," Jack teased, grabbing his pint off the table. "So, please, keep going."

Roisin grinned, slapping her son's arm. "I can see why ye like America so much if all the women look like this."

Jack caught my eye. "Not all the women look like this."

My cheeks burned, so I took my leave and joined Shannon in the kitchen, letting Jack enjoy his mother's company. When I reached the fiery little woman, she handed me a cocktail with a poignant expression.

"You'll thank me later," Shannon said, slicing a lime in half. "It's impossible to keep up with full-blooded Irish, but it'll be easier if you maintain a nice buzz and pretend."

"Just going along for the ride, huh?" I took a sip. It was her signature concoction. I recognized it from the last O'Connell party.

She rolled her eyes and started mashing the lime. "Story of my life."

I glanced at her drink, tilting my head in curiosity. She saw the direction of my gaze and pushed the glass aside.

"If anyone asks," she whispered, "it's a rum and coke."

My lips formed an *O*. "Holy shit, are you—"

She held her hand over my mouth, eyes wild. "Don't even *think* it." She went back to squeezing limes with renewed vigor, glancing at Connor, who was chatting out of earshot. "Connor is protective enough as it is. Barely lets me out of the apartment every time a body washes up in the Hudson."

"Does that happen a lot?" I asked, unsure what to say if I couldn't address her pregnancy. Apparently overprotective control freaks were a dime a dozen with the O'Connell brothers. That, and incredible looks—

although, in my opinion, Jack had them beat by a landslide.

"I went to the doctor last week." Her voice was barely audible and I was standing right beside her. "I'm almost two months along."

Not knowing what else to do, I reached for her hand. She stopped mangling the poor citrus and looked at me, happy tears pooling in the corners of her eyes. I squeezed her hand and she smiled, knowing what I wanted to say.

"Be careful," she warned as we tag-teamed another round of drinks. "You *look* at that boy wrong and he'll put a swimmer in you."

I glanced over at Jack. He stood at the other end of the room, speaking with the aforementioned brothers. The trio were quite a sight to behold. Connor wore his three-piece Brioni suit, tumbler of whiskey in hand. Then Kieran, who always appeared to be up to something nefarious.

Then there was Jack.

He was so different from the other two, with his umber hair and forest green eyes. His jaw twitched as Connor spoke to him. When he moved to muss Kieran's hair, his black T-shirt rode up to expose rock-solid abs. His jeans hung low on his hips, revealing the band of his Armani briefs. I followed the line of tapered muscle there to where it disappeared into them. He held his pint to his lips, pausing at something Connor said, his grin magnetic. Lord, I knew what those lips were capable of. That naughty pulse between my legs returned. I took another sip of my drink, trying to keep it at bay. It just worsened.

I whistled. "You're not kidding."

Sensing my attention, Jack's gaze met mine from across the room. His wide grin morphed into a suggestive smile and the tip of his tongue traced a line along his bottom lip. My heart performed jumping jacks inside my chest.

"Jesus Christ, Em," Shannon scolded, grabbing my arm to tear my focus back to her. "That's called looking at him the wrong way!"

I inhaled, adjusting myself to the present. One glance from Jack and I forgot we weren't the only two humans that existed.

"What bodies in the Hudson?" I asked Shannon, remembering what she'd just said. I couldn't discuss these things with Jack, but maybe Shannon would be more open with me now.

"I don't know." She sighed. "Connor doesn't tell me much. We're on a need-to-know basis. If he was completely truthful with me, I'd never let him leave my arms."

"How do you do it?" I frowned. "The not knowing. Doesn't it bother you?"

"I think of it like Connor is a secret agent with the CIA. I mean, they have wives, right? And they can't tell them everything about their work. Connor is so busy all the time. The last thing I want to do is force him to relive everything he's gone through in a day. Most of it is pretty mundane, anyway. Just millions being passed around from alpha male to alpha male."

When she put it like that, it didn't sound too bad. It was an adjustment for me. I was someone who craved knowledge. If I didn't understand something, I researched the hell out of it. Maybe I could learn to let this go. Like Shannon said, maybe I didn't *want* to know the ins and outs of Jack's work.

"Thanks, Shan." I gave her a small smile. "You helped me a lot."

"Any time, Em. If it makes you feel any better, I'll probably be enlisting your help in the near future." She put a hand to her belly, her face paling. "God, how the hell am I going to tell him?"

I bit my lip, floundering. A baby. In the Irish mob. That was out of my depth on so many levels.

Chapter Twenty-Eight

Jack

"You're fucking done, little bro."

Connor strode across the room to join me. The patio doors were open and I felt the need to cool off after being around Emma. It was hard enough to keep my hands off her when she was in jeans and a T-shirt. The dress she wore this evening was conservative but complemented her feminine curves well. I was so used to having her all to myself after Thanksgiving that it was easy to forget we had a small audience. Not to mention, my mum was hovering around her like I'd brought home a new puppy.

"What do you mean?" I asked, slipping my hand into the pocket of my jeans.

Connor gestured with his drink, pointing to the object of my desires. "That girl has you by the balls."

"Look who's talking."

Connor rolled his deep blue eyes. "I've accepted my fate. By the looks of it, Emma is eating you alive. I've never seen you like this. All possessive and shit. It's cute."

Groaning, I ran a hand through my hair. I studied Emma, who was speaking with Shannon in the kitchen. She looked beautiful as always, but maybe a little tired. She wasn't getting solid sleep. Not that I would know. She still wouldn't share a bed with me.

I resented the person who'd stolen her ability to sleep sound. Nathaniel Ranucci. And now his father had been added to the mix. They were taking peace from my angel's nights and I despised them for it. If they were alive, I could take my anger out on them. Instead, it had nowhere to go, incurring a deep-seated need to protect Emma from any future harm.

Still, I couldn't shake the nagging idea that I was one of them. The end-all and be-all of demons. A devil rediscovering his heart.

Could she be happy not having all of me? Not knowing my past? I hadn't given her much choice when it came to her own. Watching her work through the memories of her depression was like a soft punch to the gut. Hours passed like minutes that night, as did every chance I got to be with Emma. I could live a hundred lifetimes and never have my fill of her. The warmth in her voice was something I could no longer live without. She was innocent, honest, trusting. Like no one I'd ever met. Surviving what she'd been through would've hardened most. But Emma was malleable as ever, willing to let people like me in. People that didn't deserve it.

Fuck me. A human brimming with pure light was my darkest obsession. I could feel her in my veins, sliding closer with every pump of my heart, melting me from the inside out.

"Dude," Kieran said, joining our conversation seconds after Connor spoke. "I love her."

"Jesus, does anyone else have anything to add about my relationship?" I fumed, reaching forward to rustle my little brother's hair, jealous he was able to admit those three words aloud. He hardly knew Emma, but she was impossible not to love.

"Give your elders a minute." Connor adopted his serious tone at the drop of a hat. The one he reserved for meetings with the heads of houses or negotiations with prospective buyers.

Kieran shook his head and sauntered toward our mum, who was warming herself by the fire.

"Have you set up protection for her?" Connor asked, turning to face me.

"You know I have." I scoffed, taking a sip of my pint. He was belittling me. If anything, I'd made more enemies than the rest of my family.

Connor nodded his approval. "Shannon's getting attached. Says she finally has a friend on the inside. You better keep her around."

I cast my brother a dark look. He was grating my nerves. "I plan to."

As Connor went to join the rest of my family, I glanced at Emma. She wore a concerned expression, her bottom lip caught under her teeth while she studied Shannon. What the hell were they discussing?

Just then, the lift dinged to announce a late arrival, tearing my concentration from the girls.

"Though' you'd keep me from a family reunion, did ye?"

The sound of my father's voice stiffened my spine, like someone had poked me with a cattle prod.

"What the fuck are you doing here, Frank?" Connor was first to react, being closest to the elevator. The rest of us weren't far behind, but I paused to make sure Emma wasn't nearby.

Shannon grabbed Emma's elbow, holding her in the kitchen. When Emma looked back at her, Shannon shook her head, grave. *Good. Keep her there, sis.* She whispered something and Emma nodded her understanding before glancing toward me, consternation etched on her face.

Frank sauntered in, a bottle of Jameson with a red bow tied around its neck swinging from his hand. He held it out to me, winking. I reached for it, my face stern, emotionless.

"Nice *décor,* Shannon!" Frank boomed, passing by my brothers and me, taking in the room with his arms spread wide. "You've outdone yerself."

"If I'd known you'd be coming, I would've made more eggnog," Shannon joked, but she wore no smile.

"Don't fucking talk to my wife," Connor seethed.

Kieran stepped forward to stop Frank's march around the room. I held my hand out, halting him. He rolled his eyes and went to join Shannon and Emma in the kitchen, grabbing a pint from the counter.

"Oh, let the bastard stay!" my mum said, waving her hand at Frank as he disappeared onto the balcony. He was holding his tongue out, trying to catch the fake snow in his mouth. "He'll be passed out in his own piss in an hour."

Everyone took my mum's word for it and went back to the festivities, but I was hesitant. Frank wasn't that drunk. He had a few hours left in him at least. And my mum hadn't seen him in over a decade. She didn't know how bad things could get, even if Frank got his way. He'd pick a fight when there wasn't any need for one. And I was his favorite target.

Emma sidled up to me, slipping her hand in mine. It was cold, which meant she was on edge. Probably because she could sense I was.

"We should go," I said to her.

"It's Christmas, Jackie," my mum protested, giving my arm a squeeze. "Just enjoy us all being together as a family."

I was torn. I didn't want to leave my mum. She'd just arrived and I hadn't seen her in a year. But she was in town for two whole weeks. There would be ample time to visit without my father around.

"Jack?" Emma waited for my decision, her brown eyes wide and compliant. She would follow me, whatever I chose.

"Okay," I relented.

My mum clapped and went to help Shannon in the kitchen. Frank was still dancing on the balcony in his own little world for the time being. Emma watched him, her nostrils flaring. When she looked back at me, I recognized the hatred in her eyes. It matched my own. My little dove was protective of me.

"We can go if you want." She wrapped her arms around my torso, her lips at my ear. "Your mom will understand."

"It'll be fine." I kissed her, hoping to ease her fears. And mine. "Just stay by my side."

"Always."

The warmth in my chest—like a low-burning fire—returned upon hearing that. *Always*. It was a huge promise for such a small word.

The evening continued better than I had thought. Everyone was drinking heavily, apart from a few of us. I had ditched my pint the moment my father showed up. If things got ugly, I didn't need alcohol fueling the rage inside. Emma babysat her drinks. She was a tiny thing and couldn't handle alcohol like the rest of us. Shannon, to my surprise, hadn't touched a drop all evening.

It wasn't until we sat down to dinner that everything went to shit.

Frank, sitting at the head of the table like he'd earned it, began loading food on his plate before my mum had finished grace. I wasn't religious, but I was respectful enough to know better.

"I see ye'r still with this one." Frank spoke in between bites, pointing with his fork to where Emma sat beside me.

Emma, who'd barely taken a bite of her food, froze. I clenched my jaw, but didn't play into my father's hand. Everyone stayed silent, hoping Frank would stop at that. I knew better.

"What's yer record, Jackie Boy?" Frank continued. "Stickin' around one woman for longer'n twenty-four hours? Or stickin' it in twenty-four women in under an hour?"

My hand formed a fist on the table. Emma put her own on my leg to stabilize me. I focused on the way her touch kept me present. *Don't let him wind you up, Jack.*

"Come off it, Frank." Kieran leaned back in his chair, having already eaten his fill. "It's been twenty-four years since you've been inside a woman, anyway."

The entire table laughed, but Frank's eyes bored into the side of my skull. He was coming for me and we both knew it. *Fuck.* I had to get out of here before it got to that point. I was scared of what I would do—that Emma would see just how fucking terrifying I could be.

"Roisin, you must visit the restaurant when you're here," Shannon started, aiming to take the heat off me. Bless her for trying. "The chef has been asking for your champ recipe."

"So, Emma," Frank interjected before my mum could reply, taking a swig of his Guinness. "I hear ye like Italian sausage."

I was standing in a matter of seconds, my chair spiraling across the floor. Emma stared at me, shocked at my outburst, her face a brilliant shade of red. He wasn't going to insult her in front of me. Or ever. I'd make it so he'd never be able to speak again. If he feared Luca Nicoletti would rip out his tongue, wait until I got a hold of it.

"Frank, settle down." My mum pushed his pint away from him. "You've had enough."

"Careful, woman." Frank's sickening green eyes turned to my mum. He lifted his hand, the back of it facing her. "Or I'll remind ye why yer sons made ye stay in Ireland."

My brothers and I raced toward him, but I was fastest. I reached him first, the fury I'd been holding at bay for hours—no, decades—unleashing itself. I pushed him to the ground and pounded my fists into his face. Over. And over. And over. I knew I should stop, but it felt so good to let it all go.

"You're gonna kill him, Jack!" one of my brothers—I didn't care which—yelled. They tried to pull my arm back, but I turned and threw them off with ease.

I couldn't see anything anymore, the fury a black thundercloud in front of my eyes, but I kept hitting. Bone cracked. But I kept hitting. When my fists started to slide off from the blood, I wrapped my hands around my father's sinewy neck. I leaned forward, screaming into his face until my throat burned. I tightened my hold. He thrashed, flailing his limbs.

I was going to kill him. I *was* killing him. And it felt so fucking good to feel his pathetic existence dwindling beneath my hands. I'd never relished taking a life before. It was a duty. One my family relied on me for every so often. This was different. I wanted to kill my father after what he'd put me through. He'd turned me into this. He deserved to be destroyed by the monster he'd created.

"Jack."

The voice was soft. Quiet. But it cut through all the other sounds. The sobs. The Christmas carols. The guttural noise of a man struggling for air. They were insignificant by comparison. I loosened my grip, unaware of what kept me from finishing the job.

"Jack, it's okay," the voice whispered, closer now. Right by my side. Where I told her to stay. Where she said she would always stay. "You can stop now, Jack."

"Emma?" I looked to my right, finding her. She was kneeling in a pool of blood, her knees slipping in it. Her small hand was outstretched toward me. I let go of whatever I was holding, reaching for her.

Her eyes were wider than I'd ever seen. It was impossible not to dive into them. Like a vortex. A place where nothing bad could ever happen. Where nothing bad had *ever* happened.

"Let's go." She tugged on my arm, pulling me up and out of my darkness.

Someone behind me yelled something about an ambulance, but it didn't matter anymore. All that mattered was following Emma as she led me out of the storm of rage.

* * * *

Emma

Jack drove us to his apartment in a trance. His expression was frighteningly blank, but he never released my hand. That small amount of physical contact seemed to be the sole force keeping him from spinning out of control.

I decided then and there that I would never mention anything to Jack about my meeting with Luca Nicoletti. He worried too much about my safety as it was. How would he react if he found out I'd visited one of his rivals? He had enough on his plate with his father and the mob. God only knew how arduous it was to run an international criminal organization. I didn't need to stress him anymore.

Besides, it was over between Don Luca and me. I'd beaten him. Forced him to grant Jack amnesty. As long as he thought there was an incriminating letter in my possession, Jack and I were safe.

We'd barely made it into Jack's bedroom before he rounded on me, tearing at my dress, his mouth all over my body. Jack had told me in the past that sex was an outlet for stress. I understood his reasoning. It was next to impossible to think about anything else when he was inside me.

He pinned me beneath him on his bed, my wrists held above my head in one of his hands. His kiss was satisfying and consuming all at once, like he was giving as much as he took. I wrapped myself around him, letting him guide me wherever he needed to go.

He moved fast, eyes screwed shut against my skin. He traced his bloody knuckles along my ribs, skimming down to cup my butt. He lifted my hips, pulling me onto his arousal. I widened my legs, taking every bit of him. The soreness as he plunged deep inside hurt so good.

"You're mine," he growled through clenched teeth.

As if his words weren't enough, he coupled it with another thrust that had him hitting the end of me. He gripped the back of my hips, digging his fingers into my flesh. When I looked into his eyes, it was like being caught in a wildfire. He was beyond anger, beyond desire.

"Yes," was all I could manage, but even that word left my lungs as a sigh. He was taking his emotions out on me, but I didn't care. Whatever Jack had to give, I could take. It was an even exchange. I could be that for him. I *wanted* to be that for him.

Whenever he lost control, I managed to slip myself in a little deeper. Undetectable at first, but I knew I was making an impact on him. I would find my way inside of him, just like he was inside me right now. I ran my hands over his body, worshiping him as he savagely fucked me.

He bent over, biting and sucking on my nipple until I cried out his name, the sound echoing against the walls. He cursed, nipping at my throat. I could smell the rage burning within him. I was drunk on it, not knowing where it came from but accepting it, nonetheless. I didn't have to know the specifics of his trauma to help him through it.

As he pummeled his way into my heart, he seemed to be struggling with something. His brow was drawn. He glared at me, his eyes hooded. It reminded me of the turnpike.

"It's okay, baby," I whispered, toying with the unruly hair at the nape of his neck. I kept my gaze locked on his as I spoke. "You're falling, but I've got you. I want to feel you come apart inside of me."

He snarled, his lips connecting with mine so hard they'd leave bruises. He lavished my mouth with his tongue, devouring the love I had for him. I welcomed it. Allowing myself to pour that energy back into him was a relief. He'd asked for my heart that day in the car, whether he was aware or not, and I wasn't about to disobey. Not when it felt so good to give him what he needed.

I skated my fingers down his back, his muscles tensing as he pushed us higher into that secluded realm where we were safe. Where no one existed apart from us.

My sex spasmed with the impending orgasm, a mist of sweat covering my skin. When Jack tugged my hair, forcing my eyes to his, I came. His name passed my lips over and over. As he watched me fall apart, his pupils dilated, his jaw slack with something akin to awe. He dropped his head, flexed his hips once more then gave a low, guttural moan into my chest. It vibrated my ribcage, but I clung onto him while my core pulsed around his cock, emptying him.

"Shh," I soothed, running my hands everywhere I could reach. Goosebumps rose on his skin in response to my touch. His shoulders rose and fell with ragged breaths.

He wrapped his arms around me, rolling us so that we lay side by side. Tears pooled in the corners of my eyes while I watched his features soften. He was looking at me like he'd never seen me before, eyes roaming my face.

"Don't leave me tonight," he whispered, his voice breaking. The plea was strange to hear coming from someone as calculated—dominant—as Jack. Tonight, he was vulnerable. He needed me. If I could overcome my fears for anyone, it'd be Jack O'Connell.

I found his lips with mine and kissed him tenderly. "Try and stop me."

That night, I stayed in bed cradled against Jack's protective body. We drifted off, giving in to exhaustion. And I slept better than I could ever remember.

Epilogue

Emma

The Monday following winter break was gray as could be. A sleet storm hit the island overnight, soaking everything in its wet gloom. The buildings, the streets, the sky…it all warped together. The taxi cabs stood out in contrast, taunting me with the color of the missing sun.

Not even the weather could get me down. Although Jack and I were making a terrible track record with violent holidays, the rest of the year had been nothing short of glorious. We had celebrated Christmas Day at my apartment with my family, then gone ice skating in the park. Jack didn't know how to skate. My stomach muscles were still sore from laughing at his expense. When Ella had approached with one of those trainers reserved for children, Jack had grumbled and torn the skates from his feet.

Shannon had gotten word that Frank was recovering in the hospital. After three days, he was discharged and crawled back to Boston—literally or figuratively, I didn't care. I just wanted him away from New York. Even after Jack had assaulted his own father, I couldn't help but take his side. Jack was strong, but whatever he'd suffered as a child was Frank's doing and I didn't feel sorry for the bastard in the least.

On New Year's Eve, we went to a nightclub in Tribeca called Moon, which Kieran owned. Jack might not know how to behave on ice, but he was familiar with a dance floor. Drunk, sweaty and scantily clad, we danced into the New Year before making love in a private suite overlooking the club. Even tipsy, he knew what he was doing. Every caress, every kiss, every breath was thoughtfully placed. He could read my body like I read books.

Even now, I shifted in the backseat of the Tesla, straightening my pleated skirt across my knees. I hadn't checked my weather app before getting dressed in all black—thermal, skirt, peacoat and heeled boots. Lord, I was even dressing in the same color as him.

"Hey, Eoghan?" I asked, glancing up from the screen of my phone moments later. I had a lengthy text chain going with Ella.

His smiling eyes met mine in the rearview mirror. "Yes, Emma?"

"Can you accompany my little sister and me this Saturday? She's coming to the city and wants me to teach her how to use the subway."

Eoghan pulled to the curb outside of campus. "I'll have to clear it with the boss."

"No need," I chimed, exiting the vehicle. Eoghan rolled down the passenger window and I leaned forward, catching his ever-present grin. "I'm meeting him for dinner in Murray Hill tonight. I'll convince him."

His mouth lifted higher on one side, amused. "I have no doubt you will, Wings."

Professor Callahan's lecture was a five-minute walk from the campus center, but I made it in even less time. The sleet had started again, pounding my umbrella. My colleagues kept the same pace, running in opposite directions as we tried to find shelter for the next three hours.

My boots echoed along the prestigious wooden flooring of the hallway. There was a bank for umbrellas outside the door. I slid mine in among the others, running a hand through my hair, shaking the leftover ice out of it. I still had a few minutes to spare thanks to my hustle.

"Holy shit…" I muttered, eyes wide.

The auditorium was adorned wall-to-wall with flowers. Dark-red roses. Everywhere. Tresses along the backs of wooden seats and outlining the interactive whiteboard, dozens of baby's breath atop the desks. Some of my classmates slipped them into their hair, giggling to one another. Even a few of the guys twirled them around in their fingers, sniffing them suspiciously like they might bite.

"Yes, yes!" Professor Callahan walked in behind me. I was forced to jump out of the way. He didn't so much as glance in my direction as he strode down the steps to the pit, which was lined with the foliage. "Apparently, I've fallen victim to an elaborate prank. Either that or my husband bumped his head and woke up thinking it's Valentine's Day. Now, take a seat and ignore the decorations!"

Setting aside an elaborate bouquet, I planted myself near the back of the hall and balanced my laptop on my knees. People were still snickering, but Professor Callahan was known for his impatience. I'd had him the previous semester. He might act like this was all a big joke, but I could tell he was perturbed at the interruption to his strict schedule.

"All right, everyone should have memorized the syllabus and completed the assigned reading," the ancient but energetic professor addressed his pupils. "Ah, yes, humanities—or lack thereof—in England during the 1400s..."

As Callahan began his lecture—taking no time for introductions—I sank into my seat and began recording. Given the vacation I'd had, I knew I wasn't going to be able to pay attention. My body was still sore. A hot, glowing ache emanated from my pelvis. I smiled to myself. Once again, Jack had left his mark on me. Branded into my body, mind and heart. Maybe even my soul.

If that weren't enough, the flowers were distracting. The auditorium looked like a floral shop had blown up in it. I hoped to God it had nothing to do with me. Callahan had said someone was playing a prank on him, but Jack's deviant antics floated to mind. If this was his doing, I could be in trouble for defacement of school property. Even if it wasn't my fault, I would be in the dean's office in record time, no doubt facing some sort of reprimand. Still, who else could afford this many flowers? Jack said he wasn't romantic, but I wouldn't put it past him.

Just then, a notification appeared in the corner of my screen. It was a message from the devil himself.

You like?

Underneath the text was a photo of a medieval sword in excavation condition inside a pristine glass case. I recognized Jack's hand and the presidential gold Rolex wrapped around his wrist, cuff links glinting as he held a single red rose above the glass.

Oh. My. God.

I stuffed my laptop and belongings under the seat, hid them beneath my peacoat and ran out of the lecture. No one noticed my departure. Evidently, I wasn't the only one who'd had an exhausting holiday. Students were leaning on their hands, dozing. Or scrolling through social media on their phones.

Jogging, I made my way down the hall, losing myself in the throng of sleet-covered coats. It was frigid, but the blood pumping through my veins kept me warm as I approached Callahan's personal office. The door was ajar, which it never was. From what I'd garnered from classmates, our seventy-year-old professor hated office hours and treated everyone who used them like it was a major inconvenience.

Brass doorknob in hand, I let myself into the room. I knew who I'd find in there, but his presence still came as a shock.

"Miss Marshall, it seems you have an admirer."

My jaw dropped to the floor. *Oh, Jack…*

He stood with confidence, staring down at the English sword sitting atop an antique side table. The back wall of the office was lined with first-edition hardcovers in mint condition. My eyes traveled to Jack, who had yet to look at me. He swept his hand along the glass case that encompassed the sword Callahan so admired. He'd brought it to lecture on our first day back in September, regaling how he excavated it himself. It sat prestigiously in its case, lining the lip of the side table.

Jack, on the other hand, looked immaculate in a black three-piece suit that fit him like a glove. His dark hair was styled away from his face. When he turned toward me, he wore an expectant and downright sinful expression as he twiddled the stem of a red rose between his long fingers. His emerald eyes traveled the length of my body, pausing at my mouth, before meeting my gaze.

"I…" I started, losing my train of thought. What the hell was happening? Was I dreaming? It was quite possible I hadn't woken up yet. This couldn't be real.

"Close the door, Miss Marshall," Jack commanded, the sharpness in his demeanor speaking louder than his words. I reached my foot back and kicked the door shut, not once taking my eyes from his. As he unbuttoned his suit jacket, his lips twitched with a hidden smile. "Now lock it."

"Jack, this is insane—"

"Lock it, Emma," he repeated, his voice hinting at a delicious edge. I swallowed and did as I was told, securing the deadbolt with shaky hands.

He couldn't.

He wouldn't.

Ah, hell, he will.

Jack was eyeing me in a way that awakened every nerve under my skin. He turned to the sword and leaned forward. Resting his hand on the glass case, he unlatched it.

"Jack, that's a sword from the Crusades!" I whispered. He raised his eyebrows in a challenging manner. "My professor found it himself in the Iberian Peninsula. You can't steal it!"

A punishing look came over Jack's features. He snapped the case closed, taking a few swift steps in my direction. He held out the rose, daring me to take it from him.

"I'm not a thief, dove." There was a soft warning in his words. "At least not anymore."

I reached for the stem of the flower, our fingers brushing. My very cells sighed in ecstasy as our skin met. God, how did he do this to me? In a professor's *office* no less.

"You stole my copy of *East of Eden*," I said, recovering my ability to talk.

Jack's lips tilted upward, devious. "That's because, if you want it back, you'll have to visit me to get it." He paused, gesturing toward the glass case. "I assure you, pilfering ancient swords isn't on the agenda today. I have much more effective weapons at my disposal."

Before I had a chance to consider the double meaning in his words, Jack turned and circled Callahan's desk as if he owned it. He sat in the chair, crossing his ankles like he planned to be there awhile.

"Thank you for the roses." I bit my lip. It was thoughtful, but that had to be thousands of dollars' worth of flowers. "Just how much do you make, anyway?"

Was discussing income prying too much? He'd drawn a clear line in his past, but I never knew how close I was to toeing it.

Jack wore a playful smile, putting me at ease. "Enough to buy you billions, if you'd like."

The math wasn't hard. Even at a dollar per rose, that would make Jack a billionaire. Jesus. Being a mob boss paid well. I couldn't fathom having that much money. My stomach churned just thinking about it.

"Does that turn you on?"

I sighed, walking toward him. "The roses are lovely. But to answer your question—no, I can't be bought. I'm a trust-fund baby, remember?"

Jack leaned forward in his seat and grabbed my hand, pulling me so that I stood between him and the desk. "Well, if my off-shore bank accounts don't work, I'll just have to find another way to get my girl's attention."

With both of my hands linked in his, he kissed the part of my miniskirt where the pleats began. Right on the apex of my pelvic bone. In response, I closed my eyes, reminding myself to breathe.

"Keep calling me your girl and you'll be right on track," I answered, beginning to recognize how my voice changed when I was feeling this way. It got lower and a little raspy, like I needed water. Or maybe just more of Jack.

When I opened my eyes, his face was level with mine. His beauty, up close and personal, took my breath away. "You like that, do you?"

I nibbled at the inside of my cheek, hesitating. After a moment, I decided to be honest and nodded, glancing down at his collar instead of his enrapturing eyes.

"Mmm...and what else does my girl like?"

I tried to fight my shy smile. "I'm sure you can think of a few things."

A gasp escaped my lips when he pressed his arousal against my belly. He lifted me, setting me on the edge of the desk. His mouth was at my neck, trailing hot, fervent kisses down the sensitive skin there.

"Jack," I breathed, bracing my hands against his biceps. I made a feeble attempt at pushing him off, but he was unshakable. "This is my professor's office. I'll be expelled." Even as I said it, the inner harlot argued, *Callahan's lecture will keep him out for three hours.*

Jack leaned back. I knew by the fire burning behind his eyes that nothing could stop him. "The door's locked and I'll make sure to keep you quiet."

The promised threat had me wanton. Sensing my submission, Jack pressed his cock against my throbbing sex. He was so hard. A whimper left my body and I lay my forehead against the unforgiving expense of his chest.

"Do you really think I'd let you get expelled, dove?" he asked. The tenderness in his voice was comforting.

I looked up at him. "No."

He took that as an invitation, which it was. His mouth met mine and I was ready, granting him the entrance I'd been hoping he'd make. I slid my hands underneath his jacket, exploring his muscular torso. He shrugged out of the layer, knowing what I wanted. He pulled my body against his and traveled up the length of my tights with his fingers, suddenly stopping when he passed the hem of my shirt. He froze, breaking our kiss.

"Jesus Christ, lass." He widened his eyes. "Are you wearing *garters*?"

He'd pushed my skirt up to where my panties hooked onto the tights, holding them by a few threads of dark silk. The erotic image of his long, talented fingers toying with the delicate fabric almost made me convulse

Flushing, I smiled with mischief. "Why don't you find out?"

His jaw slackened, his tongue playing seductively along the inside of his cheek. He looked down and, with both hands, pushed my skirt up, bearing me from the waist. His pupils were blown with lust. It gave me an overwhelming sense of gratification.

"You're a naughty little schoolgirl, aren't you, Miss Marshall?" he asked, although it didn't come out as a question. His voice was husky, but he still wouldn't stop staring at my choice in undergarments. I'd planned on seeing him *after* school, but this would work too.

"I'm sorry, professor," I whispered, immersing myself in the scene. I reached up, adjusting his collar. "Maybe you can teach me a lesson…"

Jack's eyes hooded with satisfaction. His breathing was hitched, matching my own. He put his hands on each of my hips, pulling me into him. I moaned, wiggling against his erection. In response to my inability to stay still, he snapped my garter against the top of my thigh. The slight sting spread straight to my clit, the sensation bordering on unbearable.

His lips met mine and I forgot where I was. *Who* I was, even. He tasted delicious. He devoured me, his tongue teasing the ridges of mine. I swiveled my hips forward, dying for some friction. It wouldn't take much. Even his voice was orgasmic.

"Fuck, Emma." Jack hooked my legs high around his torso. "I'm so hard for you. Do you have any idea the effect you have on me?"

He traced a line with his tongue from the side of my neck, along my jaw, to the soft skin behind my ear. He pulled my lobe into his mouth, flicking the pearl earring. I trembled, seeking to please in return. I found his zipper and fumbled with it, freeing his thick length. The soft skin of his cock was like hot velvet.

He hissed as I ran my palm along him, circling the sensitive head with the pad of my thumb. Greedy with desire, I pushed my panties aside and pressed him into my swollen clit. We moaned in unison—his much more predatory than mine.

Jack snapped my garter again. "These are a fucking weapon."

I skated my hand up to his tie, grasping the Windsor knot. Yanking him down, I forced his mouth back on mine.

"*You* are a weapon, babe," I replied, biting his lower lip as he'd done countless times to me. I had no idea that it would set him off so much, but I kept that information tucked away to use for later.

He growled, cupping my ass as he thrust into me. I gasped, my channel trembling to accommodate the welcome intrusion.

"Jesus, you feel like silk," he breathed against my mouth, digging his fingers into my backside. I whimpered in response to his aggression. I was at a loss for words again. My fingertips and toes tingled, my entire body buzzing with pent-up energy.

"Shhh," he cooed, his cock pulsing inside me. I leaned my head back and was about to release another sigh when I remembered where we were. Right on the other side of the locked door, hundreds of people were walking through the halls. Milling about their day, blind to the fact that two people—one of them not even a member of the student body—were fucking passionately on top of a Pulitzer-winner's desk.

He pulled out all the way to the crown, then slid in at a pace so slow I wanted to scream. I slipped my index fingers behind two of his belt loops, seeking to pull him farther inside.

"You're going to have to learn patience, darling." Jack's voice was dark and chastising, but there was passion in its undertones. He was fighting his need as well.

"Fuck that," I bit out, balancing my head against his chest so he couldn't see the flush rising at my own words. "I want it hard and rough. Now."

"Christ Almighty," he cursed, holding my chin to face him. He leaned his forehead against mine, curling his fingers in my hair. "You ask me like that, dove, and I'll give you the fucking moon."

Before he finished speaking, I was on my stomach. Pressed against the antique desk, my legs dangling off the side. Jack drove into me hard and rough, just as I had pleaded. He gripped my behind in one hand, the other tenderly stroking my hair. As he drew us closer to the edge, he grew frantic, pulling and grasping at any piece of me he could get. The rhythm of his thrusts was chaotic. God, I loved making him lose control. His balls slapped against my clit, pummeling me with an abundance of pleasure. My muscles quivered around him, and I sank my teeth into the palm of his hand as he muffled the height of my orgasm. He bent over me, setting his jaw firm against my back as he came, a soft groan vibrating my spine.

I shuddered with ebbing contentment as he withdrew.

"For the first time in my life, you make losing control feel safe." Jack helped me to stand, placing a kiss on the tip of my nose. I blinked, trying to settle my heart. "Like I'm not such a terrible person for being myself."

"Jack…" I adjusted a strand of his hair that had come loose of its textured hold. Losing control? He looked remarkably well put together by comparison. My skin was sticky with perspiration, my hair was an absolute mess and my legs were like jelly. "I'm glad I make you feel safe…"

His brow furrowed at my obvious concern. He pushed me backward onto the desk, bending down to wipe my inner thighs with his handkerchief. He'd already tucked himself into his pants.

"Why do I feel like there's a 'but' to that statement?" he asked, turning me around with quiet force. "Hand me your hair tie."

Confused, I slipped the elastic from my wrist and passed it to him. As he ran his fingers through my hair, I felt my own insecurities seeping in.

"Are you sure you won't get bored with my lack of experience? You don't want someone more—"

He spun me again, my hair tied into a sleek ponytail by his loving hands. He wore an expression of surprise and anger. His green eyes flashed with it, making me suck in the air around us.

"Dove, I didn't even know I was looking for you until I found you." His words were gentle, in stark contrast to the hard lines on his face. "And now that I have, I know there is nothing *more* left for me. I'm the luckiest bastard to walk the earth. And lack of experience? You just rocked my fucking world. If you were any better, I'd have a heart attack."

I smiled, looking down at my boots as he straightened my skirt. My flush deepened and my chest soared at his words. Those were my own thoughts exactly. I hadn't known I was looking for Jack. Now I couldn't imagine my life without him.

"I feel the same," I said. Hand at the small of my back, he guided me into the bustling hall. "How did you even get in there?"

As an answer, Jack slid a set of keys from his pocket and locked the door to Callahan's office. He winked, slipping the keys into the professor's plastic inbox. It was used for turning in papers, but he'd eventually find his missing set.

"He's ancient," Jack jested, shrugging at the awed look on my face. "Picking his pocket was too easy."

I broke out into a wide grin while we made our way down the hall. More than a few female students tripped over their own feet as they took in the likes of Jack O'Connell. He glided through the lecture halls like a god, but his eyes remained focused on my profile.

When we reached the door to my classroom, Jack leaned forward, our lips meeting once more. The kiss was sweet and innocent. We were painfully aware of our audience. He was drawing more ogling the longer he stood around. But he was kissing *me.*

Let the other girls salivate as much as they want.

"Take this." He slipped something cold and metallic into my hand.

It was a key card. It had the address of his apartment in block letters along the bottom. But it was the engraving that caught my eye. Smoky, intricate wings had been carved into the face of the card. He was giving me a personalized key to his private elevator. The one that rose straight into his foyer.

"This key represents how serious I'm taking our relationship," he said, earnest. "I don't want to overwhelm you. You don't have to use it, but I want you to have it. Not even my brothers have unlimited access to my place, so keep it safe."

"I'll guard it with my life." I held it against my heart to prevent my hand from shaking. Before he could kiss me again, I pulled something out of the pocket of my skirt. "I have something for you as well. I was going to give it to you tonight, but if we're exchanging gifts…"

Jack snatched the bracelet from my hand, twirling it between his fingers. It was a thin leather band, simple and black. But instead of a clasp, two gold handcuffs linked together. It matched the choker that now sat between my collarbones. His eyes met mine, enamored. I took the hint, fastening it onto his wrist right below the Rolex. It matched well.

"Possessive, are we?" he asked, the corner of his mouth lifting in a satisfied smirk.

I mirrored him. "We've already discussed this. You bring out my dark side."

"Fair, seeing as you're the light of my life."

My lips popped open at his words. He caught my gasp with his mouth, nipping at my bottom lip. I melded my body against him, dipping slightly as he pressed in return.

"I'm never taking it off," he whispered, resting his forehead against mine.

"Good." I peppered that meddlesome jawline of his with kisses. "Because you're mine."

He chuckled, those emerald pools melting me on the spot. "Took you this long to figure that out, dove?"

Want to see more from this author?
Here's a taster for you to enjoy!

Emerald Mafia: Clipped Wings
Jennifer Luna

Coming November 2023

Excerpt

Jack

While entering the little bungalow, I balanced my grocery bags under each arm. They were filled with ingredients from the Mediterranean. I was excited to work with them fresh, though not as excited as I was to see Emma. I'd only been gone an hour, but a tightness in my chest had formed from the need to have her close again.

After I set the bags on the kitchen counter, my gaze found her. If anything, the magnetic force between us had grown over the past few months. I was attuned to her presence at all times, even when she wasn't aware. I stopped to stare, my breathing uneven.

The fact that a creature like her lived in the same dimension as a demon like me was baffling.

Emma was an angel, sitting on the terrace in her white, see-through cover-up. She wore nothing underneath, the little temptress. Her hair, lighter than usual, was damp and beginning to wave. She had it pulled over one shoulder in an attempt to control the wayward locks. As Emma sat on a cushioned armchair, knees pulled to her chest, her eyes were glued to the thick text in her lap. She was holding a glass of white wine in one hand, idly swirling its contents around. She hadn't heard me come in. Not much could break her concentration.

I set a jug of milk onto the stone countertop, the noise stirring her. She looked at me, that slow smile spreading over her full lips, rising higher on one side like she was thinking something naughty. Her wide brown eyes grew smaller as her cheeks lifted, her smile turning into a full-on grin at the sight of me.

Her awe-inspiring effect was in no way diminished from the first time I'd laid eyes on her.

Circling the counter and walking the length of the living area to the terrace, I knelt in front of her. As I pulled her legs away from her body, she set her book and glass of wine on the side table. With her legs down, I was able to see all of her. She was a tiny thing—average height for a woman, but thin and small-boned. She'd taken up a more rigorous form of exercise than she was used to. Her new muscle tone was slight, but long and lean. As delicate as a dove.

I kissed the inside of her knee, tasting sea salt, and admired the goose bumps that formed in response to my touch.

"I thought we said no work," I murmured against her skin, sliding my hand up her thigh to reach her hip.

"It's not for school," she insisted, wiggling.

So impatient.

I trailed kisses and little bites along her inner thigh. Her hands flew to my hair, where she sank her fingers into my haphazard curls. I groaned as her warmth soothed the ache in my chest, melting it into nonexistence.

She tugged on the crown of my head, pulling me up and in between her legs, our faces level. Her half-lidded eyes were filled with the same heat as her touch.

"I'm never going to see Santorini if you keep doing this to me." She pouted, cupping my rugged jawline.

I leaned forward to kiss the dip where her collarbones met, teasing the handcuff charm on her necklace. "It's nowhere near as interesting as you."

Her wild hair smelled like the ocean, fresh and salty. She'd been swimming, but I recognized the underlying notes of apples and lavender in it. Her skin, normally ivory, was now the color of warm honey and twice as sweet. The new freckles adorning her nose were adorable. I'd kissed them a thousand times since they had appeared.

Summer Emma might have been my favorite version, but I said that every season.

"I'm a history major, Jack," Emma argued, as she was prone to do. She was the only person on Earth I enjoyed sparring with. "My professors would kill me if they knew I went to Greece and barely even made it out of bed. Do you know how much there is to see here?"

I shook my head against her chest, watching with satisfaction as her nipples pebbled. "You'll have to enlighten me."

I had my reasons for not taking Emma into town. They were entirely selfish, and I knew it. Emma and I were both so busy back in Manhattan. We didn't see each other as often as I wanted. I could count on two hands how many times we had been able to sleep in the same bed. This was a vacation to Greece for Emma. It was a month of unfiltered access to my girl for me. I didn't give a shit about ancient history. Having Emma by my side every second of the day was the best thing I could ever hope for.

Before she could dispute further, I ripped the light fabric over her chest and pulled her breast into my mouth. Her spine arched off the chair, her body pushing into me of its own accord.

"Jack." She moaned my name. "That was expensive."

"I'll buy you ten more."

I licked my way down her flat belly, rocking my groin against her taut calf muscle. This woman had me grinding her leg like a horny dog, for fuck's sake. Emma groaned, her head falling as I approached my goal. She was ready, as I knew she would be, her pink little pussy glistening for me.

"Move in with me," I breathed against her sex.

She shuddered with pleasure, then stiffened. "No."

I flattened my tongue, dragging it through her folds in one long, languid stroke. I swirled it around her clitoris twice, then pulled back. "Move in with me."

It had to have been the hundredth time I'd asked her to move into my apartment in the city. If she lived with me, we would have every night together. It would also ease my worries about her safety. If she wasn't at school or working at Roisin's, I got antsy. Ideas of her being kidnapped invaded my mind, making me useless during work.

Alas, we'd had this conversation before. Emma's little sister, Ella, was moving to the city at the end of summer to attend Tisch, NYU's prestigious drama school. Emma wanted to be there for Ella during her first year at college, which included sharing an apartment with her.

Emma's ability to care for others was admirable, but exhausting. She was a genuinely good person. She aced her classes, was never late to work or school and emptied her wallet to the homeless. She didn't even eat meat. She was everything that I was not. When people thought of me, words like "selfish," "controlling" and "hard-ass" came to mind. Emma was soft and innocent. Everyone fell in love with her and I was no exception.

Emma churned her hips toward my mouth, desperately seeking to get off. A moan slithered from her throat, her chest rising and falling with heightening arousal. I licked and sucked, tugging her abused clit into my mouth. The moment her muscles seized, I stopped, denying her orgasm.

"Move in with me," I pleaded.

She roared—an adorable little tiger cub—and slammed her legs shut on either side of my head, pinning me to her. She knew I was taunting her with the edge, trying to persuade her to move in while she was hot and suggestible, and it was pissing her off.

"I'll smash your beautiful face if you keep doing that," she warned, her eyes flashing with frustration.

"Is that a threat, sweetheart? Because I can't think of a better way to die than suffocating in your pussy."

When a magnificent blush stained her cheeks, I smirked. Emma couldn't hurt me if she gave it her all. I could easily slip my head out from between her thighs, but I enjoyed driving her crazy. She did the same to me without trying. Even if it wasn't in a physical sense, Emma had a power over me that she was entirely unaware of. She was the only person on the planet who could put me in my place, and she just so happened to be less than half my size. My name had most men trembling in their boots, but Emma could bring me to my knees with a single glance.

"We'll go into town tomorrow," I said, my eyes roaming her delicate features. Her gaze was fixed on my mouth, greedy. "We can do whatever you want, dovey."

I bent my head, seeking to fulfill her wishes. My goal had and would always be to keep my little dove smiling.

* * * *

The setting sun had turned the sky a pinkish purple, the twinkling cliffside of Santorini a distant landscape. Emma, exhausted from hours of lovemaking, went to take a hot shower. I thought of joining her, but decided to start on dinner instead. When it came to her, I was constantly fighting tooth and nail for some form of self-control. I had to remind myself that, occasionally, the poor girl needed a break from my ever-present sex drive, not that she ever complained.

Listening to the waves rolling onto the beach, I pulled the mussels and herbs from the fridge, setting the ingredients on a large cutting board. Cooking, along with exercise and fucking, was a way for me to get out of my own head, to step back from the tightly coiled anxiety and anger that boiled just under my skin.

I hadn't experienced much inner turmoil during the past two weeks and it had everything to do with Emma. She was my own personal medicine. I just wished I could take her in pill form when we returned to Manhattan. We were halfway through our vacation, and I found myself wishing it could be permanent.

My phone buzzed from its charging station on the counter. I glanced at it wearily. We'd promised each other no work for a month, but Emma had already broken it. I knew the book she was reading had been assigned for summer break. Besides, she was in the shower. She wouldn't even know.

Leaving the cooking, I gathered my cell phone and pored over ten missed calls. Seven were from Shannon, three from Kieran, and they'd started around one in the morning New York time.

Shit.

I clicked on Shannon's picture, dialing my sister-in-law. She was two months from her due date, but anything could happen. If I missed that baby being born, Connor would kill me and Shannon would help dig the grave.

"Connor's gone dark," Shannon said by way of answering. Her voice was laced with fear and cracked as she spoke, putting me on high alert.

"How long?" I asked. It wasn't like my brother to go dark, especially without Shannon by his side. He was just as protective of her as I was of Emma, more so now that she was carrying their child. He stayed in contact with her at all times and didn't even let her out of the penthouse if things were getting dicey.

"He never showed in Boston last night." Shannon panted. I could hear her shoes clapping on the marble floor. She was pacing at home. "Tom called and asked if I was with him."

Fuck. That was over twelve hours ago. Something was wrong. Something was very fucking wrong. I spun around, turning the stove burners off.

"Who's with you?" I asked, making sure she wasn't alone while she waited for word.

"Just Guillermo," she replied, her anxiety worsening at the sound of mine.

Guillermo was their personal chef. Where was my younger brother? "Kieran?"

"Scouring the streets."

"Stay calm," I told her, although I felt anything but as I jogged into the bedroom.

Emma was just getting out of the shower, her hair still soaking wet and a plush towel wrapped around her torso. I reached into the closet, snatched the first dress I felt, and tossed it to her.

"We'll be there tomorrow," I informed Shannon, ending the call. I hoped she would take my advice. It wasn't good for the baby to feel such stress, but it was inevitable given the circumstances.

When she saw my grim expression, Emma's eyes widened. She slipped the dress over her head, yanking it down to her thighs as she stepped into a pair of sandals.

"We're leaving," I stated, throwing her phone, laptop and a few other necessary items into a backpack. I'd have the rest of our belongings shipped to us.

Thinking, as I had, that it was about the baby, Emma's nerves bled into her tone. "Charlie's not due yet."

I swung the backpack over my shoulder, grabbed Emma's hand and all but dragged her out of the bungalow. She struggled to keep up, her untied halter dress sliding off her shoulders. I bent down, scooped her into my arms, and carried her the rest of the way to the car. My brother had already been missing twelve hours and we wouldn't land in New York for another twelve. I was pressed for time.

"Get a flight plan set to La Guardia," I ordered the pilot, cell phone pressed to my ear as I buckled Emma into the G-class. "We need to be in the air in an hour."

The pilot acquiesced without hesitation. I slammed Emma's door and rounded the front of the vehicle, throwing the bag into the backseat. The tires kicked up gravel as we sped onto the small street. I dialed another number and my younger brother answered over Bluetooth on the second ring.

"How far out?" Kieran asked, his monotone voice echoing throughout the interior of the vehicle. It sent a renewed jolt of panic through my bones. I hadn't heard his tone like that in years. Out of the three of us, Kieran was the least uptight.

"Twelve hours." I swerved past an old pickup truck. Emma grabbed the side of the door to steady herself. "Call a meeting."

"With who?"

"Everyone. Meet at the northern safe house."

"Done," Kieran said, ending the call before I had the chance.

"What is it?" Emma's voice was faint. She knew something bigger was going on. This wasn't how I would react to the news of a baby coming.

"It's Connor," I gritted out, my jaw twitching as I admitted it aloud. "Someone got to him."

About the Author

Jennifer Luna is an author by night and renowned chicken nugget chef by day—just ask her kid. She lives in Virginia with her husband, son, and two cats. When she's not reading or writing, she can be found cleaning the litter box or doing just about anything for a Klondike bar. Her debut dark romance, *Dove*, is the first novel in the Emerald Mafia series, which exposes the gritty underworld of the Irish Mafia and the sacrifices one woman will make to keep her loved ones out of harm's way.

Jennifer loves to hear from readers. You can find her contact information, website details and author profile page at https://www.totallybound.com

TOTALLY
BOUND
Home of Erotic Romance

www.ingramcontent.com/pod-product-compliance
Lightning Source LLC
LaVergne TN
LVHW050930080826
845145LV00001B/279

* 9 7 8 1 8 0 2 5 0 5 4 6 7 *